ALSO BY JUNO DAWSON

Praise for **CLEAN**

Written with **verve** and **wit** ...
it's **one to just enjoy** – STYLIST

An **emotional freight train** of a novel – HEAT

Addictive – THE POOL

As **bold** and **gritty** as it is **fabulously**
glossy and readable, it's a **provocative,**
important read – OBSERVER

Compulsively readable – GUARDIAN

Gossip Girl goes to **rehab**...
Clean **hits the spot** – i NEWSPAPER

Sharp, gripping and **tender** – ATTITUDE

Compelling – FINANCIAL TIMES

Hard-hitting and **unapologetic** – SUN

Praise for **MEAT MARKET**

ıaranteed to be your **summer read** – GLAMOUR

ʌines **blockbuster appeal** with piercing commentary
ʌdelling, **body image** and **consent** – OBSERVER

A powerful **counterweight** to light-hearted
literature that still portrays **modelling as**
the stuff of dreams – GUARDIAN

Heartbreaking, painful, and **worth every second** ...
you won't be able to put it down

2400031514

Praise for **WONDERLAND**

A **radical** re-telling of
Alice in Wonderland
– COSMOPOLITAN

An **addictive** and
immersive read – THE SCOTSMAN

... much-needed **escapism** while expertly
tackling **serious themes** like self-harm,
suicide, addiction, gender and sexuality ...
dive head-first down a hedonistic
fictional rabbit hole – STYLIST

A **vicious, dark delight** – HEAT

STAY ANOTHER DAY

JUNO DAWSON

Quercus

QUERCUS CHILDREN'S BOOKS
First published in Great Britain in 2021 by Hodder & Stoughton

1 3 5 7 9 10 8 6 4 2

Text copyright © Juno Dawson, 2021

The moral rights of the author have been asserted.

A CIP catalogue record for this book
is available from the British Library.

ISBN: 978 1 786 54108 6

Typeset in Adobe Caslon by Avon DataSet Ltd, Arden Court,
Alcester, Warwickshire

Printed and bound in Great Britain by Clays Ltd, Elcograf S.p.A.

The paper and board used in this book
are made from wood from responsible sources.

Quercus Children's Books
An imprint of Hachette Children's Group
Part of Hodder and Stoughton
Carmelite House
50 Victoria Embankment
London EC4Y 0DZ

An Hachette UK Company
www.hachette.co.uk

www.hachettechildrens.co.uk

AUTHOR NOTE

This book is a work of fiction but includes subject matter
that some readers may find triggering, including conversations
about eating disorders and self-harm.

Further guidance can be found at the back of the novel.

For my sisters, Joanne and Sarah Lea

The house on Arboretum Road had seen 120 Christmases since its completion. With the ever-shortening days and a chill about its square shoulders, it knew another could not be far away.

Sure enough, as a milky winter sun set behind the rooftops of Edinburgh, for the first time that year, the house's lights came on. Ping, ping, ping! First the trees in its front garden, and then a crown of white pearls strung along its guttering, and a final set around the door. Well, didn't that look enchanting?

The house held its breath.

Perhaps, this year, the children would be coming home again.

What a sombre and muted affair last Christmas had been, maybe the worst the house could recall.

The current occupiers of the house on Arboretum Road traditionally put up their lights on December twenty-first each year. That could mean only one thing: it was four more sleeps till Christmas.

22 DECEMBER

FERN

*… WE ARE PREPARING YOUR SERVICE … PLEASE
WAIT ON THE CONCOURSE …*

Nice try, Kings Cross, do I look like a rookie? Eyes on the prize,
and I can see the train on the other side of the ticket barriers. So
close, but out of reach. It *has* to be that one. It's always platform
3. That said, we don't want to inadvertently end up in Leeds.

Outside the station, the Salvation Army belt out a chirpy
rendition of 'God Rest Ye Merry Gentlemen', but the mood
inside is bleak midwinter, despite a canopy of twinkly white
lights with which the ceiling is festooned.

We're like lemmings; surrounded on all sides by fellow
travellers, chins all tilted at the same angle towards the
information boards. Lots of twitchy suitcases, ready to roll,
and we don't have seat reservations together because *someone*
didn't book the tickets soon enough. I gave him ONE JOB.

'Come on,' I say to Thom. Gosh, my jaw is achy from
clenching too hard. 'Let's wait on the other side of the barrier.'

'What's the hurry? They haven't said yet …'

'It's that one, trust me.'

Thom sighs. 'Yeah, but if it's not, we'll have to get the guy
to let us back and it'll be well awkward …'

5

Tongue pressed against the side of my cheek, I give him a piquant DON'T QUESTION ME glare. He's pretty used to it by now. He knows what these bulging eyes mean. Thom Simpkins is so consistently, infuriatingly chill, that I have to stress for both of us. That's how it works. It keeps us alive, I like to think.

'Don't you wanna go to the Harry Potter store?'

I grimace. 'No, obviously not. One – because we'll miss the train, and two – Rowan would crucify me.'

Thom rolls his eyes. 'We have like twenty minutes to kill …'

Amateur. 'And the train doors close up to two minutes before departure. Let's roll, kiddo.' I clutch the handle of my suitcase in one hand and a Selfridge's bag full of gifts in the other. There's something pleasingly oxymoronic about buying my parents gifts with money they've given me, but it was that or no gifts. Studying in London is bankrupting us all. The gift exchange is purely symbolic, and one day I'll pay them back with a top-flight care home.

We slot our tickets through the barrier – I could really use a third arm at this point. Thom is mere inches through the gate when that strange robot voice blasts out of the speakers: *The 13.02 service to Edinburgh Waverley will depart from platform 3 …*

My tummy drops. 'Shit! Run!' I cry. Our head start is shot to shit as a seasonal mass exodus surges towards us like a scene from the *Walking Dead*. 'Go!'

We weren't the only people to pre-empt the announcement. I already see bodies boarding our service.

6

'Which coach is unclassified?' Thom asks, running ahead of me on long, winger's legs.

'I don't know! U? Or F sometimes?'

The only clue is the white cards poking out of the top of the seats. I wonder what the odds are of getting two seats together – preferably with a table – four days before Christmas. I could kill Thom for not booking the tickets sooner.

I suppose some kind soul might take pity on us, though looking around, it seems unlikely. You'd think people would be *nicer*, high on Christmas spirit, but the grim faces swarming towards us look murderous. At best.

And that's when one of the handles on my Selfridge's bag snaps and the top few presents spill on to the platform. 'SHIT. KEEP GOING. GET US SEATS.' I stop and scoop them up, unceremoniously thrusting them back in and cradling the lot like a dead body in my arms. Presents are replaceable. Standing in a draughty vestibule for the next six hours and forty minutes is not an option.

ROWAN

'I think it's time for another wee gin in a tin, don't you?' It had been buy-three-get-one-free. So we got twelve for the train ride. That's the kind of mathematics I like.

'Rude not to,' Syd says.

I could do with ice and a slice. The tins have matched the unpleasant mouth temperature of the train carriage, but I'm feeling quite *merry* now – which seems only right for December twenty-second – so I don't mind so much. I'll be nicely drunk by the time we reach Edinburgh. They all think I'm a sloppy-lush-mess-queen anyway, and I wouldn't want to disappoint.

'Are you *sure* your parents are down with this?' Syd asks nervously.

'For the love of god, yes! Chill!' I say for at least the millionth time. 'For one thing, my mother is *very* into Christmas, and would never turn a stray out into the cold, but also I think they think you're my boyfriend.'

They laugh heartily. 'A theyfriend?'

Ew. 'Is that a thing?'

'Well, Rowan,' they say in the style of Ms Randolph, our fustiest lecturer, 'speaking for my people, we tend to say "I'm your *person*".'

'OK, that's cute.'

'I know, right?' The thought of shagging Syd is ludicrous. Pure comedy. They're my ride-or-die, and I wouldn't ever fuck with someone I minded losing. And I have repeatedly told my parents that we're just friends, but they seem to think I'm lying. Why would I lie? They'd be *delighted* to have me married off.

My parents are not sitcom-level bad. It's not going to be some zany Ricky Gervais moment of falling over themselves to appear woke and getting it wrong with *hilarious results*, but I suspect they're going to Ask Polite Questions, and that can be just as cringe.

The train pulls out of Newcastle which means we're not too far away. Thank fuck. I've been low-key dreading going home, but I also need off this train. Vaping into the toilet bowl to avoid setting off the alarm is as glamorous as it sounds. It feels like we've been on this train for ever. We live here now. This is home. This seat smells of me: Tom Ford Tobacco Vanille and butt-sweat.

Staying in Bristol was not an option. With everything that was going down with Willow last year, Christmas was pretty much cancelled – cancel culture *has* gone mad – so no one minded that I escaped to France for the season. This year, attendance is mandatory, so I'm Joseph schlepping back to Bethlehem for the motherfucking census. Again, it's not that my parents are fascists, it's that they're dull. Back in Bristol, Jojo, Timo and Raheem are doing this whole 'Orphans' Christmas Dinner' and I kinda wish I was an orphan.

At least I have Syd as a comfort blanket from my new Found Family.

'They know I'm non-binary, right?'

If they didn't, they'd probably figure it out from the shaved head, hand-poked tattoos and nose ring. 'They do, but neither of them has been so bold as to ask if you were *born a girl or a boy* …'

Syd groans wearily. 'Bitch, I was born a *baby*.'

I laugh, and shove another handful of Tangfastics in my mouth. The perfect amuse-bouche to accompany my M&S Slimline Gin and Tonic. Fizzy cola bottles are god tier. My Grindr alerts keep going off. It's the best road-trip game: regional snapshots of dick in the UK. So far, the highlight was skimming up against the green, green valleys of the Wales/Hereford border. Lonely farmers. Shame I'm just passing through.

Syd plucks the Haribo out of my hands. 'So fill me in. Who am I meeting?'

I roll my eyes. They're all so aggressively drab, I might as well just use a nude eyeshadow palette for reference. God, how to describe my family? 'You know those tumours that grow hair and teeth? Just imagine one of those but it's a mass of cishet white people who shop at Next.'

They're not *that* bad. But the next six days are still going to be a *challenge*. I haven't told Syd all that much about my little sister. Willow McAllister: the world's lightest demolition ball.

All around us in the packed, moist train carriage, people are drinking and laughing, slipping nicely into holiday mode, and I'm like, what idyllic Christmas-card families are these people going home to? Are they *happy* or something? Though

10

I suppose my family do *look* like a Christmas card at a distance. It's only when you get close enough that the hairline cracks show.

You know what? I need to be a lot drunker. I down the rest of my gin.

WILLOW

I'm sure I used to like Christmas. I must have done. I remember, I think, the fizz of excitement post-Bonfire night; going through the Argos catalogue with a pen to circle things; writing a letter to Santa; giving a shit.

It got dark at half-three today.

The sky from my bedroom window is orange-black, like it might snow. If it snows, maybe I'll be able to get it up. It never snows at Christmas, even in Scotland. We've been lied to. My breath fogs up the glass, obscuring the view of the botanic gardens. It's too cold for this window seat, as much as I love it. The second Fern left for London, I took over her room, just for this spot. *Jane Eyre* fantasies.

I'm so cold. All the time. That's the worst thing. I just can't get warm, not ever. All my heat has to come from without, I'm making none within. My biological central heating is broken. I climb out of the window seat and pull an XXL hoodie out of the bottom drawer and put it on over my sweater. Layers help.

I hear the front door close downstairs. Dad shouts; says he's off to get the others. I can't remember who's arriving first – Fern or Rowan. I'm excited to see them, that's the good part, but it means the BIG DAY is almost here. My heart skitters and my stomach cramps.

Of course Mum is cooking a big dinner to welcome them home. I can smell it from up here. Chickpea and spinach curry (to be fair, only three hundred calories), but someone will be watching, waiting, observing my hands and mouth. They always are, because I cannot be trusted. There'll be an expectation that I get some rice (130 calories) or some naan bread (500 fucking calories – why don't I just inject some butter into my veins and have done with it).

Get some bread, Willow.

You get some fucking bread, you heifers.

It's so weird, it's like they *want* the demon to come out. We're not exactly new to this, they *know* what happens if they push me, and yet we do the dance.

Three times a day.

The cycle: dread, fear, panic, guilt, dread, fear, panic, guilt.

At least I'm *home* this Christmas. That's something. Being force-fed bone dry turkey by a nurse in a Santa hat was pretty wild. Six very thin girls chewing four-minute mouthfuls. Merry Christmas.

WAIT.

Welcome the intrusive thought. Acknowledge its presence. Interrogate your thought patterns. Turn it into a positive.

OK. Positives: I genuinely can't wait to see my brother and sister. Rowan is as funny as Fern is wise. I'm looking forward to meeting Thom and Syd, and watching how Mum and Dad fuck up Syd's pronouns. I will also get presents. Not mad at that.

Yeah, but you'll have to eat a fucking mountain of food and fucking Auntie Shelly is going to ask why you don't 'just eat a bit more'.

I want to scream. Everyone else is so excited. I envy them. They make it look very easy. If I could take a pill and wake up on January second, I'd swallow the whole bottle.

Or throw myself through the glass and faceplant the drive below. If I hurt myself, I wonder if they'd make me eat in the hospital?

I WAIT some more.

ROWAN

How do I forget EVERY SINGLE YEAR how fucking cold Scotland is? Bristol has a whole other subtropical climate, I swear. My satin baseball jacket isn't going to cut it. By the time we find Dad parked up in the drop-off zone, my bones have permafrost on them. Dad whacks up the heating in the people carrier. It smells of burned toast. 'Thanks for the lift, Dad.'

'You are quite welcome.' I am quantifiably shook because he is starting to look OLD, middle age descending on him like a progressive facial disease. Like, when I left Edinburgh a little over a year ago, he was handsomely *craggy*, now he's teetering perilously close to *saggy*. It's not my fault, I did tell him exactly where he could get Botox and he laughed like it was the maddest suggestion in the world.

I, personally, can't wait to grow old disgracefully. I want that scarily taut *Real Housewives* facelift look; collagen fillers injected directly into a piece of cheap ham. 'Are we not waiting for Fern and her fella?' I ask Dad.

'No, she'll not be here for a few hours yet.' He concentrates as he pulls out of the frantic station car park.

I swivel in the passenger seat so as not to exclude Syd. 'Mum was like *"get a cab"*, LOL. Do you have any idea how many hand jobs I'd have to sell to be able to afford that?'

Syd snorts from the back seat and Dad briefly takes his eyes off the road to see if I'm kidding. 'I hope that's a joke.'

'Dad!' I grin. 'As if I bother with hand jobs. Not worth the effort.'

He half grimaces. 'You'll get out and walk in a minute. I don't know why you can't get a part-time job like your sister.'

I blink pointedly in his direction. 'Father, unlike Fern, I have to work on my *craft* outside workshops you know.' This is a lie. I am not acting outside of my course at all. I definitely *could* get a job, but it'd have to be on a Saturday or Sunday and then I wouldn't be able to go out on Fridays or Saturdays, so I'd literally rather shit in my hands and clap.

I'd be a wonderful wee sex worker, as it happens. I'm good at two things: acting and sex. So far neither have made me any money whatsoever. I've had a variety of shite customer-facing jobs over the holidays. Being a sex worker is probably more dignified than the summer I did at Pets at Home. You haven't lived until you've milked a Pomeranian's anal glands.

It's only a short drive from Edinburgh to Inverleith. On the way, we pass the grim Gothic turrets of Finnians, the prison, or 'school', I was held captive at for seven years. It doesn't matter that almost three years have passed since I was last there, I still get antsy as it comes into view. I point it out to Syd, who mutters condolences under their breath. Could have been worse, at least we didn't have to board. Doubt I'd have survived that.

A few minutes later and Dad pulls the car into the drive. There's cosiness in familiarity, I guess. Home is where the home is. For the next week I don't have to worry about cooking, or cleaning, or check my bank balance. From the backseat, I hear an awed gasp from Syd. 'Ro … you said your house was *big*, you didn't say it was a *castle*.'

I make a weird lip puff I won't be trialling again. I both do and don't want them to be impressed, but I certainly don't want Syd to feel like some fucking Little Dorrit orphan. 'Haaaardly,' I drawl, already twenty per cent more Scottish after five minutes in the presence of my father.

'Rowan, it's a mansion …'

'I wouldn't go that far,' Dad says. 'But it's been in my family for over a century.'

I suppose it *is* fairly imposing from the outside, set back off the road with its sweeping drive and tower room, although the Christmas lights soften it. If I hadn't lived here pretty much my whole life, I'd be like, *Fuck this haunted house, I'll be down the Premier Inn.* 'My dad's family are pure evil,' I tell Syd. I lean in close as we step out of the car. '*They were slavers,*' I hiss.

'Thank you, Rowan,' Dad huffs. 'We don't *know* that.'

WE DO, I mouth at Syd, and they make an appropriately horrified face. 'What do you do, Mr McAllister?'

'Oh god, please, call me Dale. I can't handle "Mr McAllister" for the next week. I'm at Holyrood.'

Syd looks confused, so I step in. 'My father is that most perverse of beasts, a Scottish Tory.'

'Ew!' Syd exclaims, almost a reflex, and I howl with laughter. 'Sorry … I mean …'

'It's fine! There's nothing you can say that'd be worse than I've already heard from Rowan.' He's at the boot, unloading

17

our suitcases and my very small FUCK TERFS tote bag filled with presents. I actually put a lot of thought into everyone's second-hand books. And, hell, at least I'm here this year. Bitches, *I* am the gift. Last Christmas must have been … well, the less said about that the better.

'Thank you so much for letting me come,' Syd tells Dad.

'Not at all. Any *friend* of Rowan's is a friend of ours. He talks about you all the time.'

'We're not together, Dad, let it go,' I shout as I plough through the front door. Each year the wreath gets more elaborately bland. I'm a fan of Bad Taste Christmas: white plastic trees, glittery Virgin Marys, and metres of threadbare tinsel. Mum favours a uniform colour scheme, and the wreath tells me this year is purple and gold. Christmas at Cadburys.

As soon as I step inside, I smell fresh pine and the nasal tit-punch of Yankee cinnamon candles, and also, faintly, curry. Ah fuck it, it's Christmas. I can't be mad at a time of year where people thrust alcoholic beverages in your hand from sunrise to sunset. A glorious mistletoe bough hangs over the door in the hall. Syd, again, is wowed. I wonder what Christmas would be like round theirs?

'Mum?' I call.

'My favourite son …' She blows out of the kitchen at the end of the corridor to greet me, all beads and bangles as ever. Was she always this tiny? I loom over her like a skinny gay ogre and get a lungful of Jo Malone as I squeeze her hard. 'Is that good for your hair?' She reaches up and fingers my peroxide silver hair.

'You're one to talk.' Not one among us can remember her

natural hair colour, except, shudder, Dad who can check if the curtains match the drapes.

'And this must be Syd ...' she says, and I take a step back to see if there's a reaction. Mum lectures at the university so she's not quite as clueless as Dad, exposed to vaguely interesting people daily. That said, there's a certain *type* that studies at Edinburgh; and it must suck to not get into Cambridge, Oxford *or* Durham ...

'Nice to meet you, Dr McAllister.' Syd steps forward and offers a much-scarred, much-tattooed arm.

Mum gives their hand a firm shake. 'An absolute pleasure. Please call me Chris, everyone does, even at work.'

'I can't thank you enough for this. It was here or ... well I don't know where else I'd have gone,' Syd says sincerely. They're being polite. This is a mercy mission for *me*. Syd would have been just fine at the Orphans' Dinner.

Mum shakes her head. 'Not another word. It's Christmas, and our home is your home for the next six days.' I'm dead inside, obviously, but I'm actually quite proud of her. When I asked if Syd could come, she didn't hesitate to say yes. Didn't even need the extended *Britain's Got Talent* sob story.

'Dale, will you show Syd up to their room?' She got their pronouns right first time. She must have been practising. 'I'm afraid you've got the box room ...'

'Seriously, the sofa would have been amazing.'

Syd follows Dad upstairs, taking my bag too. Willow emerges from the shadows on the staircase, all pale and tragic, some gothic attic secret. She shies away from Syd like a nervy sparrow, only offering a timid *hi*. 'This is our youngest, Willow,' Dad saves me the introduction.

'Good to meet you.' Syd gives a hearty nod as they cross.

Willow blushes, tucks her mermaid-length hair behind her ears and continues to the hall. She looks like pure shite. I fight the urge to give Mum an accusatory *look*. A head's up would've been nice. You wouldn't think it humanly possible but she somehow looks even thinner than she did over the summer, drowning in a tent of a hoodie we could all comfortably camp in. It's always fucking one step forward, two steps back.

'You may enter my personal space.' I beckon my sister towards me with a forced grin. I fold her frail bird bones into a gentle hug. You'd snap her. 'Yum, you smell of Dead Nana.'

She laughs. 'It's lavender body cream!'

I tell her I like it. I *don't* tell her that her eyes are too fucking big for her head and I can see her skull through her peach-fuzz skin. Eat, you mad bitch, eat. 'I like your hair,' she says. 'You really outgayed yourself.'

'You have no idea. I can barely sit down.'

'For heaven's sake!' Mum slaps my arm. 'Can we *not*, Rowan?' She leads me towards the kitchen. 'And you didn't tell me Syd was Asian ...'

I give her my finest WHAT THE FUCK? face. 'Relax, Mum, they're from *Runcorn*, they do celebrate Christmas there ...'

Willow laughs, and Mum rolls her eyes. 'Oh, you know what I meant.'

'I literally don't, but whatever. Maybe later we can play an excruciating parlour game where you all try to guess *where they're really from?*' The answer, by the way, is their grandparents are Nepalese, but I'm not going to explain my friend's origin story to my mother.

'Oh, give over, I never said that.'

We reach the kitchen and I grab a Quality Street out of the decorative bowl she's decanted them into. She slaps my hand. 'Ow!'

'Don't spoil your dinner,' she says, attending to a vat of curry on the stove. It's one of those hugely aspirational Pinterest kitchens, designed to be a buzzing hive for a big family, with a hunky rustic table and enough room on the range to prepare a feast. SMEG Fridge and La Creuset pots proudly on display. What will Mum and Dad do once Willow leaves – if she ever does? They'll be haunting this place like ghosts. 'We'll wait for Fern and Thom to eat. They get in around eight.'

I shake my head and make a great show of putting a fudge in my mouth. '*A finger of fudge*, LOL. We're meeting some people at CC Blooms at nine.'

'You're going out?' Willow asks sadly.

'Rowan!'

'What?'

I know what Mum's about to say, it's one of her stock phrases. 'You've been home all of two minutes and you're already escaping?'

I shrug. Of course I'm going out. I've been escaping since the day I was born. Syd gets it – FOMO. It's *real*. I feel it, a physical affliction, like a panicky skitter in my chest, that there are memories being made without me. There's a world out there, just *writhing* with neon potential, and it's not gonna leak

21

through the letterbox into this house, is it? In fact, it would actively swerve this place.

I've always felt this itchiness in my bones – the need to *get away*. I don't even know what it is I need to get away from, or what it is I'm looking for, but I know it's out there, somewhere, waiting for me.

I just don't know exactly what *it* is.

But if I don't go hunting, I'll never find out.

FERN

As Dad pulls into the driveway, a taxi pulls out, and I briefly make out the shape of my brother – his hair now bleached – in the backseat. I crane to look out of the back window. 'Was that Rowan?'

'Yes,' Dad says. 'He's meeting some friends in town.'

A jolt of pure red rage passes through me. 'He couldn't even wait to say hello to his twin sister? I haven't seen him since September!'

'He's here for the next week, Fern, you'll be sick of the sight of him by tomorrow.'

'You always defend him,' I say sorely, although he almost certainly has a point.

'Wow, is this your house?' Thom asks from the backseat.

I grin, and twist around to look at him. 'I told you I grew up in a haunted house.'

'Seriously?' Thom – for someone very sensible – can't cope with horror films or ghost stories.

'Oh aye. Haunted by middle-class guilt and bad wallpaper.'

'Oi!' Dad protests. 'Your nana picked that wallpaper, God rest her soul.'

'It's a mansion,' Thom says, still in awe. I've been to his mum's place in Hounslow – a perfectly pleasant three-bed

23

bungalow, which – with London prices – probably costs about the same as ours in Edinburgh.

'Come on in,' Dad says. It's weird – or maybe I've been away too long – but I swear he's looking older, like legitimately middle-aged now: grey in his beard and deep lines around his eyes. Does that mean I'm officially a grown-up? Or maybe it's just that he's lost a little weight. 'I hope you two are hungry. Your mum's prepared a veritable feast.'

And it's not like Willow's eating any of it, I think to myself, slightly dreading what we're about to walk into.

What we're walking into is a brick wall of central heating. I'd forgotten what it was like to a) have central heating and b) be able to afford it. My room in Finsbury Park is heated by a crap electric heater that smells of smoke, and my housemates and I are in a standoff over who can use them the least to keep the electric bill down.

Now the hideous train journey is out of the way, Christmas can begin. I mentally twist a valve in my head and let all the excitement flood to my brain. It is CHRISTMAS.

Good lord, my eyeballs feel like they're melting. I pull my scarf off as quickly as I can. There's a plethora of Christmas cards on the side table in the hall, and I wonder who still bothers with them. There's no way my parents actually have this many friends. The house smells strongly of scented candles. And also curry.

Mum swoops out of the kitchen. 'There she is!'

She embraces me tightly for a second before pulling back to survey me. I wonder what she won't like this time. Last year, my eyebrows were *a bit much*. 'You cut off your lovely hair?'

24

She reaches out for the end of my new-ish bob. 'I did.'

'It's very short,' she says. She clearly hates it. 'And this must be Thom! Gosh, you're a tall one, aren't you!' She hugs him too. She is a hugger. Thom obliges. He *is* tall – six four, and a little self-conscious about it. I hold my breath, praying Mum doesn't do or say anything racist: touching his hair or commenting on the colour of his skin. If she does, I will die. Neither of my parents are Trump-level evil, but they are both … *inadvertently incorrect* on occasion. A Christmas with a mixed-race boyfriend and a non-binary *and* mixed-race best friend is a potential minefield. Where are you from? But where are you *really* from?

Luckily the hug ends without drama. Thom says it's good to meet her, and offers up the bag of presents. 'I come bearing gifts …'

'Wonderful. Fern, why don't you put them around the tree while I plate up? I hope you're hungry! Dale, do you want to take their things up to the big guest room?'

I'm still sour over losing my bedroom to Willow the second I left for London. I note that the attic remains a shrine to the wonder that is Rowan, while I'm now relegated to 'guest'. Figures. As much as I whine, being the Kelly to Rowan's Beyoncé has its merits. He always craved the spotlight in a way I didn't, and you can't turn it off once it's on. I'll settle for the quiet life, and anyway, while he was pulling focus, I came up on the outside and overtook him academically. That was fun. I'll gladly take The Smart One.

I lead Thom off down the hall and through concertina doors to the drawing room. I gasp as we enter, my hand flying to my heart. 'Oh wow!' The tree is *so* beautiful this year. Mum's outdone herself. I didn't think I'd like the purple and gold theme, but it looks regal, majestic. There's a luxuriant matching garland over the fireplace with our stockings hanging beneath. I see Mum has also bought personalised ones for Thom and Syd too, which is adorable. I make a mental note to thank her later. A fire is dwindling in the hearth. There's nothing like an open fire, and I feel my shoulders drop about three inches away from my earlobes.

I am home. And the fact I can share it all with Thom this year makes it even more special.

'Your house is insane,' Thom says. 'I hope I don't spill.' He grins.

'I know. We were very privileged. *Are* very privileged,' I say, kneeling at the foot of the tree. I still remember when we were little, like before Willow was even born, going to Granny McClane's flat in Glasgow. We *hated* going, her estate was genuinely terrifying, but I now fully understand why Mum insisted on dragging us back to where she grew up. Because she wanted us to see how lucky we are. 'Do you want to pass me the presents?'

He joins me. 'We didn't really go in this hard for Christmas, even when we were little. My mum never really had that much money after Dad left.'

I give him a kiss because I know that's still a sore spot even after fifteen years. His father has a whole second family he scarcely knows. I start to arrange the packages amongst the ones which are already gathered around the base of the tree. I try not to look at the labels because I don't want any spoilers ahead of Christmas morning.

Willow figured out the Santa lie when she was about six – the danger of having two older siblings – so there was no pretence and our presents are stored around the tree well before Christmas Day. 'Christmas is like *our* thing, I think.' I start to reminisce. I nod at the baby grand piano waiting patiently in the bay window. 'We are Christmas People.'

Thom crinkles his nose. 'I don't get it.'

I look at him as if he were a lunatic. 'Are you kidding?'

He smiles. 'I mean I *like* Christmas, a normal amount, but you have been talking about this trip for months …'

I think about it for a second. What's the difference between Thom and me? And then the toffee penny drops. 'Ah, your mum goes to church.'

'What does that have to do with anything?'

I roll my eyes. 'Well, she believes in a magical sky man all year round, we only have Santa, so Christmas is singular.'

He laughs. 'OK, that actually makes total sense. In our house, Jesus's birthday comes first, Santa second.'

I have a special little hearth in my heart and I light it in December. I twiddle my favourite bauble on the tree – an old one of Nana's, shaped like a spindle. In fact, I move it to a more premium spot with a better eyeline.

I don't know how to explain this feeling to someone who's apparently DEAD INSIDE. I spin the bauble around so it catches the light from the fire. 'Christmas is magic. It is. Can't you feel it?' He shrugs again. 'It's hard to explain. I love everything about it: the build-up, the anticipation, opening the little windows on the advent calendar.'

27

'See that's what I don't like,' Thom says. 'Loads of foreplay, and then it's like … meh.'

I shake my head. 'No! Every year since we were little, Mum and Dad host a beautiful Christmas Eve party. Drinks and nibbles; the neighbours come over some years, or we had friends from school or whatever. Dad plays the piano and we sing carols. It's just … the best. It doesn't matter what squabbles we were having, we all called a truce for three days over Christmas. The most perfect happiness I've ever felt. Sorry, that probably sounds really disgusting. Like the end of a Hallmark movie or something.'

'It doesn't sound disgusting,' Thom says with a warm smile. He has such flawless teeth. He swears he never had braces, but they seem too good to be true. 'It sounds like how Christmas is supposed to be.'

True, I'm sad for people who can't have Christmas like we do. I don't mean moneywise – though of course we are super lucky in that respect – I mean people who just don't *go there* festively. How awful to not let the joy in. 'And Mum ramped up Christmaspalooza when Rowan and I left home. This is the only time of year when we're all together now so she's really stepped it up a notch –' I lower my voice – 'and last Christmas was a total write-off, so …'

Willow enters at precisely the worst moment. Fuck a Peking duck. How much of that did she hear?

'Hey!' I say, standing. I rush over to greet her, overcompensating for my gaffe. 'How are you?' Stupid question, but hey-ho. She looks like a walking corpse.

'I'm OK. I like your hair.' That's one-all on the bob.

'Thanks! Willow ... this is my boyfriend, Thom. Thom, this is my little sister.'

They greet each other and my heart sinks as I get a proper look at her. She doesn't look any better whatsoever. I live in hope that each time I come home there'll have been some sort of miracle. 'Mum says to go wash up.' There's a deer-in-the-headlights look in her saucer eyes. 'Dinner's ready.'

Oh good. I'm so psyched Thom gets to witness a McAllister mealtime. I wonder if the demon will be joining us tonight.

WILLOW

I hate this room. And not just because of the decorative teapots we inherited from Nana. They all watch me, sassy, one hand on hip.

Wish we were a family who have their supper on trays in front of the TV. But no. For me, eating is An Essential Part of my Routine. We have breakfast and lunch at the little table in the kitchen, and supper in the dining room every single day. No exceptions. It's fucked. If I was allowed to eat in private, I think I'd do better. Mum and Dad on either side; thumbscrews.

Dr Finch says I can't be trusted. I am a *liar*. I am *deceptive*. He didn't say either of those things to my face, but because I am deceptive, I read my notes in the clinic when no one was looking. My weight has dipped back down to six stone nine since I left the clinic. This means I am Clinically Underweight.

I do not feel underweight. I feel like a bin bag, full of garbage and bin juice.

I have to be in this room for thirty minutes. I must consume at least 800 calories in that time before I can leave.

I'm tired.

Everything in this room feels uncannily big, all the wrong

size, like that fucking *Cats* movie. The table, the chairs, all tower over me, and I'm a shrunken gremlin, too small for everything, the knife and fork too big for my body. Almost on autopilot, I slot myself under the table.

I'm *aware* of Thom. I don't want him to see the demon.

'When do Auntie Shelly and Kara arrive?' Fern asks, home five minutes and already trying to schedule us, no doubt. She's got this fucking obsession about Christmas. People think I'm unwell, but she sends out a Christmas list in August.

'Tomorrow,' Dad tells her, and I internally shriek. I don't see how it's *our* problem that Uncle Rabbie had an affair with his twenty-one-year-old student (he *was* a driving instructor) and fled Glasgow to avoid her raging father. In fairness to Uncle Rabbie, if I was married to Auntie Shelly, I'd flee too.

'We're not fancy,' Mum explains for Thom's benefit, 'everyone tuck in.' There are serving dishes full of curry, daal, rice and naan before us, like a yellow-brown swamp. If Thom wasn't here, there's no fucking way I'd be trusted to serve myself. They don't want to embarrass me. We had a summit this morning.

I must not ruin Christmas for everyone else.

Everyone else dives for the serving spoons. Everything here is veggie, but not vegan. I'm not allowed to be vegan because that was how I first massively started avoiding calories. No one questions I CAN'T EAT THAT if you're vegan. Great way to dodge food.

I am frozen. A tiny Alice drowning in curry. 'Willow …?' Mum prompts.

'Yes,' I mutter, and reach for the rice spoon. I scoop a

gelatinous blob on to my plate. Fuck, it's a lot, but I can't put any back. Not allowed.

'So, Thom, tell us about yourself,' Dad says, dribbling daal over his curry. I see fat globules float on the surface, ready to burrow their way into my flesh. 'You're on the same course as Fern?'

'I am, yes,' Thom says, ripping apart a naan bread with his hands like a fucking king or something. 'Politics and Economics. Pretty dry, to be fair.' He's really cute, I can see what Fern sees in him. Very tall, very sporty looking, *real* sporty, not gym and steroids sporty. I should have asked to see a picture. I guess he's all over her social media, but I'm not allowed Instagram because it is Detrimental To My Recovery.

'Any idea yet what you want to do with it?'

'God, Dad!' Fern interjects, popping an onion bhaji in her mouth as if it didn't contain 200 million calories. It's like watching a circus magician. How do they do that? Make it disappear so casually? What is the secret? 'Straight in with the big life questions!'

Dad feigns innocence. 'Just taking an interest …'

'I honestly don't know,' Thom says. 'Probably not politics *or* economics.'

Everyone laughs. Is that funny? 'And what about you, Fern?'

'Get some curry, please,' Mum says quietly on my left. She has a specific tone of voice for when she wants to tell me to eat that she seems to think is a dog-whistle only I can hear.

'I *am*,' I hiss.

'I'm not sure,' Fern says. Fern and Ro are good at pretending they don't hear Mum's instructions, but Thom won't be. In

32

this house it's really normal that I get fed like a toddler. Fern goes on. 'It'd be cool to do something in policy, but I want to enjoy second year before I give it any serious thought in third year.'

Dad talks with his mouth full. It's honestly disgusting. They all morph into clothed hogs in my mind, chomping and slobbering through their troughs of gruel. 'Well, you can always come shadow me up here for a while if you want.'

Fern sips her wine, again, like it was air. Red wine might as well be a glass of olive oil. 'I know, but I want to do things on merit, not nepotism, Dad.'

'You'd be the first person in politics to do so,' Mum says archly. Another knowing titter.

'I'm still in line for a first if I keep my grade average up,' Fern says triumphantly.

'She never stops,' Thom adds. 'She puts the rest of us to shame.'

'We're all very proud of her,' Dad says, squeezing her hand over the table. Aye, Fern was on the front page of the *Scotsman* with some other pretty Finnians girls, jumping for joy on the day she got her Highers results. Cringe. It's framed in the drawing room. RIP my grades. I don't imagine I'll be on any front pages next August, not unless I die.

'Have a bit more, please, Willow,' Mum says, eyeing my plate.

My head whips around, the ends of my hair trailing into my food. I slam my fork down. '*I AM.*'

Outside voice. Emergency brakes on the chatter around the table.

A silent moment, and then everyone carries on as if it didn't happen.

It would be funny if it weren't.

Ah shit, the demon came out.

ROWAN

I wriggle my way to the front of the bar. Holy fuck, it's like Pride weekend in here tonight – guess everyone wants their pre-Christmas reunion. Billy – full-time bar manager, occasional drag queen, Mary Queen of Bottoms – screams when he sees me. 'Look what the fuckin' cat dragged in! Come 'ere ye rancid who-ure!'

I lean over the bar and kiss him on the mouth. 'You still here, babes?'

He rolls his eyes. 'Uh, you know me, they'll carry me out in a bag. Preferably a bag of M-Cat. You're looking well, darlin'.'

I thank him and order two double vodka Red Bulls. If he doesn't charge us for singles and soda, I'll curse him in my dark prayers. Syd grabs me. They are, I must admit, looking very sexy in a slouchy vest and biker boots. 'Now we're out the house, can we please discuss your Tory father?'

'I'd rather not!'

'You never said, man!'

I blink. 'Of course I fucking didn't, I want people to like me!' I exclaim before adding sincerely, 'No, I really do, it's like a pathological need.'

Syd laughs, but does look a little miffed. With hindsight, maybe I should have said something. 'I can't believe I'm spending Christmas behind enemy lines.' Syd is a devout socialist. As am I, but they have the T-shirt.

I sigh. 'OK, I'll deny saying this under torture, but he's not *that* bad.' They open their mouth to argue but I plough on, shouting over the pounding music. 'No, really, he's not actually evil. I mean it! He's pro-gay, pro-trans, pro-abortion, pro-women, he voted for free school meals … to be honest I think he's like a default Tory because his parents were. I figure with him there, there's at least a drop of humanity at the table.'

Syd looks far from convinced. 'Whatever helps you sleep at night, bro.'

Sometimes, I genuinely fret that I might have inherited a strain of genetic conservatism from my father. That one day down the line, a couple of BAFTAs in, I'll suddenly have money in the bank, and start to rabidly defend my wealth at the expense of all liberal altruism. No. I'd sooner throw myself into a vat of bubbling acid.

Billy returns with the drinks and, I'm pleased to say, charges us for singles. He's a doll and won't get cursed, at least not tonight. 'Come on, Karl Marx,' I yell at Syd, 'it's Christmas! Let's get shitfaced.'

Drinks aloft, we weave towards the sticky old dancefloor at the back. So many of the same old faces. *Bet you thought you'd seen the last of me, bitch.* Some of the glow-ups are impressive, guys my age growing into their man bodies nicely, while some of the former alphas from my sixth form days have started to lose their appeal. I see one guy I used to basically stalk around both Edinburgh and the internet, only now clearly he's calling the steroid hotline and looks like a freshly shaved testicle.

On the gay scene, youth is a cryptocurrency that depletes with age, and I'm fucking nineteen. I have so much of this left. I'm so glad I got my shit together and came out when I was an embryo. I appreciate my baptism of fire may have startled my parents, but even they must understand launching myself on to the scene with literal gay abandon is preferable to sitting at home and self-harming to My Chemical Romance.

I fully intend to milk my youth, and at least one of the men in this room. Best get started. You know what we need? Shots. I feel slightly too coherent to fully appreciate Carly Rae Jeppo's version of 'Last Christmas'. I see they have one called a Christmas Pudding – black sambuca with Bailey's on top.

Dance, drink, shots, rinse and repeat.

It doesn't matter what the music is, I lose my shit at the start of every new song – all of them remind me of somewhere, or someone, or something and they're all worth a scream.

And then Mariah comes on and my spine almost snaps with joy. Musical orgasm.

Syd finds some nice heteroflexible girl in the smoking area – here with her gay friends, but bored of being a sidekick. It is a known fact that gay men do lose interest in their female friends once the clock strikes twelve and the horn kicks in. When you've only got two hours left to find someone to take you home, it's every man for himself.

Syd, I am confident, will have their fingers in her knickers before long. The next best song EVER comes on and I drag them both back on to the dancefloor, bulldozing half the room.

My clothes stick to my back with sweat, and I'm covered in glitter, and someone spilled beer down my front, and I don't care, because I spot my prey across the dancefloor. He's not a dancer, shifting uncomfortably and clutching a beer like a talisman among his more coordinated pals. Aww, he's shy! He's quite the tattie scone: Middle Eastern, beard, lumberjack shirt. A little older than me, maybe, but not much.

And he's looking.

He looks away.

And then looks back.

I ping like a microwave.

Girl, it's *on*.

FERN

The problem with old houses is the distinct lack of bathrooms. I have a few flimsy memories of when we inherited this house. I was four or five, and it was a relic – there were actual servants' quarters. In the end, it was only my grandmother – long widowed – rattling around this huge house alone, and many of the rooms were filled with the mad stuff she hoarded: candles, tinned pears in syrup, hundreds of toilet rolls. On reflection, if she was preparing for the plague, she had it about right.

Now, after years of renovations, only the master bedroom (which I have recently become aware is a racist term) and Rowan's attic room have en suites, which means we're stuck sharing the big, family bathroom with four other people all week. Maybe I should draw up a rota in the morning to avoid any drama before it arises.

I finish my night-time ablutions. I take skincare very seriously because I figure prevention is better than cure when it comes to ageing. Skincare tutorials are my guilty pleasure. Each night, I apply serum, vitamin C and enriching collagen night cream to my face. I mean, this does mean I look quite slimy of an evening, but Thom doesn't seem to mind.

I massage my skin in the mirror. It's much better than the one back in my London flat, with a light overhead so I can really examine my pores. I prod my nose. It's *prominent*. I sometimes wish I had a cute Barbie button nose, but on other days I think my existing schnozz is quite regal somehow. I push my hair back off my face. I would be a good prime minister. I look like someone who'd be taken seriously.

I am aware my aspirations border on megalomaniacal, but I look at the stale crusts in charge – my father included if I'm honest – and think I couldn't possibly do a worse job. The bar is so low, it's a broom handle on the floor.

I flick off the light and potter back down the landing, washbag in hand. It's like being back in halls. We're in what used to be Willow's room, but is now, informally, Guest Room 1. When Willow relocated to my old room, they took the opportunity to create what's basically a hotel room: it's all very beige and inoffensive. There's a bowl with pebbles on the chest of drawers.

It feels quite grown-up – certainly much nicer than either of our student rooms. There's a king-size bed in any case, and Thom is already tucked in for the night. This is our second trip away together. We went with some of the guys on his rugby team to Newquay over the summer. That got a little messier than I liked.

'Hey there,' he says.

'I'm done,' I say, dumping my washbag and joining him. It's *Scotland* so I've brought my thickest pyjamas. I slide under the duvet, and snuggle up against him. Between the mulled wine we had after dinner, and the long train journey, I'm dead. It's after midnight and there's still no sign of Rowan. 'I'm so annoyed at my brother,' I tell Thom.

40

'Why?'

'Because I was really looking forward to seeing him. I wanted you to finally meet him too. It's a twin thing. In my head, he's important. In his head, I guess I'm an ex-wombmate.'

Thom kisses my forehead. 'I'm sure that's not true. You said he likes to party. That's all. You'll see him tomorrow, and the next day, and the day after that ...'

'I know.' I lie back, careful not to get my gooey face all over the crisp white pillows. 'It's just so Rowan. My feelings won't have even entered his head. I used to do everything for him, you know. When we were little, I reached all the milestones first: walking, talking, potty training. At one point they wondered if he had special needs or something, but no, he was just a lazy asshole and had a genetic servant.' Thom laughs. 'He suits himself, all day, every day. That's the way it goes with us: I give and he takes.'

'I can't wait to meet him.' He nestles closer. 'But, right now, I don't want to talk about your brother ...'

He runs a hand up my thigh towards my crotch and I bat it away. 'Thom!'

'What?' He kisses my neck.

I wriggle away. 'For one thing, I'm exhausted, and two – my sister is on the other side of that wall!' I point to the space above the sleigh bed.

Thom recoils. 'So no sex for six days? I didn't know the terms and conditions when I signed up for this trip ...'

He tries again, but I wriggle free. 'Thom!'

'Willow is *seventeen*, I think she knows about the birds and bees ...'

'I do *not* need my baby sister to hear us rutting. Uh, boak.'

Thom rolls his eyes and rolls off me. He instead reaches for his phone and starts a-scrolling. He's a fan of perplexing memes. 'How intense was dinner?' he says after a second, now clear of my family.

'Yep. We play that game three times a day.' I don't want to make Willow's disease about me, but living with someone living with an eating disorder is really hard. And no one ever really talks about that. Obviously it's worse for her, but her disease spread through the walls of the house like a cancer. We pretend it doesn't, out of politeness, but it affects us all. 'This sounds so cruel, and I'm probably a total bitch for saying this, but I was so glad when I left home. I was starting to dread meals.'

'God, I can see why.'

It was oddly contagious. Psychosomatic. I started to feel a little sick before meals. It was that game – Buckaroo. Anything could set her off. Dad might as well have served plates of broken glass for all the tiptoeing we had to do. 'They would never, ever admit this, but I think Mum and Dad were happy when they found her a place in the clinic ... it gave them a break for a few months. They could get through beans on toast without the Third World War breaking out.'

Last Christmas was a pale imitation. With Ro in France and Willow in the clinic, Dad had vetoed Christmas dinner at home and we ate at a fancy hotel out in the country. It was nice, but it wasn't *Christmas*.

'Do you think all that pressure makes her worse? Like everyone watching her eat and shit?'

42

A good question. 'I don't know. But left to her own devices, she'd starve to death.'

He falls silent. 'Fuck.'

'Uh-huh.'

'OK, well that killed the mood,' he says ruefully.

I give him a peck on the lips. 'We'll find a quiet moment, I promise.' We snuggle together for warmth and I feel his boner poking into my butt cheek. I pretend to ignore it.

I talked about this with Jessica a couple of weeks ago: her medical textbooks say it's totally normal for girls to have a lower sex drive than boys because of testosterone. They have more of it – usually – and it makes them horny all the time. It's not that I don't fancy Thom, because I do, he's gorgeous. When we first got together we had a lot more, but now I'm happy with once or twice a week. That's to be expected, right? It's not like I'm frantically fiddling with myself between helpings either. I'm getting enough. But I worry he's not. And after what happened last year, I of course worry about him looking elsewhere.

What else can I do? We've been doing it for over a year on-and-off, it's always lovely, but ... well, I don't know. I've jumped through the obvious hoops: sexy selfies; Anne Summers outfits; pleasuring myself and making him watch. And then ... when we went on the break ... I guess I lost all my confidence.

I know I shouldn't compare Thom to an ex, but how can I not? When I was with Hamish, he never needed inspiration. He very much took the lead. Is there a word for someone who likes to be in charge everywhere *except* the bedroom? These

43

days, I'm too tired to be in charge, for one thing, and for another it's so much more of a process for girls than it is boys. All he has to do is get hard; I have to make sure I'm smooth, and shaved, and fresh, and not on my period. I literally run a feminist bookclub, so I know I don't need to do any of those things for *him*. I do them for *me*. It's almost like the sex-prep is me switching on the engine to get it warmed up.

But, I also know … he is a boy with boyly needs. He never pressures me or anything – never – but I feel like if I don't attend to his horny needs, he might leave me for someone who will. I know that sounds like something from a cult, or the fifties, but I can't help it. The thought of losing him terrifies me.

It's odd. Maybe it's because the way we met was so fairy-tale; it's almost like sex wasn't how it got started. He was Gorgeous Monday Coffee Guy. I'd seen him in lectures of course; Introduction to Macroeconomics first thing on a Monday. Harsh. I don't need a degree in economics to know I don't have a bunch of money to be spending on takeaway coffees, but the early start felt like it warranted it. So, before the lecture, I'd go to the coffee shop in Gower Street Waterstones and get an Americano. And he was there; so tall, so handsome. Every Monday.

In films, they call it a 'meet-cute', the moment where the romantic leads come together. In *Love, Actually* it's where the prime minister first meets the tea lady. Over the first semester, our flirtation started with glances; built up to brief *hello*s; and then full discussions about the lecturer's minging armpit stains. By the time we were having conversations,

I'd already decided Thom was The One. It wasn't like with Hamish where we started out drunkenly necking at shit house parties. It was pure. It was the DREAM; the ideal; the perfect story. Sex is many things, but I'm not sure it's pure.

'I love you,' he mutters into my ear before he rolls onto his side.

'I love you too,' I say, because I do. I am SO LUCKY to have him.

CHRISTMAS EVE EVE

ROWAN

The room smells weird, and it's toasty warm. This is not my room. And then I remember that I'm not in Bristol. The second thing I remember is that I'm not alone.

The worst moment, by far, in any hangover is the OH FUCK WHAT HAVE I DONE NOW moment.

I groan and roll over to face him. I remember him being really cute, but sometimes my eyes tell porkies after a few drinks. Oh, no, he is cute! Phew! Well done, me. He looks adorable, armpit exposed, hand resting over his head on the pillow. He has a fuzzy chest and tummy. And his name is Amir, so I wasn't *that* shit-faced if I can remember the minutiae.

I quite want to lick his armpit, but I'll not. In fact, I need to smuggle him out. I honestly don't know what's worse: the potential of Mum's fury at bringing a lad home, or her being Cool Mom and offering him breakfast and shit. I'm not quite sure how she'll react. I never really brought boys home – mainly because I was like fifteen or thereabouts when I started meeting guys online so a lot of them were technically nonces. Sure, I *told* them I was seventeen or eighteen, but not once was I asked for ID, so I don't really see how that's my fault.

She'd probably *pretend* to be fine but then give me a lecture later when my hangover really kicks in. The older I get, the worse they get. I'm sure they never used to be this vicious. Vodka makes my jobbies green, I swear. I reach for my phone – which I did not lose last night, wonderful news – and check the time. It's almost eight-thirty. Fuck, they will definitely be up.

I do my best Kylie Jenner. 'Riiiiise and shiiiiine …' I sing, wary of my breath which smells like cat shite. He doesn't stir, so I give him a shake. He'd better not be dead.

Although that would make for a funny story in like a year or so.

Luckily he stirs, also looking a bit confused re his whereabouts. Why didn't I kick him out last night? I remember it being fun, though. It was funny too, both of us giggling like naughty schoolboys as we tried not to make any noise. I love that PrEP has made random hook-ups less guilt-ridden. I don't regret the sex one bit; I regret not giving him a moist towelette and sending him on his merry way. 'Morning, sleepyhead,' I say.

'Hey,' he croaks.

'You OK?'

'Aye,' he says, rubbing his face. 'What time is it?'

'Almost half-eight.' It's so weird having a guy in my high-school bedroom. I wonder what he makes of the *Monster High* doll collection lining the windowsill over the bed, or the framed Princess Diana shrine on the dresser, surrounded by candles.

'Och, hell. I feel like pure shite.'

'Right there with you, buddy.' I run my hand over his chest. He works out, clearly. I am obsessed with his body. If we were back home, I'd be well up for Round Three, but not today, Satan. 'Do you wanna shower before you head out?'

He laughs. 'OK, I get the hint. Gimme a sec.'

'Well, it's that or you can come and meet my entire family …?'

He sits bolt upright. Yep, that ought to do it.

FERN

Well, of course the lock on the family bathroom isn't working. That would be just too easy, wouldn't it? Thom said he couldn't do his morning poo without someone guarding the door, so I'm presently on sentry duty while my boyfriend takes a shit and a shower.

Must be love.

At the end of the corridor, I see a flash of platinum hair poke around the top of the stairs to the third floor before it ducks out of sight like a timid squirrel. Did I imagine that?

'Rowan?' I say, going to investigate. 'Is that you?' I hear light footsteps scurry back up to the attic. 'Rowan, what the hell are you doing?' I call after him. What has he done this time?

A moment of silence, and then a hushed voice says, 'Will you please stop shouting?' My twin brother creeps on to the landing in sweatpants and a T-shirt. 'Is it just you?'

'Yes, it's just me. Are you on crack or something?' I wouldn't put it past him.

He gives me a hug and our odd yin and yang come together for the first time in months. He will always be my dark half; the pepper to my salt; the spice to my sugar. I hold him and, for a second, feel that bit more whole. I never have and never will have a connection like this with anyone else.

It's, as Rowan would say, *witchy*.

'I like your hair,' he says in my ear.

'I like yours too. Why are you being weird?'

By way of a response, he lets go, and arches his back to look up the stairs towards his room. 'Coast's clear …'

A handsome Arab-looking guy skulks down the stairs like a comedy burglar. I follow Syd on Instagram, so know this is not them. 'Are you for real?' I aim that directly at Rowan.

Rowan, for a certified wrong-un, has the most angelic face. 'What? Early Christmas present to myself. Are Mum and Dad up?'

'Well, someone's in the kitchen, and it's not going to be Willow, is it?'

He turns to his new friend. 'OK, that means we need to be quiet …'

Behind us, the bathroom door opens and Thom emerges, just a towel around his waist. God, this is turning into French farce and we've been home for less than twenty-four hours. Thom freezes, rabbit-in-the-headlights style, and Rowan is no doubt delighted at seeing a half-naked man – his eyes almost pop out of his head. 'Rowan, this is my boyfriend, Thom. He normally wears more clothes than this.'

They're both tongue-tied. Hardly an ideal first meeting. 'Um … hi,' Rowan says, clearing his throat. 'This is … Amir, was it?'

Amir offers a shy wave.

Thom says nothing, gripping his towel for dear life.

Amir smiles and I think he might be quite taken with Thom too. Who wouldn't be? I know he's way out of my

53

league and fear for the day Thom figures it out.

'Come on, loverboy, let's get you out of here,' Rowan says, dragging Amir towards the stairs. 'Nice to meet you, Thom.'

'Um, yeah,' Thom says, mortified. Oh, bless him.

'Come on, let's get you some clothes before someone else sees your nips.' I poke his chest and hustle him towards our bedroom.

We'll laugh about this later, Rowan and I. I will say this for my brother, I don't know anyone else like him and I wouldn't change him for the world. I feel that little glow in my tummy. It's not just a *day*. Christmas is in foods, and songs, and places, and more than any of those things, it's in people. *Now* it's starting to feel like Christmas.

ROWAN

This can't be happening. It just cannot. It can't. It's too fucking stupid.

I hustle Amir out of the front door, literally pushing him, because that encounter on the landing has well and truly messed with my head. He lingers on the threshold. What's he waiting for? It's Baltic out here. 'Great sex!' I say. 'Thanks! Bye now! Have a nice Christmas!'

'I'm Muslim,' he says.

I shrug. 'OK ... have a nice life?' I need him gone right now before my head explodes all over the hallway.

He grins. OK, he is really exceptionally hot, I chose well. He should consider a career in porn (if he hasn't already). 'Is that it?' he asks quizzically.

'Is what it?'

'Can I get your number?'

'Oh!' I say. 'I'm finding it hard to focus. *Was that really ...?* A headache feels like it's trying to poke my right eye out of my skull. I feel re-drunk. Maybe I hallucinated?

Focus, Rowan. On the one hand, good sex with a competent top is not as easy to find as people like to think, so maybe I am throwing the baby out with the spunky tissues, but on the other ... I really do need to address what just happened upstairs.

'That's cute, but I'm travelling four hundred miles in a few days.'

'Maybe next time you're home ... or later this week?'

Urgh, did I promise him something when I was drunk? There's something very cursed about men. If *I* was acting all needy, he'd have left an Amir-shaped hole in the wall on his way out. If I act aloof, they rub up against me like I'm catnip. What is the cure for men, please? 'I ... um ... if it's meant to be ... let's leave it up to the Fates. On Grindr.'

He gets the hint. He smiles, a little disappointed perhaps. 'Last night was really fun.' He gives me a slow kiss on the lips. 'Take care, Rowan,' he says, finally leaving.

I close the door and turn to see Mum hovering in the kitchen doorway, the Ghost of Slut-Shaming Present. 'Who's your new friend? Is he not staying?'

'Don't be tacky, Mother, you know exactly what that was.'

She looks a little wounded. I haven't got time for this ... I need to speak to Syd right this second. 'I'm not running a hotel, Rowan.'

I wince. 'Mum, it was here or in a toilet cubicle, which would you rather?'

I dart for the stairs before she can launch into the full lecture. I creep past Fern's room, hearing dull voices within. I ignore them, heading straight to Syd's room – in reality, the sofa-bed in Mum's 'library'. I don't even knock, I just barge straight in. I strongly feel Syd is going to want to hear this. I step over their discarded clothes and throw myself down at the side of the bed. 'Syd! Wake up!'

They groan and pull a pillow over their head. 'Fuck off, Ro.'

'Wake up. Wake up right now! This won't wait!' I pull the pillow off.

They make a familiar chewing noise, suggesting the dry-mouth is real. 'What the fuck, Ro? I'm dying. How much Molly did we do?'

'Not nearly enough, are you listening?'

They open bleary eyes and squint at me. Ooh, they do look *rough*. 'What is it, Rowan? This better be good, my mouth feels like sandpaper.'

I mean, maybe I should go back and check, because I just don't understand how this is happening.

Syd sits up, now looking a little concerned.

'Ro? You good?'

'Oh, it's good! OK, it's not *good*, but it's huge,' I tell them. 'You're not gonna believe this …' My head is reeling. You know when you think you must still be asleep? God, maybe this is all a fucked-up, MDMA-induced dream; a rogue dollop of serotonin causing me to see things that aren't real.

'What?'

'So I just met Fern's boyfriend …'

Syd flops back down. 'So what? Can this wait?'

I grab hold of their arm and roll them over. 'Syd … it's *him*.'

'What? Who?'

Why are they being so dense? The only HIM that ever mattered. 'Him! The boy! The boy from France!' I sigh. 'Do we need to do a fucking flashback?'

LAST CHRISTMAS

ROWAN

There are worse places I could be, I suppose. Home, or an anorexia clinic, to name but two. Les Monts Blanc is by no means the most bouji resort in Courchevel, but I prefer that. I've been in some of the five-star hotels and it's wall-to-wall wankers. Les Monts Blanc is far more bijoux, and at least vaguely affordable to mortals who might have a passing interest in skiing as well as posing. Downside: I have to dress like an extra from *Peaky Blinders* – a burgundy waistcoat and matching bowtie. Chim-chiminey, cor blimey, Mary Poppins.

The light outside the windows is blindingly white; sun on snow. The hotel lounge is quiet, and won't get busy until après ski. I've got The Carpenters Christmas album on repeat because never before has a woman singing about Christmas sounded so fucking sad. Today is a tad different however, because it's not every day you have an actual A-lister in the bar.

I say that, but we did have Liz Hurley last week.

This is better, though, because he's hot. Liz Hurley is undeniably hot, but I don't want to shag her, you know what I mean.

I can't actually remember his name because he is a footballer and I use that part of my brain to remember the forgotten drag queens eliminated first from *Drag Race*. Like, I need that mental space for Alisa Summers and Soju. I do recognise this guy, though, because he was all over the news for his charity work. Like he raised money for kids in poverty or something? Anyway, it's *him* and he's broken his leg.

There's always one, and it's always early in the stay. Bad ski juju. I decide to take pity on him because he's exceptionally cute, very famous, and most importantly, he might give me the biggest tip of my life. 'Hi,' I say, approaching the sofa he's taken near the fireplace. 'Can I get you something, sir?'

He looks up and blinks, almost like he thinks he's hallucinating. 'You're English!' he says.

'Scottish, how dare you, but yes, I speak much better English than I do French, look at it that way.' I nod at the cast on his ankle, currently elevated on to the coffee table. 'Broken?'

'Yep.'

'Sorry 'bout that, sweetheart. I just wanted to say congratulations on the campaign thing.'

He squints up at me through almost indecently thick lashes. 'Sorry, what?'

'Your charity work. Like, totally impressive. Feed the kids! I mean, it's a tragic state of affairs when a footballer has to remind the politicians that children in one of the richest nations in the world are starving but ...'

'I think you've got the wrong person ...'

Oh, you get this a lot with celebrities. They're all incognito. Like, chill hun, I'm not going to pap you for the Sidebar of Shame. 'Oh aye. I get you ...' I give him a conspiratorial wink.

'Do you think I'm Marcus Rashford?' he asks with a broad smile. Oof. I feel the smile.

This could be a test. 'If that's your name I do …?'

He laughs. 'I'm not him. Man, I wish. My name's Tom. I don't even play football, I play rugby.'

Well, that's awkward. 'Are you for real?'

'I swear.'

'Oh shit, that's so racist. I swear to god I don't think all Black people look the same.' I can feel *some of my best friends are black* on the tip of my tongue. Oh god, no.

Luckily, the guy – Tom – laughs it off. 'No, it's fine, I hear it a lot! A lot a lot. It's a huge compliment, but I don't really see it. Also, not to brag, but he's only five-eleven.'

It's hard to tell how tall he is half reclining on the sofa, but he's very tall. I'm a little disappointed he's not famous, I'd have considered going back on Insta temporarily for a selfie. I'm now also doubting if the very glam brunette was Liz Hurley.

Regardless of whether he's Marcus Whatever, he's definitely hot. I wonder if I stand more of a chance with a mere mortal?

Tom keeps talking. 'I think it'd be front-page news if Marcus Rashford broke his leg, don't you?'

He has a point. And a sense of humour, to boot. Hardly fair for someone so cute to be witty too. 'First day here?'

'Yep. Figures. Sod's law.'

'You ski before?' I mean we're both trapped here all day, so it can't hurt to make polite conversation, can it? I perch on the sofa opposite him. My boss, Delphine, is a proper twat, but she's downstairs in the restaurant, flirting with the chef who is very much not her husband.

'Yes! Loads! That's the irony. I'm actually good, I swear.'

He's very cute. *Straight though*, I think, reeling myself back in. 'I believe you, thousands wouldn't.' I offer what I hope is my most beguiling smile. 'Nah, I see it all the time. It doesn't matter how experienced they are, there's always one poor bastard sat here keeping me company all afternoon.'

'I can't believe I don't get to ski.'

'I'm deeply grateful for your generous sacrifice. I might let you help me chop the fruit if you play your cards right …' I say somewhat suggestively. Straight guys LOVE it when gay guys flirt with them. It's a harmless freebie for all involved. They get their ego stroked and I get … well, fuck all actually. 'What you drinking, babes? It's on the house.'

He asks for an oat vanilla latte (do I fucking look like a Starbucks?), so I go make him one and give him a piece of (probably quite stale) biscotti as a bonus. I also select for him some tawdry paperbacks that have been left behind on the wee bookcase. I've flicked through them all on quiet days and they fall into three categories: thrillers where rich white ladies think their husbands are murderers; mildly racist SAS versus the Taliban stories; and what I call "Wallpaper Historicals" because they are set at some point in the past, and have covers that look like flock wallpaper. Oh, and it doesn't matter how many times I chuck *Philosopher's Stone* into the fireplace, another copy appears on the shelf like literary herpes.

I take him one of each genre. 'Here you go,' I tell him. 'Something to pass the time.'

He has a computer game device thing, but accepts the books nonetheless. He reaches over, with some difficulty, for his biscuit. 'How'd a Scot end up working here, then?'

Ladies and gents, we have a talker. Fine. I sit back down.

This is *not* flirting, it's honestly a mercy mission. Who was it who said bartenders are the cheapest therapists in the world? Or did I invent that? Again I am reminded that flirting with straight boys is a spectacular waste of time. I want the entirety of S5 back, Hamish Bell.

I'm hardly going to tell him the truth am I? *Hi, random, stranger! My sister is wasting away in a mental health facility and I can't bring myself to watch, so I booked the first flight off Brexit Island.*

'I'm in witness protection,' I lie. 'Don't tell anyone, but I'm Marcus Rashford.'

He laughs loudly this time and I soak up the applause. I learned very young that there's a currency in making people laugh. I may well have been gay as the day is long, but at least I was funny. I added value.

'Will you get some turkey here?'

'I certainly hope some stuffing if nothing else …'

He laughs again. 'Can I ask a personal question? Are you …?'

'Gay? What was the first clue?' Yes. After all these years, it is tiresome, having to turn myself into a comedy routine so straight men can stomach me, but it's easier. You sort of castrate yourself into the fey eunuch clown so they don't get scared you're gonna rape them or something. Poor Tom; it's not his fault he's been told being gay is a fate worse than straight. Truth is, it's a fucking *gift*; once you let go of the balls and chains of masculinity, you can do literally whatever you want.

'I dunno. You can't always tell,' Tom says. 'Gibbo – one of the guys I'm here with. He's straight – so he says – but he's camp as ...' He nods at the monster Christmas tree at the foot at the stairs.

'I'd be interested to meet this Gibbo character and maybe we'll put that to the test ...' I toss my tea towel over my shoulder and prepare to sashay away on a saucy cliffhanger.

'Nah, I think you're more my type to be honest,' Tom says, looking me dead in the eye, and I swear I almost gasp like a Disney princess. Don't get me wrong, Grindr is POPPING OFF out here with guys away from their girlfriends and wives, but lo, my gaydar has failed me here today. I actually look around for witnesses to make sure I didn't imagine that.

'I ... what?' I ask, not quite daring to believe what I *think* I just heard.

He smiles, and honestly my throat is the driest it's ever been. He looks up at me, bashful. 'I'm ... um ... I guess I'm bi or something.' He doesn't look too sure of that, and lowers his voice, but I'm shook to hear the word 'bi'. It's been a while. It feels quaintly old money in the current economy of queer, fluid pansexuality.

I hope I don't look shocked. I like to think I'm unshockable. 'You don't hear a lot of bi these days. I like it, it's retro.'

'Well ...' he says with a big sigh, 'it feels weird in my mouth too.'

I settle in because I'm not going back to the bar now. I lower my voice. 'I'm not the first person you've told ...?'

'Oh, no. I told my ex-girlfriend actually. And that's why she's an ex.'

'Well, she sounds like a cunt.'

He laughs before regrouping with a hint of melancholy.

66

'Nah. It's for the best. I've met up with a couple of guys on Grindr since, nothing serious, but I'm not gonna pretend it's not happening when it is.'

I'm oddly jealous of those faceless Grindr hook-ups. Like, I wish he was fresh snow and I was the first on the slopes.

Today just got a million times more interesting. He goes on, 'I like girls, I like guys.' He leans in and lowers his voice further. 'Trans girls ... hot. I even told my mum a few months back, well not that last bit. I just couldn't be fucked with it becoming like a big secret or something, you know what I mean?'

'I never really *did* secret,' I muse. 'When I was six, I had a stuffed Hulk toy and told everyone he was my boyfriend.'

'The Hulk? Is that your type?' He grins.

'Yeah! Green. Anger management issues. Hot.' We laugh together, and it feels like a date, which I have to remind myself it's not, because *I wish*. This guy is leagues out of my league. I'm self-aware enough to know I have internalised some homophobia regarding my own campness, but – in this instance – I'm literally just using my eyes. We don't *match*. If he's Disney Channel, I'm Pornhub.

Although he did say I was his type so ...

The door swings open and I almost leap behind the bar like a cat. It takes me a second to realise Delphine wouldn't be coming into the lounge through the door. Instead it's a stocky ginger guy with a nose ring who *would* be much more my usual type. 'Simper! You OK?'

Tom stiffens on the sofa, a little caught out. I'm guessing this guy *isn't* one of the people who knows he's bi. 'What you doing?'

His friend flumps on to the sofa too, padded out in ski gear.

'Aw, I felt bad, man, and the others wanted to do the Red Run, which I am not fucking with after what happened to you yesterday.'

'Fair enough … Zach, this is …'

'Rowan,' I say at the exact same time as there's an enormous crash downstairs in the kitchens, reminding me where I am and who my boss is. 'I better get back to work,' I say breezily. 'I was just keeping your friend company.'

'Thanks, dude! Hey, do you know where the best place to go tonight is that doesn't cost a million quid per beer?'

I nod. 'La Douche Folie is a must in the afternoon, and it's shots night at Pub Le Ski Lodge tonight. Have fun.' I turn back to the bar.

'Thanks,' Tom says. 'I'll catch you later, man.'

Sure. That was fun for a minute.

It's funny, though, as soon as my back is turned, I can't help wondering if I'd imagined a little bit of one of those science metaphors: chemistry, magnetism, the *spark*.

I'm on a split shift so I don't even think about him because I'm too busy. The idea is that seasonal staff have a couple of hours in the afternoon to ski, but I'm honestly too knackered. I have a wank and a nap in my room and then return to the bar for round two.

The restaurant here is *fine* but Courchevel is full of Michelin-star places so people tend to meet here for cocktail hour and then piss off elsewhere to eat. The gag is I can't make cocktails FOR SHIT. Babe, I literally make it up as I go. I learned early on that if you set fire to a bit of citrus peel, the basics think it's pure witchcraft.

For whatever reason, the bar is carnage tonight. There's a very specific noise that posh people make when they're drunk, sort of like braying donkeys. Tonight, they've turned their attention to Christmas songs. I do not, and I cannot stress this enough, wish it could be Christmas every day.

But I smile and nod because I can live off the tips alone for the next year. Make it rain, you dicks. Class is a funny old beast. Like, objectively, I understand I am privileged. My dad is a Tory MP for fuck's sake, and I grew up in a massive house surrounded by lovely things. BUT, and here's the key difference, my mum grew up in a skanky council flat in Glasgow and somehow *became* middle class. Even though she has plenty of money, she lives frugally – and hammered into us the value of money – because she has no intention of going back.

The people in this resort ... you'd have to tumble down many, many branches of the family tree to find a pauper. And they all have, dare I say it, the tell-tale gums of the aristocracy.

They launch into 'Fairytale of New York' and I brace myself for the delirious, foaming delight of straight people screaming CHEAP LOUSY FAGGOT at the top of their lungs. Can't get enough of that.

Only then the crowd parts, like Moses with ... whatever sea Moses parted, to allow a man on crutches to the bar. It's a cliche, for sure, but I do feel a funny skip in my chest when I spot him. He catches my eye and gives me a nod. He's a vision in plaid and denim, a mirage in this hideously dry room. I don't see anyone but him.

He came back.

'You came back,' I shout over the din.

'I did,' Tom says.

But *why* did he return? My mind starts whirring. I want to believe it's for me, but maybe he's just waiting to meet someone else or … I don't want to get my hopes up.

Does he have any idea how sexy he is? He can't because knowing you're sexy automatically reduces your sexiness by about five per cent, and he might be the full hundred.

I check there's no one waiting to be served. 'And why's that?'

He smiles again. 'I wondered if you'd be here.'

Oh wow. OK. My massive balloon heart. 'Well … here I am.'

'Is it cool if I hang?'

I don't want to appear too keen, but fuck it. 'It definitely is.'

My night, as they say, has taken a TURN.

There follows ninety minutes of exquisite foreplay. I keep catching his eye across the bar as I flit backwards and forwards, fixing drinks for idiots. I feel his eyes on me when my back is turned. I like it.

When one a.m. comes, the bar empties out. We talk as I clean the bar down; load the glasses; wipe the tables and put the chairs up. The cleaners will take care of the rest in the morning. As I finish up, he takes over the music. I didn't have him down as a Motown fan, but he selects Marvin Gaye, Stevie Wonder and The Supremes.

'This is retro,' I say, stowing the spray and blue roll behind the bar.

'It's what I grew up on,' he tells me. 'It's what my mum likes.'

'Your mum has good taste,' I say, ducking underneath the bar.

He looks at me a moment longer than normal. 'Can I kiss you now, please? It's been hours.'

Well, as it's Christmas. I lean over the bar and it's every bit as good as I'd hoped.

We kiss in the lift, all the way to my tiny single room upstairs. Staff get rooms in the eaves of the lodge, and we certainly don't get a cleaner. I quickly kick a week's worth of dirty laundry under the bed before I flick on the reading lamp next to my bed. 'Come in,' I tell him.

'This is ... cosy,' he says, hobbling in behind me.

'It's a shithole.'

'At least it's private. I'm sharing a room with two other guys. I only got promoted from the sofa bed when I broke my leg.'

'Have a seat.' I find a half-finished bottle of Jack Daniels and take a swig. I am stone cold sober – we're forbidden to drink on shift. It's odd; I'm not normally bashful around guys – I can even fake cockiness around straight lads usually – but tonight, I'm ... I dunno, mustard keen to impress. Some nights, some guys, matter. 'You want a drink?'

He looks up at me from his perch on my bed. 'No, I've had enough, I think.'

'Caller, hold the line while I have a wee snifter, if you don't mind ...'

'Come here.' He holds out his hand.

Oh god, here we go. I take another shot and go to him. I sit next to him. He runs a hand along the inside of my thigh and I shiver. 'Is that OK?'

He's nervous, I get that, but what's weirder is how nervous I am. Top of the roller coaster, ready to plummet. It's so, so silent. I swear I can hear the snow. I can't bear the anticipation any more so I lean in for a kiss.

We kiss and kiss for ages. I'd forgotten how much fun just snogging is. I always go in for the kill too fast. And he's a great kisser, and where's the rush? Dawn is a whole new day away.

It's also quite challenging to do *anything* quickly with a leg in a cast.

When I can't wait any longer, when I'm so hard it feels like it might snap off, I go into his boxers. He says nothing, but shivers and moans as I take him in hand. He's insanely hard too, a little wet patch already on his pants.

Moonlight reflects off the snow and through my thin curtains, making everything silver blue. He looks up at me as I straddle him, a question mark in his eyes, like he's waiting for me to show him the ropes. He is so, so beautiful. I'm going to cherish him.

Forgive the fade-to-black, I was busy having ALL THE SEX. The sun was up before we went to sleep. Turns out, he knew exactly what he was doing, needing very few pointers although he approached events with a beginner's enthusiasm, face full of awe. Stamina too, stopping only to take brief naps. Some nights you get so tangled up in someone, it's like you're one thing.

Thank god it's my day off. It's weird. Normally I'm not a cuddly-sleeper, but I can't seem to let go of him – not that we have much choice in this little bed. I fucking love nights like these. Nights where the sex is so mind-blowing, you tell yourself (and believe) you've fallen in love.

It is a drug, let me tell you. I can feel a candy-colour cocktail of hormones and shit flooding my brain, and it's making me loopy. If I were a cartoon, my eyes would be swirling around, all lovesick.

I don't think either of us have really slept, dipping in and out of hazy sleep and kissing. All morning I'm half waiting for him to make up some bullshit reason to leave now he's run dry. He doesn't, though, and we don't wake up properly until around eleven.

'Morning,' he says, and I scan him for gay-panic. Sometimes the morning after brings a whole new, sober, man. But if he is freaking out, tripping on dick regret, he's hiding it well.

'Hey.' I leave it at that, not willing to show my hand just yet.

He says nothing, but kisses me again, even with morning breath. Wow, I must really be dynamite. It's funny how you just *know* when you're good at something. Fern was always great at maths and English, while I can pleasure men into a coma. I know who got the better gift. 'Do you mind if I clean up?' he finally says.

'Sure.' I untangle myself and look for a clean towel for him. My dreary cell looks even worse in the light of day, covered in dirty laundry and old coffee mugs. I nod at his leg. 'Can you manage by yourself? Do you need a sponge bath?'

He chuckles. 'I have a system. Then, you wanna get breakfast or something?' He checks his phone. 'My friends are already heading for the slopes so …'

'Don't they have a million questions about where you are?'

'What happens on tour ...'

Huh. OK. So he's either after a little holiday romance, or is trying to justify a night of non-stop shagging with sausage and eggs. 'Yeah. I could eat. There's a cute place just around the corner.'

We get ready and head down the street to the cafe, hobbling along at his speed through the Christmas card toy-town that is Courchevel. It looks exactly how I imagined it would before I got here; like a Winter Wonderland, Sylvanian Families snow-capped playset, but instead of a twee boulangerie, it's actually Chanel. I am living my best Belle, Provincial Town, Bonjour! fantasy. *That girl is strange, no question!*

I certainly wouldn't want to live somewhere like this. For one thing, I thrive on city life. If I want a packet of Beefy Monster Munch at 4 a.m. I want to be able to get that. Moreover, Courchevel is painfully straight and cis. The looks I get around town, you'd think they'd never seen a guy in an acid-lime faux-fur coat before. Prudes.

As we stroll through the village, I wonder if people think we're a couple as we pass them. I hope they *do*. This provincial little town could do with a bit of queering.

I peep at him from inside my huge woolly scarf. 'So, what is it you do in London?' I ask. I'm wary of doing date-chat because what's the point, but what else am I supposed to say? *So, have you always had a lovely willy?*

'Student,' he says.

'Of what?'

'Well, I might be changing it next year. I think history.

That was always my favourite. And also, my ex is on the same course as me so …'

'Oh wow. Awks.'

'You have no idea.'

We pass some carollers on the corner, singing 'Silent Night' *en Francais*. I normally really hate their smug little faces, but today I'm maybe ready to let a bit of Christmas in. I was all set to write it off this year, but I find myself in the mood. I did used to love Christmas. When school was painful, I'd count down the weeks, starting in September. However bad Finnians was, Christmas was always on the horizon.

'What about you?'

'What about me?'

'What do you do?' He motions at the dainty town. 'This isn't for ever, right?'

'I'm at theatre school right now.'

'You're an actor?'

'I am indeed.'

'Have I seen you in anything?'

I'm the star of countless self-taped audition pieces. I am so good at getting down to the final three, it's quite the forte. "*They went another way*". I especially enjoy the casting calls for the Gay Best Friend that invariably go to a straight actor. Love that for us all. 'I was Edmund in a regional touring production of *The Lion, The Witch and The Wardrobe* when I was like twelve. I fell in love for the first time with the guy who played the back end of Aslan.'

'You gonna be famous some day?' he asks me, and it's triggering.

'Fuck you, I'm already famous in my head. I'm a motherfuckin' star!'

He grins. 'I don't doubt it.'

We arrive at the cafe. It's a hole in the wall really, but their food doesn't cost a fortune and the coffee is good. There are only four tables inside and we manage to get the corner one. He orders coffee and croissants, his French better than mine. He brings the tray to our table and puts three heaped spoons of brown sugar in his coffee, which surprises me because he gives off a very 'clean eating' vibe.

Over breakfast, I pour out my heart. All my frustrations as an actor bubble up. I don't know *why* it all spills out, maybe it's his kind face. There's an openness to him and I feel oddly safe. I don't feel the need to impress him any more than I already did with my mad bedroom skillz.

'There are like ten roles for every ten thousand actors,' I say. 'It's hard for everyone, but I have been told – to my face – that I might struggle to get cast as the straight male romantic lead that TV and film so craves. I don't "pass" as straight.'

He blinks. 'People told you that? Brutal.'

Oh, aye. *Watch your posture; more manly; less OTT; can we do something with the voice?* One of the coaches at school once singled me out to teach me, in front of the whole seminar, how to *walk like a man*. All synonyms for 'less gay'. 'Yeah, pretty much.'

'Well, fuck 'em.'

'The casting couch is one option,' I say grimly.

He laughs. 'I meant write your own stuff. Write characters like you.'

76

Well, that'd be a novelty wouldn't it? A story about a young gay man; unapologetic, not dying of AIDS; has a love-hate relationship with gender norms. A story where his gayness wasn't the only thing that defined him. A gay policeman, a gay doctor, even a gay guy just falling in love, and his relationship being of equal importance to the straight people's around him.

A nice idea, if I weren't so tragically unable to stick at a project for more than a week. I get bored so easily. And it's so hard. And a better idea always creeps up behind the one I'm working on. 'I don't know if anyone is screaming out for that story.'

'I'd watch it.'

'You would?'

'I would if you were in it ...' He flashes me another megawatt smile. It'a a shy smile, like he's embarrassed of his teeth. He needn't be, he's perfect.

After brunch we potter through the streets, Courchevel's bizarre mix of twee and designer. The pavements have been shovelled clear of snow, so it's easy enough for Tom to get by on his crutches. I'm starting to wonder if he's humouring me by sticking around. I suspect he's probably looking for the right time to ditch me and go find his mates.

Suddenly he stops.

'Are you OK?' I ask turning back.

He's stopped to look at a poster.

'They're showing *It's A Wonderful Life* in ten minutes. You wanna watch it?'

I didn't even realise we were outside the Cinéma Mégarama

until he pointed it out. Sure enough, Fern's all-time favourite starts at one o'clock.

'C'mon,' he says jovially. 'It'll be fun!'

As he goes to push the doors open, I gently hook his elbow. 'Wait. Like … *why?*'

'Why what?'

'Tom, it's fine. I know what this is. I know how it ends. It's fine to call a One Night Stand a One Night Stand. I'm not going to cry, or start leaving heart emojis on all your Instagram pics like some secret code.'

He looks a little hurt. 'I'm not *that* guy, you know.'

'What guy is that?' I say as an older lady pushes past us to get through the door.

'The douchebag who'll say anything to get into someone's pants.'

I hold in a wry laugh. 'Babe, they're all *that* guy. *I'm* that guy.'

He's cute, but I'm not sure what he wants from me. He's leaving soon, what's this all about?

'You're overthinking it. I wanna spend time with you. You're fun.'

'That's me. Superfun!' I say sarcastically. Gay men are SUCH GOOD FRIENDS.

'It's just one day. C'mon … go nuts.'

I'm supposed to be skiing with Aussie Louise at three, but I like to think she'd understand my dilemma. This is bonkers, but I … guess I like him or something? I'm not ready to let go just yet. 'Sure. OK.'

Cinéma Mégarama is the one cinema in town. I've never actually been, but it's a dinky wee thing with curving art deco features in cool green and gold. The smell of freshly popped corn hits me as soon as we enter the foyer. Every now and then, I get a twinge of homesickness, and the sheer normalcy of a cinema really kicks me in the 'nads. Popcorn reminds me of Christmas Eve Eve movies with Fern and Will.

Tom thinks it's wild that I've never seen the film before, but I've always been of the opinion that if a black-and-white film is worth it, they would have remade it in colour. He is appalled by this sentiment. Apparently it's his mum's favourite too.

I buy the tickets and he buys us a king-size popcorn to share. 'Sweet or salty,' I ask, testing him.

'I guessed sweet?'

'You guessed correctly.' I pluck a kernel off the top. 'Meant to be …'

We file into the theatre, one of only three couples here. Well, who comes to a ski resort to watch films in the afternoon? We take a spot on the back row. Presumptuous, I feel. That said, he's right to be, because about forty-five minutes into the film I give him a surreptitious hand job. One to check off the to-do list. We both dissolve into giggles as the dude in the film tries to throw himself off the bridge and from a few rows in front the old lady angrily shushes us over her shoulder.

By the end, however, Tom has a little cry (although he tries to hide it) because everyone loves George again and gives him a load of money, which is nice I guess, but I'm dead inside so my eyes remain dry.

After the film – his jizz now a crusty patch on my scarf – we go for pizza slices and drinks at La Douche Folie. There's nothing quite like Ibiza house music in the snow. 'Are we dancing?' I ask.

'How?' He gestures at his broken leg. He's perched on a bar stool while I lean on our corner table.

'You stand still, I'll dance around you. Like a pole dancer.' He laughs, checks no one's looking, and gives me a kiss.

'That's brave,' I say.

'You think I'm soft?'

'I *know* you aren't,' I say, nodding at a tell-tale bulge in his jeans. 'I just meant, here we are, in public, in daylight. Some guys I've been with don't even tell me their real names.'

'Those guys sound shitty. Why don't I tell my mates where I've been? You could come to dinner! That feels like an easy way to—'

I'll stop him right there. 'Babe, you don't have to tell them anything you don't want to tell them,' I say, finishing my mulled cider. The outdoor heater feels like it's toasting the top of my head. 'Don't you head home tomorrow?'

He nods. He must do because tomorrow is Christmas Eve, and he said earlier he'd be spending Christmas Day with his mother.

'So this is what it is,' I say.

Tom looks into his beer. 'Yeah, I know,' he says mournfully.

'What?'

'I dunno. I just had a really good couple of days with you. I hope I proved you wrong. Not all men are awful.'

I reach for his hand over the table. As the more experienced queer, I have an opportunity here. Some rancid scene queens in Edinburgh were so disparaging of me in the early days, and I turned some of the hatred in on myself. It doesn't need to be the same for Tom. 'Babes. You are stunning.' I loop my arms around his neck and stand in the space between his knees. 'Last night was a *rarity*. I felt it too. I've been with a fella or two and … it's not always like that. It was different.'

'Yeah?' His whole face lights up. I knew I didn't imagine it. The *spark*. 'I just …'

'Just what?' I want to let him down gently, but I'll also have to be the Grinch who Stole Sexmas. A lot of boys made me promises they couldn't keep too, and that hurt more. I'll rip off the waxing strip. Painful for a second, but better than an agonising slow-peel. 'Let's not make this something it's not. It's not a puppy, sometimes a gift really is just for Christmas.'

He laughs but the light goes out of his eyes. 'Savage.'

Maybe we *could* make this work. No, what am I saying?? We categorically couldn't. He'd freak out and realise I'm not the only fish in the sea, and I'd inevitably get bored because I already know about the abundant fish population. And what, I'm gonna go to London every other weekend? How? I could barely afford one journey.

Syd once told me that holiday romances never work. Because real life is no holiday. I can be the doting little *Love, Simon* boyfriend for twenty-four hours, but so can anyone.

'Last night was amazing.' I brush a snowflake off his eyebrow with my thumb. I tell him that because it was. I've had maybe … actually no, I'm not sure I've ever had a night quite like that one. I remember us waking up and woozily going again as dawn broke. We couldn't keep our hands to ourselves; it was almost like we melted into one entity, all molten gold. 'And now nothing will ruin it. It's like a snow globe. It'll be perfect and sparkly for ever. When we're sixty, wherever we end up, we'll still talk about that Christmas in Courchevel when we had the best sex ever.'

He looks disappointed, but resolved. 'True.'

'Bitch, as if I'm gonna make it to sixty,' I add with a smile.

The sun is setting, both physically and on our glorious, if brief, romance. It's time to wrap it up. I think we both feel it. I pay for the drinks while he texts his friends to find out where they are, and then we walk slowly back towards the hotel, eking it out for as long as we can.

The snow is falling heavily now and all the town will no doubt be discussing whether or not it's the 'right type' of snow for optimum skiing. Either way, it looks very beautiful. We really *are* in that snow globe. It's getting dark, and the Christmas tree lights come on in the town square as the clock strikes five. The Christmas market is buzzing, the smell of mulled wine and gingerbread and roast chestnuts in the air. There's a carousel right outside Santa's grotto at the heart of the plaza, the calliope playing a merry tune.

I want to hold his hand, but they are full of crutch. He has to meet his friends at Bar L'Equipe. 'So this is it,' I say as we stand on the crossroads – the hotel in one direction and his friends in the other.

'This kinda sucks,' he says. 'Can I get your number?'

'Why?' I say gently. I've never been a fan of endless dick pics and three a.m. phone sex. Even at Christmas, you gotta go cold turkey.

He nods, understanding, before leaning in for a proper kiss.

82

And in front of a carousel full of kids. I'm dimly impressed. If I *was* going to get a boyfriend, I'd want one like Tom. Where literally everyone looks at us and thinks, *How the fuck did Rowan McAllister ensnare him, it must be witchcraft.* Goals.

'I think I love you a bit,' he says, his lips millimetres from mine.

I laugh. 'A bit?'

'Is that mad?'

'Yes!' I kiss a snowflake off his lip before it can melt. I allow myself to dwell on Niall. Sweet Niall. Oh yes, I once got perilously close to love. I didn't like it. 'There is nothing scarier than love.'

His phone keeps ringing in his pocket. 'Man, I gotta go.'

'Go.' I do not want him to go.

He sighs deeply. 'I'm not gonna forget you.'

I grin at him, backing away. 'How could you *possibly* forget me?' I turn on my heel and start back towards the hotel. *Don't you dare look back.* As I walk away, I get heavier inside with every crunchy stride in the snow. A sob grips my throat. I want to cry.

Fuck.

I exhale a big, sad cloud into the cold air and try to get my shit together. This is not sad. It's not. It is a *good* thing. If a falling piano lands on me tomorrow, at least I'll know … I had one perfect day.

CHRISTMAS EVE
EVE

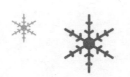

FERN

'Are you OK?' I ask Thom. He looks grey and weird, like that one time we smoked some really strong weed and he somehow turned paler than me.

'Yeah,' he says, stiffly waiting at the breakfast table in the kitchen. I much prefer eating in here, far less formal than the dining room. Next to Thom, Willow bravely battles a bowl of Cheerios without Satan leaping out of her mouth, *Exorcist* style. This morning, Dad is in charge of breakfast. Mum has gone to Waitrose to get some goose fat for the turkey tomorrow and some double cream for the trifle.

'Welcome to McAllister's Diner!' Dad says in the weirdest American accent I've ever heard. 'Thom, how do you want your eggs?'

'Um … I don't mind,' he says. He seems a squillion miles away.

'Sure you're OK?' I ask. Is he sick or something? How much did we drink last night?

'I'm *fine*,' he says, getting a little huffy. 'Um, poached, please.'

Rowan bursts into the kitchen, with Syd right behind him. They're even more striking in the flesh, even with a hangover. 'I'll take scrambled!' Rowan loudly announces.

'Morning! What can I get you, Syd?' Dad asks.

'No eggs for me, thanks …'

Dad slaps his forehead. 'Chris did say, I'm sorry! Avo on toast?'

'Perfect, thanks.'

'I'm not allowed to be vegan,' Willow says pointedly.

Trust Rowan to bring home a vegan for Christmas. It's like he actively set out to make life harder for Mum and Dad. Syd really should be a Calvin Klein model. The shaved head, the tattoos, the piercings – they really have nailed that whole Gen Z aesthetic. I know there isn't a 'non-binary' look, but Syd has truly mastered the equilibrium of masculinity and femininity. 'Aren't you going to introduce us?' I ask.

'Shit, yeah, soz,' Rowan says. 'Syd, this is my sister, Fern, and her boyfriend, Thom.'

We greet Syd as they and Rowan seat themselves on the other side of the rustic kitchen table. I'd love a table like this someday, and a family of my own to go around it. Thom and I will make exceptionally cute babies.

Rowan seems to stare Thom down. 'So this is Thom? Thom with an H? That's notable. Do I pronounce it *Fom*?'

His eyes dip, bashful. 'No. It's … just short for Thomas.'

'Thomas Simpkins.' Rowan says theatrically and I wonder why he's being even more extra than normal. 'Don't suppose your mates call you Simper?'

I sit up straighter. 'How did you know that?' I butt in. On his rugby team, he's always been Simper.

'They do actually,' Thom says.

Rowan rolls his eyes. 'What a coincidence! I once knew a Simper, that's all.'

88

Thom just shrugs.

'So we know how Ro got on last night … we met the detritus in the hallway,' I say archly, picking at a bit of toast. 'How was your night, Syd?'

Syd nods, helping themselves to coffee from the pot. 'Wicked, thanks. Cheesy, but very fun. You should have joined us. It was sick.'

I smile. They seem much friendlier than the fashion-school exterior suggests. 'Rowan doesn't like me to cramp his style.'

'That's not true!' he argues. 'You just always get tired by midnight! You're fucking Cinderella!'

'Language, Rowan!' Dad interjects, somehow making three types of egg at once like some sort of brunch squid.

'Are we doing Christmas-Not-Christmas Movie Day today?' I ask. I want to pin Rowan down. After last night, he's not ruining all the traditions through being a hot mess.

'What's that?' Syd asks.

Thom is being super quiet and I don't know why. I guess he *is* shy around new people. I need to bear in mind that this week is really intense for him. I wouldn't want to spend a whole week with his mum if I'm honest. She's very lovely but Jesus keeps finding a way into our conversations.

I explain the concept for Syd. 'On Christmas Eve Eve we watch movies that are *tangentially* Christmassy, but not Christmas movies *about* Christmas – those are for tomorrow.'

'You know,' Ro says, '*Die Hard*; *Batman Returns*; *Frozen*; *Gremlins*; *Tangerine*; *Edward Scissorhands* … there's an argument for *Home Alone* too. I'm fully here for a chill day. I feel rough.'

'Cool, I'm down,' Syd says.

'Me too,' Willow adds.

'Can you believe Rowan has never seen *It's A Wonderful Life*?' I say to Thom. It's our mutual favourite. 'He refuses to watch black-and-white films, like a total philistine.'

'I have, actually!' my brother announces with relish. 'Last Christmas in France. I thought it was so boring, I stopped watching halfway through and gave the guy I was with a—'

Dad plonks a plate of scrambled eggs in front of his face. 'Thank you, son, can we try to keep things PG until after six p.m.?'

Rowan starts to protest his freedom of speech, when Thom pushes his chair back, the feet shrieking over the kitchen tiles. 'Excuse me,' he says quietly.

'Are you OK?' I ask.

'Yes. I'll just be a sec.' He leaves the kitchen and heads for the stairs. I guess that second coffee prompted a second poo. Dad hands me a plate too and leaves one for Thom.

'How long have you and Thom been together?' Syd asks.

'On and off for about two years,' I say, grinding some pepper over my eggs. 'We took a break for a while.'

'And why's that?' Rowan asks.

'None of your business,' I snap, because it isn't. Also, I don't come off too well in that story and don't need Syd to think I'm a bigot. I'm not a bigot.

OK. Picture the scene: one sunny afternoon the summer before last, there we were chilling on Primrose Hill, drinking Echo Falls rosé out of plastic cups, when Thom hurled this huge brick of information through my window and just expected me to not even have an opinion. Like, if I'd told him *oh, I'm bisexual*, I'd fully expect him to at least want to talk about that.

'He's very handsome,' Ro says. 'If he were *my* boyfriend, I'd post more pictures of him on my social media.'

'I do! You don't even use social media,' I fire back. 'You think it's basic.'

'It is. But you're basic.'

I offer him a blistering glare. As much as he hates posing for them, there *are* pictures of Thom on my Instagram, but it figures that Rowan is too self-involved to care what my boyfriend even looks like. 'I take it from your guest last night you're not seeing anyone in Bristol?'

'Oh, I'm seeing lots of people in Bristol, thank you very much.'

Dad sighs. 'How early can I start drinking?'

The front door closes and Mum clatters down the hall, tote bags swinging. She dumps them on the counter with a sigh. 'Well, that was a disaster. *Of course* Waitrose has run out of goose fat on Christmas Eve Eve. Fern, hen, you might have to pop down to the Metro for me later …'

'Me? Why me?'

Mum kisses the crown of my head. 'Because, frankly, I don't trust my other two children to return.'

She has a point.

WILLOW

OK, this is weird. How did this happen? I am sitting in the lounge with only Syd for company. I know Fern has gone to Tesco, but I have no idea where Rowan or Thom are. I can't leave now, that would be rude, but I also wish I'd got out of the room before it was just the two of us. The second hand of the clock echoes between us.

Syd is very cool. They should probably be in magazines. I've never seen anyone make Adidas pants and a polo shirt look so good. What am I supposed to say? *I like your sweatpants*?

'You got a preference?' they suddenly say, and I actually jump a little in my seat.

'What?'

'For the film? Fern's shortlist isn't that short.'

Ah, OK, I can do this conversation. I'm freezing, so I slip off the sofa and sit cross-legged by the fire. 'I don't mind. Let's face it, Rowan will pick in the end.'

Syd laughs. 'Yeah. He likes to get his way.'

'So does Fern.'

'Did you ever get much of a say?'

Another of Dr Finch's many theories. His 'map' of my disorder. He believes, that with a high-achieving sister and attention-whore brother, I fell between the cracks. Sometimes, children – without even knowing it – realise sickness is a real headline grabber at home. Did I starve myself to get Mum and Dad's attention? No. Did it get their attention? Fuck yes. Do I want the constant monitoring? Absolutely fuck no. If I in any way unleashed this curse upon myself, consider the lesson learned.

'Not really,' I admit. I used to have more fight. I remember giving as good as I got – and the baby of the bunch usually triumphs. When I was really sick, I rationed out what little energy I had for exercise. I'm better now, but I'm still tired a lot. My illness is like an app running constantly in the background, draining my battery. Mum is always on at me to *do more*: go for walks, or join in with her yoga classes – it'll be good for me, so she says – but I just don't have the strength. I usually nap for most of the afternoon. 'I'm the runt. I let them take charge.'

Syd pulls their legs under their body in the armchair. They look so out of place in our stuffy living room. 'I learned how to manage Rowan last year. You just say NO in a very definite way. My therapist would call it being "boundaried".'

I wonder why Syd needs a therapist. Rude to ask. I guess being non-binary in a binary world must be pretty gruelling. 'I remember this time when Mum left Ro screaming on the floor in Marks & Spencer. He wanted some Percy Pigs. She just walked away. It was pretty funny. He stuck to his guns, though. We were at the top of the escalator before he ran after us.'

Syd laughs. 'The problem is that if *we* leave him screaming on the floor, he'll end up going home with five guys for a chill-out.'

I don't think that's a joke. My illness is so noisy in my head, so time-consuming. I forget everyone else is out there, living life. 'Should I worry about him?'

'Probably. Should he worry about you?'

I recoil. I wasn't expecting that. 'What do you mean?'

'He talks about you all the time. You know what he's like, he makes a big joke out of everything, but you're on his mind. He was pretty scared.'

I know, and I feel bad about it, but as if I'm gonna talk about it with a total stranger. I feel the demon swell in my stomach. I hate the idea that Rowan is telling people about me. Especially Syd. I thought they were really cool, but they must think I'm insane like everyone at school does. 'I'm fine,' I say.

Syd sort of half smiles and fuck knows what's so funny. 'You don't have to be fine! That wasn't like a threat: *get better so your brother can stop sweating it.* I guess I meant: *I know Ro can be a dick, but he really, really loves you.*'

The demon really wants to jump out and tell them to mind their own fucking business. I quash it down. 'I know.' I force out nice words. The skin on my hands goes blotchy with salmon pink hives. That happens when I get flustered.

'How do you feel about *Home Alone*?' They change the subject and the demon slinks back to its lair.

'I love *Home Alone*. Obviously. His mum is Moira Rose.'

Syd's eyes light up. 'You watch *Schitt's Creek*?'

'Of course! Obsessed.' It sounds batshit, but after pills, doctors, group therapy and being fed through a tube, a gentle sitcom about a family living in a motel cured me more than any of those things.

'I have the biggest crush on Alexis,' Syd says. I thought they liked boys. But that might be because Mum and Dad were so convinced they were dating Rowan. Guess not. Or maybe they're bi. Or pan. Like David Rose said in *Schitt's Creek*: red wine, white wine and rosé. I don't really know what to say.

It's been … so long since I had a crush, I can't even remember what one feels like. Anorexia is a cancer that spreads through your body and your life. My friendships and my schoolwork went first, then my periods stopped, then I just stopped feeling. Nothing is funny; nothing is sad. There's certainly nothing as spicy as a crush. I dimly remember going through a *5 Seconds of Summer* phase because my friends were. But I was eleven.

Syd leans in. 'Why don't we make a pact now that we start with *Home Alone*? If we get Thom on board, the twins are outvoted …?'

And that's when I know I really like Syd.

FERN

It's the day before Christmas Eve, so of course the supermarket is carnage. Not a sprout in sight. I wonder if Mum is going to be out of luck with goose fat and custard. Outside, the Salvation Army are singing 'God Rest Ye Merry Gentlemen' and it becomes a mash-up with 'Christmas Wrapping' on the sound system as I cross the threshold into the store. I love this song. I love *all* Christmas songs – oh, except that homophobic one.

God Tier: Mariah, Destiny's Child, and I personally have a special place in my heart for the Leona one.

Crap Tier: the ones Mum and Dad like ... the screaming seventies ones and the aforementioned ode to domestic violence.

A little boy is having a sit-down tantrum in the vegetable section and I remember the time Mum fully abandoned Rowan in M&S. Glorious. To this day I wonder how far Mum would have got before relenting. Or is there a parallel world where Ro still lives feral in Marks's food hall, surviving on punnets of melon slices and sushi?

I quickly establish Mum will have to make do with powdered custard for the trifle. It's only Dad and Ro that eat that rank slop anyway – both are averse to traditional Christmas pudding.

It'll do. I throw a packet into the basket and grab an extra two pints of milk, just in case.

As I turn the corner into the next aisle, a couple are basically having sex next to the bread and cake section, having a full fumble. She looks quite close to climax judging from her face. Her boyfriend has gloved hands on her *area*. Bold, I think, for Tesco.

'Were we that bad?' a voice mutters in my ear.

I whirl around and find myself face-to-face with the past. My brain needs a second to compute. They always say when you finally stop worrying about running into an ex, they'll manifest.

I didn't think I'd ever see him again.

'Hamish! Oh my god!' I don't know what to say. Do we hug, do we not hug? He spreads his arms wide and we clunkily embrace. It takes a second to realise my face is resting on a blue Tesco fleece.

'Miss Fern McAllister! Long time ...' he says. He is the same, but different. Older – he is a man now – but the scooter-accident scar on his top lip is as cute now as it was then. The curl in the lip gives him a permanent naughtiness. He's a wee scamp. He *finally* cut his hair too. It's still long, but when we were going out, his was almost as long as mine. 'How are you? Looking good!'

'I am ... shocked!' I say. 'You're working here?'

'No, I just really dig the jacket.' He grins, stroking the fleecy fabric. 'Yes, I'm working here! My name is Ham and I am happy to help.' He taps his name badge, the letters peeling off.

'I somehow doubt that ...' Understand I take no pride in asking this, but ask I must. 'The band broke up?'

'No!' he says very quickly. 'We're still together for now. I just do this part-time; you know.'

'Sure ...' I say, because he knows what I'm thinking and I know what he's thinking too. I was right and he was wrong. That band, that sodding band, broke us. At least if they put the album out, it would all be for something.

'You just up for Christmas?' he asks. He casts a glance over my shoulder, no doubt on the hunt for whoever his manager is. It figures he'd be shit even at this type of work.

'Aye, my boyfriend and I came up together for the week.'

He smiles again. 'Easy, tiger, I'm not tryin' to get in your pants. Stand down!'

'No!' I gasp, 'I just meant— '

'Fern, I'm kidding!' He always could play me like a fiddle. I've never met anyone else quite like Hamish. He's a *star*, and by that I mean he is a fireball, and I should know, I got burned. 'I've seen him on your Instagram. He's a wee looker; you make a gorgeous couple. You seem very happy.'

'We are.' How on earth did we end up having this conversation next to the luxury shortbread tins?

When did I last see Hamish Bell? The summer before I left for London I suppose. We have some friends in common, so couldn't cut each other off cold turkey. And very much like a drug – I imagine – he was hard to quit. The problem with Hamish, although it was a nice problem to have, was that he was always very much ... a *giver*, and, well, even after we officially called it quits, we kept winding up ...

Friends with Benefits. Has that literally *ever* been a good idea? Every time we ... it just kept him in my system. And like any desperate junkie, I wanted more and more. I kept trying to badger him back into the relationship. I imagine all the nagging was *very* sexy.

In the end, I sort of had to pretend he was dead for my sanity. I was done trying to make us something we weren't. I did all the work. Wishing he was the perfect boyfriend didn't cut it. So I set him free to make as many mistakes as he wanted.

'London is great, the course is going well.' That's what you do with an ex, isn't it? You blind them with how gleaming your life without them is.

'And here I am, right where you left me.' I don't think there's any malice in that. Two years ago, I'd have given anything for Hamish to come with me. I think I knew, though. Some of us leave our hometowns, and some are stuck to the flystrip. 'Between you and me, this job *sucks*.'

'At least blue is your colour …'

He laughs. 'I better do some work; my boss is such a nightmare. She's a real Nazi. Like, I mean that. Her boyfriend has the tattoos on his face and everything.'

'Wow … OK.'

He scoops up his plastic crate and stows it on a trolley thing. 'Hey. What are you and your very tall fella doin' tomorrow night?'

'The big Christmas Eve at home thing.'

'Oh aye, the McAllister Family Christmas, I remember it well. If you get bored of carols and mince pies, there's a massive rave down Leith Volcano.'

'Where?'

'That derelict church that they turned into a venue for the

Fringe? It's gonna go off, you should come down.'

I literally can't think of anything I'd like to do less on Christmas Eve. 'Yeah, maybe. I'll see what Thom thinks …'

'Sure you will!' He knows as well as I do that I won't be raving tomorrow night. 'It was good to see you, Fern. I have the maddest dreams about you sometimes, you know …'

'Right.' I roll my eyes.

'It's true! I do!' He leans in very close, so only I can hear. 'And some of them are pretty fucking mucky, too.'

Despite myself, I bark with laughter. 'Well, now I know you're lying.'

He looks a little wounded. 'I'm not! You ever get lonely on a cold winter night, call me up. I'll describe them to you. In detail.' With that, and a devilish smile, he backs away.

I cannot pretend something in me doesn't stir. A little bit of Hamish is *still* in my system, and probably always will be.

I try to shake the weird encounter off, drifting down the aisle past the selection boxes and drums of Cadbury's Roses. So he's had a haircut, and literally nothing else has changed. It's strangely comforting. I used to want to kill him, but I'm actually really glad I ran in to him. I'm not angry any more. Sometimes an epilogue is good value. Two years later or whatever. I watch him get back to his job and instead feel a little sad. Hamish, however messy he was, *is* a star. He needs his stargazers, and he won't get them stacking shelves.

I almost go back to him, offer him advice, before realising that's some very bad habits trying to return. Oh no. Been there, done that.

ROWAN

Thom is sitting on my bed when I emerge from my en suite. Luckily, I'm wearing a towel. I suppose we're even for earlier.

'You're taking your chances,' I tell him, and drop the towel, going one better. Not like he hasn't seen it all before. I pluck some turquoise camouflage Aussie Bums out of my holdall and step into them.

'What was that in the kitchen?' Thom says, angrier than I've ever seen him. 'Was that supposed to shame me or something?'

And then I see his eyes are red. He's been crying. Fuck, I'm just the worst.

'I'm sorry. I can't help myself. I see a weakness, I exploit it. It was the only way I survived school. I became worse than my tormentors. I had to be smarter, funnier, deadlier. Straights were the enemy. Not that you're …'

'Was that funny to you? Like, watching me squirm?'

Someone's not seeing the funny side, are they? 'No … I … look; I am sorry. I'm not going to tell Fern if that's what you're worried about. The skit in the kitchen was just for you and me. This doesn't have to be a great big twist or anything. It's just … a mad coincidence.'

He rests his head in his hands but his shoulders creep down a couple of inches, which makes me think he was worried chiefly about me confessing all to Fern. I mean, no one wants to hear their boyfriend bummed their twin brother, right? Funky Pigeon dot com don't do a card for that. I'll fucking say.'

I retrieve my jeans from the back of my desk chair and pull them on. 'I gotta say, though, didn't you put two and two together when Fern said she had a brother called Rowan? Like, how many Rowans do you know?'

He looks up at me and scrunches up his nose. 'I always thought you were called *Ryan*,' he says sheepishly. I stare at him agog for a moment before we bother erupt into giggles, unable to sit on the stupidness of that. We both try to muffle the noise.

'*Ryan*? What the fuck?'

'Back in France I didn't hear what you said and then I was too embarrassed to ask again after we'd …'

'Fucked.'

'Exactly. All I knew was Fern has a twin brother, he's not on Insta, and he's gay. I think she did once show me a picture of you two together, but you were like ten or something.'

'And you were broken up last Christmas?'

'Yes. Hundred per cent. What I said was true.'

I join him on the bed and cross my legs, facing him. I'm suddenly very aware we're both sitting on my sex sheets from last night. Gross. I cast my mind back to the ski slopes – one piece of the puzzle is really bugging me. 'So my sister dumped you for being bi?'

Thom nods. 'She freaked out.'

Fern is hard work, but I didn't think she was a bigot. 'Well, that's disappointing to say the bare fucking least.'

Thom seems to relent. 'It's not entirely her fault. I kind of

102

sprung it on her without warning. You know that bit where you're psyched because you've figured yourself out at long last? I sort of reckoned she'd be excited too. Got that one wrong. I assumed it wouldn't change things.'

I'm irrationally angry on his behalf and jump in, both feet. 'It shouldn't have! Unless you were cheating on her with a dude, with *anyone*, in which case you're an asshole.'

'I wasn't cheating on anyone with anyone!'

'Good.' I say sulkily. 'God, I'm so mad at Fern.'

'What about us?' Thom asks.

My vintage Tas of Tasmania sweater smells funky, like I packed it when it was still damp. I get up and find my washbag. I douse myself in Tom Ford as a precaution – the final dregs left from last Christmas. 'What do you mean, what about us?'

He looks genuinely confused. 'I … didn't think I was ever going to see you again.'

Well, so what? 'That was a safe assumption. This is a freakish occurrence. This is like when … the Segway inventor was killed *on a Segway*.'

'Is it?'

'No. But you know what I mean. The odds of a guy randomly shagging a set of twins in different countries in the space of twelve months have to be … well, whatever impossible odds are.' He looks like a man on the edge. 'I guess you have a type. On a genetic level.'

'That's not funny,' he says. But he smiles a little, and I suddenly remember exactly how hot he is. He is so much better than the memory of him.

I remember in graphic detail how good our night in

Courchevel was, and not just the obvious bit. It's odd; I remember how *warm* he was, how I couldn't keep my hands off him. My autopilot reflex is to kiss him, but if this situation is *kinda* not OK at present, that's *definitely* not OK. Any jury in the land would convict. HE IS MY SISTER'S BOYFRIEND. I stamp that firmly on my brain. There are some lines even I won't cross.

'C'mon, cheer up …' I tell him. 'It is a *bit* funny, you have to admit. It's very … Christmas movie. Like the cheesy ones on Channel 5, where some frosty bitch from the city breaks up with a smarmy lawyer, and has a breakdown, so has to go home to Leafy Glade, Alabama, where she reunites with the humble carpenter she dated in high school, and ends up working as a mall elf, and rediscovers the true meaning of Christmas.'

'How is this like that?' At least he's properly smiling now.

'Well, it isn't. But I got carried away. I would watch the shit out of that movie, though.' I join him on the bed again. 'Thom, between you and me, I had the biggest crush on Fern's actual high school boyfriend – this guy called Hamish – and I managed to be vaguely chill around him for like two years. I think I'll get through six days with you guys.'

Thom looks like he's about to say something and then changes his mind.

'What?'

'I … nothing …'

'No, go on. And quickly because if anyone catches you up here, there will be questions.'

He shakes his head. 'I was gonna say … I think you're better at this than me. I thought about you a lot last year. I tried to find you online. I … even called the hotel.'

'You did not!' I gasp. That's so extra.

'I did! They said they didn't have a Ryan working for them, which makes sense now.'

'Why? Like, why call?' What was he hoping to achieve?

He can't look me in the eye. 'I don't know … you were just in my head a lot. It was before I got back with Fern and … I dunno.'

'Wow, was I that good?' He blushes.

I *could* tell him the truth and say he'd drifted into my head all year too. Everyone has melancholy moments. Valentines; those Saturday nights when no one is free because they're doing couply stuff. On those lonely nights, all alone in bed, I'd warm myself with the parallel world fantasy where I'd met this amazing boyfriend in Courchevel and we'd somehow made it work. It'd send me to sleep all gooey inside like a Pop Tart. But that's the thing with fantasies – they're always, *always* better than realities. So instead I say, 'You're so cute.'

He tries not to look hurt, but that has to sting, right?

I grip his shoulders, and even that contact feels slightly verboten. 'Thom, you massive sexy giant. Do you want to be with Fern?'

'Yes!' he says at once.

'Exactly. You are dating my sister. There is no "us"!' He flinches again, but I need to kill off any lingering dick-nostalgia right now if we're going to sit across from each other at Christmas dinner. 'Bleach me out of your head. I can tell you right now that if we'd tried to do some long-distance thing, it wouldn't have worked. You don't know me. I'm *awful*.'

He looks up at me and frowns. 'No, you're not. I think you want people to think you are, though, which is weird.'

We really don't have time for therapy. 'OK, Freud. Go on, get out. I don't wanna go downstairs with you, Syd will think I've noshed you off.'

'Syd knows?'

'Yes. But they're cool, I promise.'

'Dude!'

I steer him towards the door. 'Thom, I say this in the kindest possible way: get your shit together. I mean it. She is my sister and I love her. I don't want Fern to find out. Not ever.'

WILLOW

This is weird. I linger at the bottom of the stairs to the attic, trying to make out what they're saying. Male voices really hum the walls. They're talking like old friends one second, and the next it sounds kinda aggy. But I thought they only met this morning? Is Rowan getting it on with Fern's boyfriend? He's a dickhead, certified, but I didn't think he was *that* bad.

I came upstairs to use the loo, and thought I'd see what was taking Ro so long. I guess now I know.

I wish I could hear *what* they were saying.

'What's good?' Syd appears behind me. They move like a ghost cat. My heart jams.

'You scared me!' I whisper. 'Thom's in Rowan's room for some reason.'

'I know,' Syd says earnestly, taking my hand and dragging me down the landing. 'Leave them to it, trust me.'

'What? Why? What's going on?'

'It's nothing. Really.'

I pull my hand back. I didn't *actually* think Rowan was shagging Thom. *Now* I do. 'Well, it obviously is …'

Syd sighs deeply. 'OK, I'll fill you in, but you cannot tell Fern. OK?'

FERN

I plonk the tote bag on to the kitchen counter, along with today's mail. Mum is rolling out pastry. 'Did you make pastry? What is this? Who are you?'

'I'm baking a pie for dinner.'

I give her an impressed look.

'What?' she says. 'I cook!'

'Where's Dad?' Dad is the usual chef, it has to be said. The penny only recently dropped as to why. Mum grew up on frozen fish fingers and tinned peas. Dad, with his loaded parents, ate in lovely restaurants all his life. It figures he'd have the more developed palate.

He makes the most extraordinary mince pies. I see a gang of them waiting for me in a Tupperware box. I don't know what the secret ingredient is – it may well be crack cocaine for how moreish they are – but he fills the shortcrust base with a gorgeous zesty filling and then caps it all off with a sugary crumble topping. He should quit politics and go on *Bake Off* on the strength of them alone.

'Mum?' I ask again when she ignores me.

'He is ... out,' Mum says vaguely. She's being a little weirdly evasive. I assume it's something to do with presents. She's probably sent Dad on a mission. With Rowan in the house, they've always been very good at hiding the gifts. From September on, he'd go prowling around the house, trying to spoil the surprises. Mum slides the mail back towards me, casting a brief glance over the stack. 'Do you want to open those cards and put them with the others?'

'Sure.' I flick through a pile of glossy envelopes. Rowan and I used to scrap over who got to open the Christmas cards, even though we didn't know who half of them were from.

Mum nods at the groceries. 'Did you get everything?'

'Yep,' I say. I found goose fat, eventually, in the posh deli cafe thing around the corner on my way home. 'You'll never guess who I saw in Tesco.'

'The Virgin Mary? Shakin' Stevens?'

'Who? No. Guess again!'

'Oh my days, Fern, I am a bit busy here!'

'Hamish!'

Mum rests her rolling pin and frowns. 'Hamish Bell?'

'Aye. Apparently he works at Tesco now.'

The snobbery leaps off her face. 'Permanently?' I shrug. 'What happened to the band being the next Biffy Clyro?'

'I don't know,' I say. 'He said they're still together …'

My days as a garage-band groupie feel like they happened to some other girl. A much younger, far more clueless, girl, even though it was only two years ago. I still remember that day, though; the day he suddenly announced, halfway up Arthur's Seat, he was deferring his university application to focus on the band.

Oh, how I used to love watching him play from the side of the stage. *She's with the drummer*. God, I could die from cringing. He had a place at *Oxford*, though. I guess he charmed even the entrance panel. His poor parents, what must they think? *Our son's going to Oxford, oops no, my mistake, he's actually got a job down Tesco.*

'Who are the cards from?' asks Mum.

I hadn't really even looked. 'Um Denise and Ralph; someone called Jean; Steve and Ed, and Auntie Rachel.'

'You two were always chalk and cheese,' Mum says.

'Me and Auntie Rachel?'

Mum tuts. 'You and Hamish! Maybe you need to have one entirely inappropriate boyfriend so you know how to spot them in the future.'

I grin. 'Wasn't Dad your high school boyfriend?'

Her eyes glaze over like she's staring down the time tunnel. 'Aye. But that's not to say he was the *first*.'

'Gross. I don't wanna hear it. Do you need a hand with anything or can I go watch the film with the others?'

'No, thanks, but you're an angel for asking. It's more than your brother or sister did. Your aunt and cousin will be here shortly, so you can keep them entertained while I get dinner ready for tonight.'

Won't that be a joy. My cousin Kara is terrifying. My Auntie Shelly is even more terrifying, but somehow Kara's switchblade eyebrows make her worse.

I leave the kitchen with the pile of cards, and follow voices – mostly Ro's – to the drawing room. Everyone is gathered around the TV, Netflix already fired up with *Home Alone*. I snuggle up next to Thom, who's still giving off a weirdly thorny vibe. 'Are you OK?' I ask quietly.

He sighs. 'Yeah. I … I wonder if I'm coming down with something?'

I feel his forehead with the back of my palm. 'You don't feel hot …'

'I dunno …'

'You should have a Lemsip.'

He gives my hand a squeeze. 'Nah, I'm OK.' I go to give him a kiss on the lips, but he pulls back. 'I don't want you to get sick too.'

I stroke his hair. Hamish wouldn't have thought twice about something like that. I congratulate myself on making good choices.

'Are we all ready?' Willow says, giving me a weird look.

I scowl back at her. 'What? I was doing a job for Mum! You could have started, I've seen it a hundred times!'

She presses play and I nestle further into Thom's nook. I curl my feet up and let Christmas wash over me. I want to enjoy this family moment while I can because, if Shelly and Kara are on their way, things are about to get *noisy*.

ROWAN

'It's so good of you to keep me company while I smoke,' Syd says very loudly before passing me the fag. I take the deepest lungful of my filth career. Sweet Satan, that's good. I pass them the cigarette back before Mum comes to the kitchen window again. There's a firepit in the back garden that, much like *Love Island*, has been designated as the smoking area for 'out' smokers Syd and Aunt Shelly.

Syd blows second-hand smoke into my face. 'So, you'll tell your mum you had a threesome with twins, but not that you smoke? Sure, that's logical.'

'She's very anti-smoking,' I tell them. 'Her father died of lung cancer when she was little. It's a whole thing.'

'I hear that, and take it on board,' Syd says, blowing a smoke doughnut.

'Anyway, I heard if you quit before you're thirty, you basically grow new lungs ... You brought some pot, right?'

'Of course.'

'Thank fuck for that. I'm gonna need it.'

'The Thom sitch?' Syd says.

'Give me another drag, queen.' I get another hit. 'I feel like shite for teasing him; he feels like shite because ... well, I don't really know, actually, but he's sitting there with a face like a smacked arse. At first I was like, *LOL, I shagged my sister's boyfriend*, but it's actually a major downer, to be honest.'

Syd nods sagely. 'Who knew?'

I take another, more measured drag. 'Right? Do you think this is karma? Like you can only have so much hedonism before fate fucks you over?'

Syd laughs. 'What? You finally burned through all the men, and the last one left was your sister's boyfriend?'

'Keep your voice down!' I snap. I look back at the house. It's only mid-afternoon, but it feels like night is nudging in. The SAD struggle is real. I am *not* a winter soldier: I like day drinking in parks; and Pride; and festivals; and road trips to the beach. 'You know, it doesn't matter. I had a holiday fling. It happens. I honestly never thought I'd ever see him again. I'm over it! I was never under it! He's Fern's boyfriend and that's that.'

'But …'

I hold up my hand. 'But nothing.'

'Ro, I see you. You go on about him a lot …'

I forget that Syd can read me better than anyone else. They see into me, I swear. It's true I talked about Thom a lot, in a way that most guys don't even get a footnote. 'Those two days in France were … like a film or something. But it wasn't real. It's dangerously easy to fall in love with someone when you're in a cute, snowy village with no one else around.'

'Boy, you said the L word …'

'Oh, fuck off. You've known me for like two years and how many guys have I had?'

Syd smiles slyly. 'I don't think I know numbers that great, Rowan.'

'Exactly. I get bored, or I get needy, or I get drunk and shag the guy who works at H&M in the changing room. I would have fucked it. I always do.' Syd looks at me with sympathy, a flavour I'm allergic to. 'Oh, don't look at me like that, I own my unseemly lament.'

'Timing, man,' they say.

We had two blissful days together, but we also live two hours apart. 'Time *and* space. It wouldn't have worked. He's a nice *idea*, and that's all. And anyway. Let's say we *had* got together after France – what do we think would have happened if Fern had found out I was dating her bisexual ex?' I prod a finger into their cheek. 'Whatever you do, don't say anything to anyone, OK? As far as you know, Thom and I met for the first time this morning. That is the Alternate Universe we're in now. Christmas is Fern's thing, and I'm not gonna let my chaotic penis ruin that. Got it?'

Syd holds their hands up in surrender. 'Loud and clear.'

In the distance, I hear the front door slam shut. I guess that means Aunt Shelly's here.

WILLOW

We have always hated each other. Kara used to nip me when no one was looking. She would steal my toys and take them home with her. She gave one of my Barbie dolls a crew cut. She was like four and I was five. I think there's a demon in her too.

While Auntie Shelly hugs Mum, Kara hangs back, her expression sour. Poundshop Kardashian. Bum and boobs. Fake ponytail; fake lashes; fake tan. Her face is so contoured it looks slightly stripy, like a tiger or something. I note she's put on weight, because of course I do.

I have beaten her, my demon tells me.

Shelly greets Rowan first. He's everyone's favourite. 'Hi, wee man, Merry Christmas,' she says. I always forget how strong their accent is. I have to adjust my ears. To begin with, they could be speaking a foreign language. Shelly always makes fun of how Mum has trained herself to speak in our 'posh' Edinburgh dialect.

'Och, get that door closed,' Mum beckons them into the hall. 'How was the journey?'

'Aye, wisnae tha' bad.'

Mum quickly introduces newbies Syd and Thom as we congregate in the hall. 'I like yer tatts,' Shelly tells Syd. That could have been a lot worse. I doubt Shelly and Kara are down with the Trans Thing.

Mum asks if they want a drink and they both ask for Irn Bru. Of course they do. That's the demon talking: I am vile. It is interesting, though. If Mum hadn't done so well at school, and gone away for university, would she have ended up like Shelly? Or is she just lucky? Mum – as repulsive as this is – was always regarded as something of a MILF back at school. Shelly looks like Mum, but … worse. Shade, yes, but also true. Her cheeks are sunken and her teeth are fucked. Even her hair is thinner than Mum's. Mum gets really cross if you point this out.

I get that. They're sisters. I can slag off Rowan and Fern, but I'd cut someone else if they shit-talked them.

After Shelly has greeted everyone else, she turns her attention to me. Here we go. Brace, brace. 'How are ye, Willow? Ye feelin' any better?' She gives me a stiff hug. 'Och, yis all bones, hen.'

Straight to the point then. 'Yes, thanks.'

I see Kara look me over. I'm so good at seeing it: the *disgust*. You see it in a flinch, or a frown, or the curl of the top lip. Fat bitch. In the clinic we had to do this exercise where we looked at pictures of celebrities and models and had to identify what a 'healthy' body looked like. Spoiler: none of us were very good at it. I don't know how I look to other people. I don't know how I look to myself.

There is a point, though, about a millimetre of flesh, between the ideal thinness for girls – "slim" – and being repulsively thin – "skinny". Fucked if I can tell, but there was about a week between people telling me how good I looked, congratulating me on the weight I'd lost, to *holy shit, are you OK?* By that point, my head had gone and the demon had got in through the cracks.

Shelly pats my hand. 'Christmas, though, eh? Loads of nice food. Ye'll be right.'

I look to Mum, sending a silent SOS, and she steers Shelly away. 'Carry on with your film. I'll get your drink, Kara.'

'We're watching *Home Alone*,' Fern says.

'Which room have we got?' Kara blurts out.

Mum turns back. 'You're sharing the back guestroom because we needed the office for Syd. I hope that's OK? There are twin beds in there …'

'It's like yer runnin' a hotel,' Shelly says.

'Aye,' Kara says. 'Rowan, can you show me where it is?'

Rowan looks puzzled but agrees. She knows where the room is, she's stayed here enough times. Something's up, but there's always some drama with her. I guess it's something to do with her dad running off with that girl. I can't find it inside me to care. I'd be happy to ignore her all week.

Such a downer. I wish they weren't here. I wish it was just me and Ro and Fern and Mum and Dad. I feel like I'm doing cosplay: Normal Girl. But I'm not normal. I'm holding the demon back and it's making it mad. I feel twitchy, like there's static electric crackling under my skin.

'Will?' Syd calls me from the lounge. 'You coming?'

I nod. OK, the rest can go, Syd can stay.

ROWAN

I do love Kara. She's a snazzy glimpse into the world of normal people who didn't spend their childhood terrified of what they were becoming. While I was having various identity crises, Kara was perfecting her contour and watching *I'm a Celebrity …*

Her life is pure drama, mind. If I'd been born a cisgender girl, I often think my life would have been like Kara's; a non-stop flurry of hand-jobs with neds, stealing mascara from Superdrug, and nail extensions. She is such a hun, and she looks like a Bratz doll, always.

I walk her down the upstairs landing. 'You're in this one …' Kara hustles me into the smaller guestroom. 'Kara! What are you doing?'

'Oh my god, Rowan, shut up for a second. I'm pure mess.'

'What? What's up?'

She closes the door, her mental Ariana ponytail swishing out of control. 'You cannae tell anyone.' Her eyes bulge.

'I won't …'

'Rowan, I think I'm pregnant.'

See? Drama. 'What? No, you're not!'

'I swear on Nana's life.' Nana has been dead for eight years, but go off. 'I'm over a week late.'

I look at her aghast. As if I know my way around a fallopian tube. Although I'm impressed I know what one of those is. Actually, I did pay particular attention during sex ed lessons. If they'd have used sex problems in maths, I'd have done a lot better than a C. *It takes Raheem ten minutes to complete a handy in the toilets at CC Blooms. If he's there for three hours, how many handies can he perform?* 'Don't look at me! How do I know if that's normal or not? Shall I get Fern?'

'No! Mum will kill me, I'm nae kiddin'. She's always sayin' if I get knocked up, she'll drag me by my hair to the abortion clinic.'

I don't tell her that that ponytail isn't going to hold fast.

She lifts up the rim of her sweatshirt to reveal a surprisingly toned tum. Someone's been doing their HIIT. 'Can ye tell?'

'Kara, I don't think it works like that. Who are you even shagging?' If Willow is seventeen, Kara is sixteen. At least it's legal, I guess. The slimmest of silver linings, there.

She rolls her eyes. 'Well, it's either Craig Rooney or Allie Bristow, but he didnae nut inside.'

I'm not gonna judge that because I've had a great many more nut inside me, and I don't have to worry about this particular outcome. Teachers, churches, doctors, parents: always trying to make sex scary, but in different ways for the gays and straights. What would they do on TV? 'Have you taken a test?'

'No. I was worried Mum would find oot if I did it in the hoose, like. Will ye help us?' She hops from foot to foot, obviously freaking out.

I take a deep breath. 'Of course I will. Let's not lose our shit until you've actually done a test.'

Kara wraps her arms around me. 'Thank you! You're the best cousin ever.'

'I know.'

'Can you go now?'

I sigh. There goes *Home Alone*. I also need a convincing excuse. I delve into my local knowledge to scout where I can discreetly get a pregnancy test in the vicinity. I have my queer cred to consider. I don't want to go anywhere where they might think I've somehow got someone pregnant. Ghastly.

FERN

Mum has – against the odds – made three passable pies: two chicken-and-leek and one mushroom-and-leek for Syd.

Here we all are, around the table. It's only at Christmas we have to extend it to full size. There's a pretty poinsettia arrangement at the centre with tapered gold candles. Tomorrow will be the traditional Christmas Eve buffet; then Christmas dinner served at two p.m. and then leftovers curry on Boxing Day.

I've changed into a leather skirt and roll-neck, and I forced Thom to put on some chinos and a shirt. Show Christmas some respect. Syd, Willow and Rowan haven't made the same effort, the heathens.

In the hum of candlelight, everything looks perfect. We could be a John Lewis ad if you played a damp minor-key version of an eighties song in the background. You can't really see that Willow is trembling, locked in a staring contest with her tiny wedge of pie; you can't see that Aunt Shelly is drinking Buckfast instead of wine; I don't hear Kara refusing to eat vegetables because they make her boak. But it's all there, bubbling under the surface.

Even Mum and Dad, normally the calm centre, seem on edge tonight.

Dad is seated to my left. 'Where were you today?' I ask him, pouring him some wine – a nice Merlot. I like red wine because it makes me feel instantly sophisticated. Rowan is necking Prosecco like a stripper or something.

'I was at work.' He looks to Mum. 'We don't all get three weeks off for Christmas.'

Mum purses her lips. 'The chance'd be a fine thing. I don't even want to think about the dissertation proposals I have to start reading ...' Mum is one of the world's leading authorities on the poetry of Robert Burns at Edinburgh University. I didn't realise quite what a rock star she was until I went to watch one of her guest lectures at Roehampton.

I am, and I'm aware this is a mature stance for someone my age, very in awe of my parents. They met when they were seventeen, married at twenty-three, and had Rowan and me when they were twenty-six. Dad took a career break to look after us so Mum could finish her PhD, which I think is very cool.

Most of my friends at school didn't have this sort of family around them. I'm very lucky. This is goals. It's much too early to talk about houses, marriages and babies with Thom, but I can see it. If we could get through all that shit last year, I think we're good. Thom is, unlike Hamish, woven from husband material. I never could see a future with Hamish, everything was too chaotic.

But somehow, even Mum and Dad's united front looks to be under strain right now.

Then, speaking of united fronts, Scottish independence rears its head. Dad is firmly against (*I believe with the rise of*

China and Russia, now is not the time to make our domestic union weaker ...) while Shelly, loudly, thinks it's time to make the move (*Tha eejit is nae prime minister of mine, we didnae ask for Brexit up here*). Oh, this one will last until Hogmanay.

Mum, on Willow's left, keeps whispering *encouragement* in her ear until even I tell her to lay off. Rowan sips a centimetre off the top of his flute before topping himself up. Kara chews with her mouth open.

I squint my eyes and stare into the candle. They will not ruin Christmas. Never. I fill my ears with the Christmas lift musak streaming out of the Google Home. Aye, it all *looks* perfect.

At least I have Thom. I want to offer him something, a reward for his compliance with my dream Christmas. I turn to him and whisper in his ear. 'Hey. Let's have an early night tonight ...?'

WILLOW

'Stop right there, young lady. Where do you think you're going?'

I was so lost in my head, I didn't realise Dad was in the kitchen, loading the dishwasher. 'I just want some air,' I mutter. My whole face feels tight. My jaw aches.

He looks up at the big clock over the door. 'Nope. Not for another half an hour.'

I'm not allowed to the bathroom or out of the house until an hour after a meal. This is bullshit because I never had the stomach for bulimia anyway. 'Dad! Auntie Shelly and Syd are out there. I'm not gonna do anything.'

He ponders on this. 'Aye, OK, go on then.'

I slip out into the night and quite welcome the cut-glass cold. It's a cleaner cold than the constant chill in my marrow. I slurp in a couple of deep breaths and remember one girl in the unit who told me, sincerely, that a deep breath is as nutritious as a meal.

There's a basket of throws in the porch and I wrap one around myself like a cape. Auntie Shelly is trotting towards the back door. 'Ooh it's Baltic, hen … see yis inside.'

Syd is still smoking. I join them at the firepit. 'She's fun,' Syd says.

'You think?'

'She was very keen to tell me about Michelle, the trans woman who works at the Springburn Job Centre. Can't think why.'

'Oh god, sorry.'

Syd smiles. 'She was cool. You know what? Transphobia is very middle class. I think people with circumstances like your aunt have bigger things to worry about, don't you?' I hadn't thought of it like that, but it makes a lot of sense. 'You smoke?' they ask.

'No.' I gave it a whirl, but I genuinely didn't like the headrush.

Syd lights another, and I perch on the bench built into the garden wall. 'So, dinnertime is intense,' they say.

I look up at them, already panicking. 'What?'

'Christmas when you have anorexia ... that's gotta be intense?'

My first instinct is to tell them to fuck off and mind their own business. I hate it when people say the word *anorexia* like they know. Just because you know its name doesn't make you an expert; doesn't mean you lived in its universe. I know the word *astronaut* but I've never been to space. I feel my neck vanish inside my body, tortoise style. 'It's fine.'

Syd sort of laughs a bit, and I wonder what's funny. 'Is it?'

I don't want to come over as a stroppy little kid, so I try keep my voice chill. 'Look, um, I don't know what Rowan said, but we don't talk about it, OK? It only makes things worse.'

'Fuck that noise,' Syd says, and it's like a slap. What? Are they allowed to talk to me like that? I think I know myself better than a random stranger. I open my mouth to argue but they jump right in. 'No! Willow, no offence, but you gotta talk about the elephant in the room. It's a bullshit saying, but it's true. If you ignore it, the elephant ... just sits on shit and breaks stuff.'

What's the non-binary equivalent of mansplaining? 'It's not the same.'

'Isn't it? Is not talking about anorexia making you less anorexic?'

I spring off the bench. I can't have this conversation. 'It's got nothing to do with you.' I grip my blanket around my shoulders and sweep across the lawn. So it turns out Syd is a massive wanker. There's a type of person who, despite never having had an eating disorder, thinks they're an expert because they read about it in a magazine at the dentist. Shame. I thought Syd was different. Turns out it's just some tattoos and a haircut.

ROWAN

As I exit the bathroom, I find Thom waiting to get inside. 'We have to stop meeting like this,' I purr, although he looks tense. 'Oh, dear god, can you please relax? Syd has some weed somewhere if you want.'

He exhales through his nostrils. 'Sorry. Today has been a lot.'

I see he needs a bit more salve for his soul. 'It doesn't need to be. It's nice in a way. Now my sister and I finally have something in common.' This time he laughs a little. 'See? It's already getting funny … told you.'

He leans against the landing wall, his shoulder resting underneath a framed photo of my dad's parents on their wedding day. He keeps his voice low, like he's at confession. 'I'm trying to unpick it. Why this has got me so spun. Fern already knows I'm bi, so it's not like I'm scared you'll out me, is it?'

I don't really have an answer for him. 'Aye, but I doubt she's told our parents that, so maybe do keep it down.' I know they're cool with me being gay, but people can be really cunty about bisexuals. All those myths about them being sneaky or promiscuous are very of my parents' generation. Maybe that's exactly what his disquiet is; the terror of feeling his privilege slipping away. Not a single person on this earth ever thought I was straight, but Thom has something to lose.

'That's exactly why I told her in the first place! I don't *want* secrets. Why would anyone want secrets? Maybe we should just tell her. If you think it's funny, maybe so will she?'

I look at him like he's high. 'Are you on glue? Have you met Fern? Do you want me to take you to the storage cupboard and show you how she used to write her name on individual Lego pieces so she knew which were hers?' He nods like he can well believe it. 'Twins don't share, Thom. It's bad enough we were forced to share a womb.'

'OK. That makes sense in a messed-up way.'

This isn't about him, in the end. It's about Fern and me. She has always had this idea in her head that I'm the golden child and she's the *spare*, which couldn't be further from the truth. It was always *why can't you behave like Fern does*. 'She will lose her shit, trust and believe.'

'OK, I'll take your word for it. I'm just trying to work out why I'm having such a meltdown,' says Thom again, looking down at me.

I examine his earnest face and it hurts to have to tell myself that he is, sadly, off limits – now and for ever. I wish he *was* just a random and our paths had crossed again. There's so much of him. I want to climb him like one of those cat trees and sit on his face.

'I'm sorry,' I say, looking away. 'Spending Christmas here would have been intense even without all this drama. But we have to be cool. Fern has this weird obsession with Christmas, and I don't wanna spoil it for her. I hope we can be friends?'

Thom's long lashes dip. 'Of course.'

Fern's head appears at the top of the stairs. 'There you are!' she says, and I'm not sure exactly which of us she's talking to.

'What's going on?' I say. 'Are we going out tonight?' I check my phone. It's like nine-thirty. I still feel full from dinner and, truth be a told, a bit twatted on Prosecco. Also, last night ended up costing more than I thought it would. Was I buying drinks for that guy I brought back? Why would I do that?

'No, we're gonna have an early night,' Fern says, taking Thom's hand. 'We'll get drunk with you tomorrow night, though, obviously.'

'You mean you're gonna *fuck*?' I say, instinctively. Something tugs at my small intestine. Is it the thought of my sister having sexual intercourse – vile in itself – or the fact of who she's doing it with?

Why am I having feelings on this, please? I must get rid of them, immediately. He's HER boyfriend.

'Rowan!' Fern hisses.

Thom looks deeply embarrassed.

And I do what I always do: roll the turd in glitter.

'Go!' I say with a flourish. 'Enjoy yourselves, you crazy kids, but don't forget: wear a condom …' Then I add in a whisper as I walk away, 'Kara thinks she's preggo.' Switch and bait; pull the spotlight away from me onto someone else's drama.

'What?' says Fern's eyes almost pop out of her head. 'For real?'

'Seriously,' I say over my shoulder. 'Let that be a lesson to you …'

And I swan off down the landing as if I hadn't a care in the world.

FERN

I can act out 'sexy', although my body does not feel sexy. Still, I made sure I was wearing matching underwear and I shaved my legs and made sure my pubic landing strip was neat and tidy. I refuse to go pubeless; I think that's weird, and encourages men to lust after pre-pubescent girls.

I stand before Thom at the foot of the bed, fighting the urge to dive under the covers and hide myself. Despite being very well versed in all things Body Positivity, I sometimes think there are two types of sexy body for girls: underwear model (rake thin with inexplicably big boobs) or bombshell (perfectly proportioned bum and bust with tiny little waist). I clatter between these two stools. When I see myself in the mirror, I see a tube – I'm straight up and down with no curves, a human chorizo. Sturdy ankles may have been great for hockey at school, but don't make for perfect Barbie pins unfortunately. It doesn't help that Thom is an actual Adonis.

All this being said, via Willow, I have seen the Dark Side of body obsession, and will gladly take sausage body over mental illness.

Thom waits on the bed in his Calvins. I note, however, he isn't as yet pitching a tent. Something's been bugging him all day, although he won't say. I hate when he clams up like this. 'Are you OK?'

'Yeah, just had a bit to drink.'

I try to panther prowl over the bed to him, but it probably looks insane. I swear I used to be good at this. *How can he fancy me and also boys? Do I look like a boy?* I push that nagging voice right out of my head. That's a mood-killer right there.

We kiss for a minute and then I go down on him to get him going, and because I know he likes it. I do too, because I think I'm quite good at this, so that makes me feel sexier. He groans and I take that as reinforcement. He likes it when I'm on top too, but all the bouncing around on him makes me feel weirdly self-conscious.

Moreover, I'm only just over an especially brutal episode of cystitis, so I'd rather not.

Thom is, I'm pleased to say, very into giving head too, and off he bobs. It's good, and he knows what he's doing. I try to drift away on it, ride that wave of pleasure, but I can't help but think my magical O may be some way out to sea tonight. I don't know if we'll get there. We don't always, and that's fine. It's the taking part that counts.

We go into the sex part of the sex, and he closes his eyes as he rocks on top of me. It bugs me. I don't need him to hold rigid eye contact throughout, but I always wonder if he's lost in the moment or picturing someone else. And is that someone else a boy or a girl? Any tingliness I was feeling subsides.

If I'm going to achieve O, I might need to do the same. I love watching Thom at work: his body is long, lean, muscular. The little buds of hair on his chest are super cute and I like the grooves that run over his hips. That said, I've been having sex with the same person for a year and a half, and variety is the spice of life.

Who shall I think about tonight? I love spinning the fantasy wheel of fortune. Fantasy is free, and also judgement-free, right? Sometimes I think about a muscular, sweaty, but highly problematic builder who catcalled me from a building site. My libido is not politically correct. Sometimes I think about Dr Jenkins, my politics lecturer, with his wolfish blue eyes. Somehow, the fantasy now morphs into Hamish.

And this one isn't a fantasy.

I'll credit him with this, he was always, *always* able to find my O. Hamish Bell is a wrong-un, make no mistake. Always so naughty. I recall the time he slipped me a finger on the back row of the bus; or the time he did me in the kitchen while his parents were in the lounge; or just how he'd take control in bed, flip me over and pull my leg up and—

And would you look at that. It's my O.

I grip hold of Thom's arm. 'I'm going to …' And I do.

CHRISTMAS EVE

WILLOW

My sleep is a mess. My insomnia has flipped one-eighty. It used to take me hours to get to sleep, my legs almost buzzing as soon I climbed into bed, no matter how exhausted I was. Now, I fall asleep fast, but wake up in the early hours. I ping wide awake. No chance of going back to sleep.

I roll back and forth in bed until about six, when the heating clanks on and I give up. I pull a sweater over my pyjamas and head for the kitchen. It's still pitch black outside the windows. I like these secret hours, just the house and me.

I put the kettle on the Aga and tuck myself in at the kitchen table. All I want to read at the moment are old Agatha Christie paperbacks from Dad's study. I'm presently on *The Mirror Crack'd from Side to Side*. Miss Marple is on the hunt for a village poisoner.

The kettle starts to whistle and I choose a lemon-and-ginger tea (two calories).

The back door opens and I very nearly drop the mug. 'Oh my god!'

Syd enters the kitchen, dressed in sporty running gear, and pulls out their earpods. 'Sorry, did I scare you?'

'Um, yes.'

'Sorry. I woke up early and wanted to get a run in today.'

I was not expecting Syd to be a runner. Like, that's so dorky and they are so painfully cool. I'm kinda embarrassed about the demon jumping out at them last night. Now both Thom *and* Syd have seen me at my worst. The way I stropped off like a little girl. Pure mortifying.

'You run?' I ask. They seem willing to talk so maybe we can just pretend it never happened. That's a perk of being sick – people don't stay mad at you for long in case they accidentally tip you over the edge and finish you off.

'Yeah.' They fill their water bottle at the sink. 'It keeps me sane, man. Endorphins or serotonin or whatever. Years back, my doctor suggested exercise when I was having a total mental health meltdown and they couldn't up my SSRIs any more. I was like, I don't think so, but he convinced me to try yoga first, then kickboxing, and then I started running. And, tell you what, that shit works.'

I sip my tea. It's way too hot. I lean past Syd and add a drop of cold water to the mug. 'I'm not allowed to exercise,' I admit. 'I think yoga's OK, but that's it.'

Syd nods. 'I get that. I had to be careful not to swap one obsession for another, but life is all about coping strategies, you know. Some of them are healthier than others. Like running is better for me than cutting my arms to shit, right?'

I agree. I force myself to keep my eyes locked on theirs and not on the silver scars on their arm.

'I'm gonna shower, but I'll have a brew if one's going?' they say and I grab them a mug. As they leave the kitchen, they turn back to face me. 'Hey. I just wanted to say sorry for last night, yeah?'

I stare into the cup, embarrassed. OK, we're not pretending it didn't happen then. 'It's OK.'

'No, it's not. I was out of line, and you were right to call me out.' They lean on the doorframe, skin shiny with sweat. 'Because my mental health fluctuates, I sometimes think I *own* mental illness, does that make sense?'

'It does,' I say, because I did not like those other anorexic girls in the unit stealing my specialness.

'So yeah, sorry I dumped unsolicited wisdom on you. It's like, I've had toothache, but I'm not a fuckin' dentist.'

I offer a meek smile. As they head upstairs, I return to the table. I pick up my book, but now my head is booting up. One of my doctors was always taking about insight – or being aware of your illness. Knowing you're nuts when you're nuts is way better than being nuts but thinking you're sane. Accepting help is better than pretending you don't need it.

Syd seems to have insight. And unsolicited wisdom is still wise.

ROWAN

I open my eyes to see Kara looking down at me. 'Oh my god!' I say and roll over, burying my face in the pillow. 'That is so freaky! How long have you been there? Are you a fucking sleep paralysis demon now?'

She ignores me, staring at me intently. 'Did you get us the test?'

'No, Kara, I did not! I was with you literally all afternoon yesterday, when do you think I had a chance?'

'Rowan!' she whines.

'What time is it?'

'Almost nine.'

That does not count as a lie-in. It's Christmas Eve. I wish I cared as much as I did when I was like twelve. I remember almost bouncing off the walls with excitement and waking up at about five-thirty. Now, it feels like any other day, but worse, because I have nowhere to be and nothing to do. A day with a very specific Prosecco hangover.

Christmas is cancelled. John Lewis and Coca Cola can try to sell me the MAGIC (to sell me shit) but I'm not buying it.

Unless it's Mariah. I'll buy that literally every year. In July.

I push the duvet off. 'OK, I'm up.'

'Will ye go now? I'm goin' oot me heed.'

'Now?'

'Aye!'

'Won't it look suss if I go to the shop before breakfast?'

Kara shrugs. I'm obsessed with the fact she's already glued on her lashes by nine in the morning. Dedication right there.

'Whatever.' I scour the floor for yesterday's clothes. 'Is there a particularly reliable brand I should get?'

'Just get whichever's cheapest.' She offers me a five-pound note that's evidently been through a spin cycle. I pluck it from her fingers. I'm not footing the bill when you can get free condoms literally anywhere.

I throw on some sweatpants and tell everyone I want a 'real coffee' which sounds more believable than telling them I'm going for a run. That would literally never happen unless I was running away from a murderer, and even then I'd try to reason with him.

It's effing freezing, the pavements and car windscreens sparkling with frost. The sky feels white, low and heavy. Do Tescos do pregnancy tests? I don't know but it's at least five minutes closer than the nearest pharmacy, so I head there first.

What if Kara actually *is* pregnant? If it were me, I'd get an abortion at the first opportunity, but that's easy for me to say because I'm never going to be pregnant.

To me it's simple: Kara's a kid. She shouldn't have a kid. Aunt Shelly is a hot mess too, so it's not even like she'd be much help. I'm suddenly furious with Kara for being so sloppy. I've had to spend my whole sex life worrying about condoms, lube, PEP and PrEP, so why shouldn't she? Wow,

I guess we all truly have a tiny *Daily Mail* reader in us, just waiting to manifest.

I enter a pleasingly toasty supermarket and head for the toiletry aisle. I don't know where else it would be. Sure enough, they have two pregnancy test kits next to the condoms and (what I call) the 'Straight Lubes'. I wouldn't want that strawberry-tinged 'play' gloop anywhere near my rectum, thank you kindly. Also people who call sex 'play' need to have a word.

One of the test kits is a lot more expensive than the other, so I compare the boxes. Does one contain toxic fumes or something? Does the more expensive one also provide the aforementioned termination if desired?

'Is there something you want to tell us, Rowan?'

I recognise that voice. I turn and see Hamish Bell, resplendent in navy Tesco uniform, behind me. Oh, just fuck him, he's getting even better looking as he gets older. Which motherfucking attic is his haunted portrait hanging in, and can I rent some wall space? His beard is filling in and very much suits him. 'Oh my god, Hamish. Loving the stubble!'

'Thanks man, how are you?'

'Good. Not pregnant! At least not yet! I'll keep trying, though!' Uh, I hate myself. I wish I didn't get tongue-tied around cute straight boys. What sort of curse is this?

'Not for Fern, is it?'

I give him an incredulous look. 'Have you met Fern?'

He laughs and nods sagely. 'She does take contraception quite seriously, yes.'

Every boyband has the boring talented one, the cute one,

the one who stands at the back and doesn't do much, and the one you just know is secretly a bit filthy: Robbie, Harry, Joe Jonas. *That* one is Hamish. 'So you work at Tesco? That's depressing. Did the band flop?'

He laughs again. 'This is just a part-time gig! Didn't Fern say she saw me yesterday?'

'She did not,' I say and wonder how that slipped her mind. Maybe she didn't want to mention an ex around Thom. 'Is there any difference between these kits?' I waggle them at him.

'I had a very reassuring moment last year with that one,' he points at the more expensive one. 'I guess they bank on you not being tight when it comes to unplanned pregnancy …'

'You are so right.' I put back the cheaper one.

'But, like, who is it for?'

'Did you ever meet our cousin Kara?'

His eyes widen. 'Isn't she like ten?'

'Sixteen.'

'Yikes. We got old.'

'Speak for yourself.' I bite my lip. Oh god, I want to have sex with him right here next to the selection boxes. Why am I so keen on men my sister has boffed? There's one for the therapist I can't afford. 'Well … you have a nice Christmas …' I back away down the aisle.

'Did Fern mention the rave tonight?'

'What do you think?'

'I thought not. Well, if it's more your thing, there's a big rave at Leith Volcano. You know the old church?'

That might be cool after we've done the nice family bit. 'I'll see what my friend says.'

'Friend? You met someone?'

'Not like that.' I bid him adieu again before turning back. 'You knew I had a thing for you right?' It's a mark of two years passing that I'm bold enough to ask that now. I used to be so scared of boys. I see now that they're scared of me, and how sad that is for them.

He smirks slightly, and I'm reminded of how oddly paired he and Fern were. *Definitely* filth. 'Aye, I knew. Fern too. It was sweet.'

I give him my most powerful come hither and bum me look. 'I was many things, but never *sweet*, Hamish ... maybe I'll see you tonight.'

I head for the checkouts. I will *not* look back.

I look back, and he's still looking.

Now, wouldn't he be an amazing Christmas present. What? He and Fern broke up like two years ago. *He's* fair game.

FERN

The kitchen looks like Mum's gone to Iceland, which would be plausible if Mum wasn't a certified Waitrose shopper. The counter and table are piled high with various canapes in various stages of defrosting. 'Do you need help?' I ask, cradling my tea at the table. I left Thom to sleep. He'll surface when he's ready. I can't lie, after a powerful O, I slept like a baby.

Mum wipes her brow, midway through preparing some potato salad by the looks of things. 'Yes, Fern, I need help. Mental help for offering to host nine people for Christmas. Next year, we're eating out.'

She says that literally every year. 'Where's Auntie Shelly?'

'She hasn't done her Christmas shopping yet; she's gone into town. Can you imagine, on Christmas Eve? She must be out of her mind.'

'Well, I'm not going anywhere. I can help.'

Mum's shoulders creep down a couple of inches. 'Thank you. You're a star. I'm OK right now, but I'll give you a shout.'

I note once more that the chef is absent. 'Where is Dad? I've hardly seen him since I got back.'

Mum says nothing for a second and then carries on chopping potatoes. 'Work.'

'On Christmas Eve?'

'It's a Friday, Fern,' she says tersely. 'In the real world, people don't get almost a month off for Christmas.'

True, but he's a *politician*. They do precious little work at the best of times. In fact, I remember Dad being around all last Christmas – he was the one who'd drive us out to the unit to visit Willow.

They're up to something and I don't like it. I never did like surprises.

ROWAN

I got almost all the way home before I remembered my cover story and doubled back to one of the cute indie coffee shops that have sprung up all over the area like middle-class chickenpox. I see a latte has crossed the three-pound mark in Edinburgh. Thieving fucking bastards, honestly. I definitely can't afford a croissant too.

It *is* great coffee, mind.

I arrive home and enter via the front door. Kara is waiting at the top of the stairs, silently beckoning for me to join her. 'Did ye get it?'

'Aye.' I slip it out from inside my jacket.

Kara gasps and shoves it inside her hoodie. 'Will ye help us?'

'Ew no! Gross!'

'Rowan, please! I've never done one before!'

'Oh, for crying out loud!' We check the coast is clear and both head into the big bathroom on the first floor. 'I'm not watching.'

She looks rightly horrified. 'Too feckin' right, yer not.'

I sit in the bathtub and read the instructions while Kara gets on with it. The pamphlet unfolds to a sheet of paper the size of a wall map. Who knew pissing on a stick was so complex? 'Is it your first wee of the day?' I ask.

'No,' she replies.

'Hmmm. You're meant to go first thing because that's when your piss is extra juicy with pregnancy shit.'

'Is that what it says?'

I roll my eyes, still not facing her. 'Obviously not.'

'Will it still work?'

The instructions say it's a suggestion, not mandatory. 'Aye, should do.'

Behind me, the toilet flushes. 'How long will it take?'

I recoil as she approaches. 'Wash your hands, you vile tramp!' She does so. 'It'll take two minutes to detect the presence of human chorionic go ... nado ... trophin, whatever that is. A distinct blue line should appear in the results window.'

Kara places the test on the rim on the bath and we wait. They say a watched pot never boils and a watched pregnancy test is similarly dry. We wait. And then we wait some more. 'Maybe we shoulda set a wee timer?' Kara says.

She makes a point. After what *must* be two minutes, longer even, we both stare at the results.

'Can you see that line?' she asks.

'I ... can't *not* see a line ...' It's incredibly faint, but I think I can see a line. I can definitely see a line. I think.

'Well, is it a line or is nae?'

I tilt it to the light coming from the window. 'I don't know ...'

'Well, what does the pamphlet say?'

I scan the *Your Results* section again. 'OK. A positive result is accurate ninety-seven per cent of the time. It says a negative result is less reliable because: *you may be in the very early stages of pregnancy and have not yet started to produce significant levels of* ... that hormone stuff. If the result is inconclusive you should take another test in a few days or see your family doctor.'

Kara clutches her hair. 'This is a 'mare. Rowan, ye'll have to git me a new test.'

'Kara, I can't – it'll look hella suspicious that I keep running out. And anyway, it says to wait a few days. Why don't we try again on Boxing Day?'

She nods. And then her face squidges up and she starts to cry. 'I don't want a baby, Rowan ...'

'Hey, don't cry.' I climb out of the bath. 'It'll be fine.' I wrap my arms around her.

'How will it be fine?' she sobs into my shoulder.

I hadn't got that far with my reasoning. It was one of those nice lies you tell people; anaesthesia from the toxic reality of life. It absolutely won't be fine.

FERN

I stand in front of the TV. Someone has to take charge. In the dining room, I can hear Mum and Shelly getting things ready for the big buffet later. Kara looks puffy-faced and isn't wearing her trademark stripper make-up. I'm dying to ask if she's all right, but that would land Rowan in the do-do. All I can really do is try cheer her up through the medium of cinema. 'OK,' I say. 'These are our options: *The Muppet Christmas Carol* ...'

'Yes!' Rowan says at once. 'Sorted.'

'We always watch that one,' Willow moans.

'So why break with tradition?'

'Rowan. This is a democracy, not a Rowocracy,' I tell him. 'Our other nominees are *A Christmas Prince*, *It's A Wonderful Life* or *Let It Snow*.'

My brother looks at me as if I were simple. 'But Fern, literally none of them have Muppets and/or songs in.'

'How about *It's a Wonderful Life*?' I suggest.

Thom and Rowan bark NO at the exactly same time.

'What, why?' I ask Thom. You love that film.'

'I'm ... just sick of it,' he mumbles.

I ignore him. 'Let's take a democratic vote ...' We do so. Syd opts for *Muppets* with Rowan; Thom goes for *Let It Snow* because he's never seen it; Willow and Kara both vote

148

Prince. So it comes to me to decide. 'Let's do *Muppets* ...' I say, for a quiet life.

As Rowan rejoices, I settle in next to Thom on the sofa for an afternoon of gentle Christmas movies. The fire is crackling and Thom and I made hot chocolates with whipped cream and cinnamon for everyone – even Syd has one with oat milk. So far, it's the picture-postcard perfect Christmas Eve. I nuzzle into Thom to get warm, and pull a tartan blanket over my lap. This is *much* more like it.

There's a clatter from the hallway as the post arrives. Rowan leaps up from his position in front of the fire. I don't know how he doesn't melt, he sits so close. 'It's my turn! You did them yesterday.' He glares at me and scurries to the front door. He returns a moment later with a pile of cards. 'Mum?' he yells. 'Can I open the cards?'

'Yes!' she calls from down the hall.

The film starts and the credits roll over the snowy rooftops of a Victorian Muppet London. Yes, it's Rowan's choice, but I won't deny that it's the best version of *A Christmas Carol* I've seen.

Rowan tears into the cards with an energy he normally reserves for tearing off jockstraps. 'Who the fuck are Eileen and Kenneth?'

'Who the fuck sends Christmas cards?' Willow adds quietly. 'Why not just go burn a forest down?'

'Old people,' I say.

'God, imagine buying a stamp,' Rowan says.

I focus on the film as Rowan continues to make his way through the pile. 'Oh my god,' he mutters after a minute or two. I look over and see he's holding not a card, but a letter.

'What's that?' I ask, picking a marshmallow off the top of my hot chocolate.

'I thought it was a card,' he says, his face an even milkier white than normal.

'Opening other people's mail is a criminal offence,' I tell him because I'm sure I heard that somewhere.

'Fuck,' Rowan says.

'What is it?' Willow asks.

I realise he's not kidding. 'Are you OK?' Rowan stares blankly into space. 'Ro?' I prompt. I sit up a little straighter. He's not playing and, if I'm honest, he's not *that* good an actor. I feel a weird falling feeling in the pit of my stomach. His aura tells me this is something serious. Something cancer serious. My mind starts racing through all of the worst-case scenarios. Death, bankruptcy …

'It's a letter from a solicitor.' His voice sounds strangled. 'They're getting divorced.'

My head hadn't got to that one yet. The word hangs in the air like a mushroom cloud. None of us need to ask *who*.

ROWAN

It's all very formal, like an episode of *The Crown* or *Game of Thrones* or something. We gather around the half-set dining room table for some sort of war council. The WAGs are relegated to the living room. This conversation isn't for them.

Mum has summoned Dad home from the office *if* that is indeed where he was. I mean, who the fuck knows any more. He might be shacking up in Falkirk with Nicola Sturgeon or something. 'What on earth were you doing opening my mail?' Dad asks.

'I thought it was a card!' I argue. 'It was in a posh envelope!' I was barely paying attention; I just worked my way through the pile with one eye on the telly.

'Is it real?' Willow asks, looking worryingly pale. With the lank hair and the skin, she looks like your wee girl from *The Ring*.

Mum and Dad are stiff. They're sitting next to each other but also seem to repel each other like magnets.

'Well?' Fern demands. She looks manic, eyes unblinking.

'Yes,' Dad admits softly. 'Your mother and I are separating.'

'Fuck off!' I snap.

'Language, please,' Mum appeals.

'What? Why?' Fern shouts.

Willow says nothing.

'We didn't tell you because we didn't want to spoil your Christmas,' Mum says. 'We were going to tell you everything in the new year.'

'I don't think it's great news at any time, Mum,' I say.

Fern turns on Willow, always picking off the weakest member of the pack. 'Did you know about this?'

'No.' Willow sighs. 'How could I?'

'Are you blind? You live here. How could you not know something was going on?'

'Fern, that's enough,' Dad says. 'We made sure Willow wasn't aware of anything while she's been focusing on her recovery.'

Well, that figures, I think to myself. There's so much cotton wool wrapped around her; she wouldn't hear anything anyway. Fern doesn't say anything else, tight-lipped.

'I don't understand,' Willow says, every move, every word laboured like she's moving through tar. 'Everything is the same ... like, why?'

There's a moment of silence as they seem to psychically agree what to say. 'Oh for crying out loud, just tell us!' I say. 'That's the cat all the way out the bag. A shitty, dead cat, with maggots.'

'Things are not the same,' Mum says. 'But like your father says, we wanted to put Willow first.'

Fern chunters something indecipherable.

'Fern, if you've got something to say, say it to my face.' Willow glares at her. Ooh, the mood in here is sour. This ... isn't great, though. Yeah, we fight and bicker and rip the shit out of each other, but we stick together. I never thought the wheels would come off.

Fern ignores Willow's demand and instead focuses on Mum and Dad. 'Well? How can you be getting divorced? Have you had therapy? Taken a break? A trial separation? Why would you jump to divorce?'

They are sheepish again. There's a horrible pause and my brain fills some of the blanks in the crossword. After so long there's only one thing that'd end their marriage. 'Someone had an affair?' I say, the sentence becoming more solid as it progresses. There's another, even more horrible pause.

'No way,' Willow breathes.

'Chris?' Dad, in his most petty voice, defers to Mum, and I instantly know he's torturing the guilty party.

Mum begins. 'When you are older, you'll understand that ...'

'Mum!' Fern explodes. 'You didn't! How could you?'

Mum looks like she's going to go off, but controls herself. 'Like I said, sometimes adults ...'

'Mum, you know we're adults, right?' I say. 'Like, we have had sex ...'

Mum glares at me. 'Yes, Rowan, I am *dimly* aware because you persist in trying to get some sort of a reaction out of us with sordid details of your love life, which tells me you aren't nearly as mature as you like to think you are.'

Well, shit, that tea is scalding. I grumble under my breath. 'You're the one who had an affair, harlot.'

Despairing, Mum's head falls into her hands.

'Rowan ...' Dad warns.

'When did this happen?' Fern is now pacing the floor like

she's auditioning to play Uptight District Attorney in a courtroom drama.

'I don't think going into the details is helpful,' Dad says.

Fern's eyes blaze with fury. She looks possessed. A different demon from the one that lives inside Willow; there's a real *Karen* brewing inside her, and one day she will verily ask to speak to the manager. 'I do. If we're going to come from a broken home, I'd like to know which man was worth throwing her family away over.'

'Aye, it better be fucking George Clooney coming round for espresso pods,' I add.

'Can everyone take it down a notch, please?' Mum pleads. She sounds more resigned than upset. I guess that's better. 'And I am not throwing my family away, Fern.'

'She's not,' Dad says, unexpectedly defending her. 'We are still your parents and we love you more than anything in the world.'

'More than each other?' Willow asks. There are tears on her cheeks now.

Dad reaches over the table and squeezes her hand. 'It's not as simple as that, sweetheart.'

'So who is it?' Fern demands again.

'Do you really want to know?' asks Mum.

'Yes, I do.' Fern demands. I both do and do not want this McNugget of information. I don't see what good knowing will do, but I don't want the unanswered question either.

'A man from work,' Mum says, her voice brittle with shame. 'A PhD student.'

'A *student*?' Fern will be speaking to that manager now.

154

'So you're getting fired as well? Great!'

Mum looks so weary. 'Not *my* student, and he's a mature student.'

'Are you, like, leaving Dad for *him*?' I ask.

'No. It's over. It's been over for a long time.'

'Then why do you have to get divorced?' Willow says.

Fern tuts at her. 'Don't be naive, Will, she cheated on him! A total betrayal of trust! It's not about the ...' she can't bring herself to say sex, 'it's about the lie.'

'Fern, leave her alone! We've been through all this, we don't need an interrogation,' Dad says. 'But you're right. And we *have* had couple's counselling, actually, and a lot of trust has been broken. We have tried to fix things, but ...'

'But we can't,' Mum finishes. 'You are not children any more. We can't stay together and pretend everything is fine to make you happy. The last twenty years have been all about you three. Now it's time to think about us. I'm sorry, but it is.'

I look to Fern and Willow in utter disbelief. Man, I thought we'd dodged this bullet. Most of our friends' parents got divorced when we were between like seven and twelve. There was seemingly a point where all the dads had affairs when the mums stopped shagging them on the regular. Or when the dads traded in the mums for younger, sexier versions of the mums.

I did not see this one coming. And neither, judging from their faces, did my sisters. 'This is so clapped,' I say, desperate to break the silence. It has barbs.

'This can't be real,' Fern adds. 'You've been together for almost thirty years. You have to be able to fix this for *you*, not us. You've been through so much.'

Between us and Willow there was a baby that died; a boy called Ash. Stillborn. Fern's right. How can you survive that and then give up eighteen years later?

'We just wanted to give you this Christmas,' Mum says, closing her eyes.

Willow pushes herself away from the table and storms out of the dining room, slamming the door so hard one of the decorative teapots slips off the shelving and shatters on the floor. Yep, that's about where I'm at too, suicidal teapot.

The dust is settling and I think about what this means in real terms. It's not *not* going to affect Willow, is it? In any other family, this news would be shit. In our family, this news might be deadly.

FERN

The three of us needed a debrief. Willow glares at me from what used to be *my* bay window. I sense the demon is about to jump out. Her eyes darken, I swear. 'You think it's my fault,' she says bitterly.

Of course I do. What they don't tell you about eating disorders in Year 6 PSHE circle time is how *boring* they are. For three years all any of us in this house have talked about is her bloody food consumption. All day, every day. It's so tearfully dull. I dread coming home. 'No, I don't,' I lie.

'It's not your fault, Will.' Rowan says, although I'm not sure his heart is in it.

'It's Mum's fault,' I add, with a similar absence of gusto.

'I'm sure it's not that simple.' Rowan falls back on the bed. 'It takes two to tango.'

'How is it Dad's fault that Mum had an affair?'

He looks at me as if the answer were the most obvious thing in the universe. 'Maybe she wasn't getting the D.'

Revolting. 'Jesus, Rowan.'

'Gross,' Willow says.

Rowan turns his face to Willow. 'Well do you ever hear them shagging? You're next door to their room.'

Willow winces. 'No … oh my god, this is so rank.'

There you go, I think to myself. If I lived in constant fear of my youngest child dying, I'm not sure I'd be able to get it up either.

Life is not sexy. I remember when I first got together with Thom, we couldn't keep our hands off each other. I remember surprising him naked, or kissing him before he could get through the doorway. But then life trickles in; all the *we have to be somewheres*, or *this assignment is due*, and yeah – *I'm really worried my sister might die*. Passion killer.

'It's not about sex,' I say uneasily.

'So it *is* about me.' Willow looks out of the window. The sky is already indigo blue. 'It's my fault.'

'Fuck's sake,' Rowan groans.

'Not everything is about you, Willow,' I say with more venom than I intend. Wow, *my* demon jumped out.

'What's that supposed to mean?'

I do *try* to be gentle, but my feet are cut to shreds from stepping on all the eggshells and I'm very much over that. 'I get you have a lot of shit going on, and maybe that's why you haven't seen … what's happening.' Because, really, it's not even about her. It's about her *illness*, which has mutated into a corporeal creature almost autonomous of Willow McAllister.

She rolls her eyes. 'Thanks, so I'm self-involved?'

'Oh my god!' I cannot *deal* with her when she gets into these pity ruts. The more you try to dig her out, the further she sinks.

'Squad, can we focus, please?' Rowan says. 'Can we please discuss the fact that next Christmas we might have to split

158

shifts between two houses? Can you imagine Dad in a sad bachelor flat with black ash furniture and leather recliners? How is this real? It's such bullshit.'

I perch my bum on Willow's desk. 'When we were kids everyone's parents were getting divorced. I sort of thought Mum and Dad had made the decision to stick it out to the bitter end.'

'She fucked someone else,' Willow says.

'Yes, thanks, Willow, I got that.' I snap.

'I dunno,' Rowan says. 'It's encouraging that we'll still be having sex in our twilight years.'

'She's forty-six, not ninety,' I remind him. This doesn't quite feel real. How can our mother and father possibly break up? There are some things you just take for granted: the sun will rise in the morning; night will follow day, and Chris and Dale McAllister are a couple. It is one of the pillars holding up the world. Does that mean our world is about to fall in? 'At least we have each other,' I accidentally say aloud.

'What?' Rowan says.

'I don't know,' I say, wishing I hadn't said anything at all. 'That's something. We can't divorce each other, can we? So there's that.'

'Group hug,' Willow mutters sarcastically.

Rowan rolls his eyes. 'I guess it means they have to at least be civil to each other. We're a bridge between them.'

'No.' Willow jumps off the window seat. 'This is fucked. I'm not doing all that shit. What happens if they meet new people? What if they already have kids? Stepdads and stepsisters and all that shit? No way. And am I meant to choose which

159

one I live with for the next year? Or do they share me? God, I bet they're fighting over which one gets rid of me.'

'Willow,' I say, 'as if that's true …'

'Just fuck it.' Somehow, Willow storms out of her own room and slams the door behind her.

'Well, where's she gonna go this time?' Rowan asks mischievously.

We share a wry, twin smile, and follow her downstairs. Sometimes, Willow detonates and all you can do is stand by with a dustpan and brush. She storms past the lounge, where Mum and Dad are handing out cute cups of mulled wine to everyone.

'Willow?' Dad says. 'Can you come in here, please?'

Willow does as she's told, but her spine is up like an angry cat. Rowan and I file in behind her. Everyone else is gathered like we're at the denouement of a murder mystery. It was Mum, in the university, with the PhD student. I perch on the arm of the sofa next to Thom. He quickly fires me a *WTF?* expression and I just shake my head. Not now.

'This is so embarrassing,' Mum says. 'I don't know what you must think of us.'

'Christine, what's goin' on?' Shelly asks, on the Stella instead of mulled wine.

Dad steps in. 'Chris and I are separating in the new year,' he says on one long sigh. 'The idea was to keep Christmas as normal as possible before dealing with the ugliness in the new year.'

'Typical Tory,' Rowan breathes.

For once I agree. 'I don't think turkey and sprouts are

160

going to make this OK, but whatever.'

'Fern, you told us you were bringing Thom home in September,' Mum says. 'Willow and Rowan didn't even have a Christmas at home last year. We just thought it would be … nice.'

Dad interjects. 'And it would have been if Rowan hadn't opened our post …'

'Don't blame me,' he says. 'We're grown-ups, you should have told us.'

'We wanted to avoid this awkwardness.' Mum gestures at the cringe scene. Syd and Thom must be cursing the day they chose to come up. The extended Jesus Is Born club remix in Hounslow with Thom's mum is looking really good right now.

'I cannae believe yev said nuttin,' Shelly says. 'Wos brought this on?'

'I tell you later, Shell.'

'She fucked someone,' Willow says.

'Willow!' Dad shouts her down so loudly I fear he might blow the windows out. 'Apologise for that NOW.'

She scowls, her face twisted. 'Why are you defending—'

'Willow, so help me god, you will spend the rest of the week in your room alone. You hear me?'

Willow goes to strop off again, but he drags her back by the wrist. I wince; he'll snap her if he's not careful. 'Get off me!'

'No. If you behave like a child, I'll treat you like one.' She wriggles her arm free, but stays put. For now. I'm quietly impressed at Dad. So long as she eats, Willow has been doing exactly what she wants for years. About time someone stood up to her. 'You will *not* speak to your mother that way. Understood?'

'I'm sorry,' she hisses in a way that suggests she really isn't.

Mum continues, speaking directly to the tourists. 'Syd, Thom, the last thing we want to do is ruin Christmas for you.'

'It's fine ...' they mumble over each other.

'It's really not,' Mum reiterates. 'Needless to say, Dale and I, and the kids, have a lot to sort out, but we'll do what we always do ... we'll sweep it under the rug for now and deal with it later.'

'How?' I say and I very nearly burst into tears. But I don't. 'How can you expect us to pretend this isn't happening?'

'We may need to get very, very drunk,' Rowan suggests.

'No!' Dad now snaps at Rowan. I wonder if he's finally had enough of our shit too. We've certainly given them enough to compost. I say *we* ... I've done little wrong. 'If your mother and I can get along, then so can we all. No one is *pretending*, Fern, we're having a family Christmas because we are still a family. We will always be a family, no matter what.'

What is anyone supposed to say to that? Mercifully, a timer goes off in the kitchen. 'Ah,' Mum says. 'That'll be the prawn tempura.'

It breaks the glass dome over the room, and everyone breathes freely. Shelly goes to help Mum, and I take the opportunity to drag Thom out of the room while Rowan and Syd go for a cigarette. Willow skulks out with them. Thom and I head to our room.

Once there, I very quickly fill him in on everything he's missed. While we were discussing our parents' divorce (god,

162

I can't get my head around it) he was playing Monopoly with Syd, Kara and Shelly and it absorbed the time successfully. Good old Monopoly, training innocent children to become *landlords* since 1903.

'What now?' he asks.

'What do you mean?' It's still Christmas Eve, I WILL still wear my special Christmas Eve outfit. I slip out of my jeans. When we were little, Mum would always buy us special outfits for Christmas Eve and I never grew out of it. This year I've got a chic black dotty dress with a cute pussy bow collar. 'Are you changing?' I ask/tell Thom. I grab my wine glass and take a big swig. I feel jittery and need to calm down.

'Are we still seriously gonna have this party when all this stuff is going down?'

'Of course!' Even I hear a hysterical sharpness in my voice. 'Get changed.'

'All right …' He rummages in his holdall for a shirt. 'I mean … that was intense down there. Are you OK?'

I can feel myself about to scream at him – *of course I'm not bloody OK* – but I hold it in. I say nothing. This isn't his fault and I won't take it out on him.

'Hey.' He comes over as I fumble with the buttons on the dress. 'Never mind me. *Are* you OK?'

I bat his arms away. 'I'm fine.'

'Fern …'

I look up at him. 'I am *fine*. It's Christmas.'

WILLOW

The dining room. They can get fucked if they think I'm eating. One day won't kill me. They cannot make me. I cannot process Dad (or Mum? It's *his* house technically) moving out *and* the creeping horror of a mealtime ahead.

I am a house made of straw. One huff and I'm fucked.

I'll just have some fruit. I will eat *something*, but not now, not in front of people.

All piled up on the dining room table, it looks like some sort of horror film. I remember once, the headmaster at Finnians told this story in assembly about how – in hell – there are mountains of food, but everyone starves because you're given chopsticks the size of barge poles. In heaven, everyone has the same giant utensils, but feeds a friend, and there's some moral about helping others. This dining room is my hell. It's a beige feast of vol au vents and sausage rolls and mozzarella sticks. It stinks of puke.

Mum thrusts a side plate into my hands. 'Get some food, please, Willow.'

All I see is shimmering fat dribbling off the table and pooling on the floor. I can't do it. I'm shivering. My bones are jangling like windchimes. I once tried to describe it to Dad – how this feels. He is very scared of heights. I asked him if he'd climb to the top of the Eiffel Tower. He said no. What if someone had a gun on him? He said he'd do it, of course, but he'd struggle.

Well, that's me and food. And the gun is the phrase *Willow, you'll die.*

I do not want to die, but that doesn't make food less terrifying. And I know what's real and what's fake. We're so far past this being about me being skinny or fat. Now it's just a terror that lives inside me.

'I can't,' I say.

They all hear. I can see that disappointment. *Oh, here she goes again.* There's a pause before everyone pretends I'm invisible and continues to help themselves at the buffet. 'Willow, just have a bit,' Mum says softly. 'If you need to, we can eat in the kitchen, just us two.'

This is one of the techniques we learned in the unit, and one we'd discussed before anyone got home. But why should I? Everything I've done has been for nothing. Snakes and ladders, and I just slid down the mother of all snakes. I don't see how I'll get through this. I've clung to routine for years. They're going to take it all away.

'No,' I say. 'I don't want anything.'

Aunt Shelly pretends to clear her throat. Dad looks over, concerned, chewing on something. Rowan is too busy helping himself to pizza. Syd offers something that *might* be a sympathetic smile.

'What's going on?' Fern swoops into the conversation uninvited, her eyes loopy.

'Nothing, Fern,' Mum says. 'Let me handle this.'

I turn to leave the dining room, but Mum catches hold of my elbow. 'Willow,' she whispers in my ear like a bad ventriloquist, 'I really don't want *another* scene today, do you?'

'Mum, please. I don't want anything.' Just an hour or two off. I cannot do this now. My heart is beating way too fast and I feel prickly hot all over.

Mum sighs. 'Just have a bit ...'

I want her to see that I mean it this time, that right now, eating is impossible for me. 'No, Mum, please ...'

I don't even see Fern move in. She's so fast. She grabs my wrists and pulls me over towards the tables. I'm too shocked to make a noise. 'JUST EAT SOME FUCKING FOOD,' Fern demands. She seizes handfuls of stodge and slams it down on my plate with such force, I drop the lot on the carpet.

'What the fu—'

'Not every day is about you, Willow. I'm so sick of your whining. Now just eat something and *shut the fuck up*.'

She looks insane, hair all in her face. She picks up my plate and tries to shove it in my hands, but I knock it back to the floor. I dimly hear Mum and Dad trying to break us up, below a high-pitched ringing in my ears. Uh-oh. It's coming ...

I feel the demon coming out ...

'Get off, Fern!'

Dad holds Fern back but she carries on screaming. 'I'm so over your shit! I'm so over people not saying it! I'm so over all of the silence in this house!'

It jumps out. **'WELL, WHY DON'T YOU ASK**

166

ROWAN ABOUT THE TIME HE SHAGGED YOUR BOYFRIEND THEN?'

The ringing continues, but it's like the temperature drops as everyone else falls silent. The room turns to ice. Oh fuck, what did the demon do this time? Why is everyone staring at me? No, wait ... everyone is staring at *Rowan*.

Fern looks from Thom, to Rowan, and then back to Thom. 'What?' she asks either, or both, of them.

'That was a dick move, Will,' Syd says.

I think that inadvertently confirms whatever I said, though.

Fern looks to Ro. 'Rowan?'

A thick silence stretches like toffee. 'I ... Fern ... you weren't together ...'

'It's true, though? You two?'

'*Rowan* ...' Dad says. A bit late for a warning.

'They weren't together!' Rowan shouts.

I can't take it back. It's out. It's a gas and I can't stuff it back in the lamp. What the fuck have I done?

'Fern ...' Thom says. *I can explain.*

Her mouth curls down at the edges. She's going to cry, I can tell. Thom reaches for her, but she turns and makes a beeline for the door. Ro immediately follows her, but Thom stops him. 'I'll go.'

And now all eyes turn to me. I look to my brother. 'I'm sorry,' I say.

He looks madder than I've ever seen him, his face almost not his face at all. 'I can't believe you did that. Are you satisfied? Now we're all as fucking miserable as you are.'

167

FERN

'It was while we were broken up.' Thom chases me up the stairs, but I can hardly hear him for my heart drumming up in my skull. 'I swear to God I had no idea he was your brother or—'

'Or *what*?' I whip back to face him. I couldn't care less who overhears us.

'Or I'd have never …'

And then I throw up on the stairs. It's a purple mixture of mulled wine and the mini vegetable samosa I just ate. I watch a whole, unchewed, pea dribble off the edge of the step.

'Fuck,' Thom says. 'Let me get a towel …'

I continue to stare at the sick as he moves past me towards the bathroom. And then I vomit again. The first release was just a sneak peek. This time the entire contents of my stomach explode out of my mouth and nose, my back arching.

I need air. I step over the lumpy puddle and run downstairs. I go out the front door and the December evening hits me like a slap. It's like diving into the ponds at Hampstead, so cold it snatches my breath away. It's actually good. I feel less dizzy, more *here*, at once.

My mouth tastes of puke and my teeth are furry. I spit up on to the front lawn. Inside the house someone – maybe Mum, I think – calls my name.

I can't be here. I cannot talk about this. I need to physically get away from that house, it's like I'm having an allergic reaction to it. My body wants out.

They're going to try to make this OK, aren't they? They're going to make me the unreasonable one. Rowan can do no wrong. It will somehow be *my* fault that he shagged my boyfriend. *If you hadn't broken up with him for being bisexual …*

Fuck that. I'm already walking down the drive away from the house, my boots crunching through the frost. I have no idea where I'm going, but I'm gone.

WILLOW

I think Taylor Swift once said that famous people stop mentally developing at the age they become famous, which is why so many celebrities behave like kids. I wonder if that's also true of anorexia sufferers. Am I stuck at thirteen? I rarely get my period; I throw tantrums; I'm the same size I was then.

They've 'removed me' and brought me to the kitchen. Time-out. Mum and Dad loom over me like gods, and my ragdoll body feels very tiny at the breakfast table.

'That was totally unacceptable, Willow,' Dad says. 'This is not the end of the conversation either, by the way.'

'Where has she gone?' I ask.

'We don't know,' he goes on. 'I'm going to take the car out in a second. She can't have gone far.'

'I'm sorry,' I say. 'I don't know why I did that.'

'This stops,' Mum says. 'You are almost an adult now. We have babied you for long enough. From this day forward, you are an adult with an illness. You either help yourself or we get you help.'

I know what that means. The unit again. 'No …'

'No more excuses. No more "demon", Willow. There is no demon, there is only your behaviour, and we won't tolerate it any more.'

I scowl. 'Who's we? You and my new dad?'

'Grow up!' Dad barks and I flinch. He never raises his voice. 'Your mother and I will continue to support you equally. We've come too far.'

I feel tears burn my eyes. 'But how am I meant to … everything's gonna change!'

'Welcome to the world, Will! You cannot sit in your room reading until the end of time. The world is scary and full of challenges. It's full of unkindness, and unfairness, and you just have to deal with it.' He takes a second to cool off. 'Take responsibility for your own recovery. Neither me nor your mother can make you well, Willow. If only it were that simple. You have to decide you want to beat this thing. And it makes no difference what we do.'

I've heard all this before. He knows his lines.

But how can I pick myself up? The floor keeps shifting, tilting, turning. It's a funhouse. I can't get up. If I could have one day off, I might be able to get on my feet, find something to hold on to.

'We are still here for you,' Mum says. 'No matter what.'

Then why does it feel like I've just been given an ultimatum? Get well or get out. I can't see a future. Everything is close and black.

ROWAN

I jab a fag in Syd's face. 'This is very not acceptable. How could you tell her?' It's so cold in the garden I can hardly breathe between drags.

'Mate, I am so sorry … she was listening to you upstairs and kinda guessed. But I did fill the gaps. She swore, man. I thought she was cool.'

'Syd! She's certifiably insane. Literally.'

Now they scowl at me. 'Get fucked, Rowan, you have no idea.'

'All you had to do was lie. Just a little one.'

'I don't lie, bruv.' They finish their cigarette. 'But I'm sorry. I messed up.'

I can't be mad at Syd for long, and I've done much worse. I once stole their debit card to pay for Lana Del Rey tickets because I knew I was overdrawn. 'Dear god, you owe me one.'

'I owe *Fern* one.'

No one does sanctimony like the queers. We're so evolved. 'Fair. I better go clean up my mess, hadn't I?' I throw my cigarette butt into the bushes. 'Will you do me a favour?'

'Yes.'

'Just keep an eye on Will while I look for Fern? She's a

dickhead, but I bet she feels like shite.'

Syd nods. Ride-or-die.

I head back to the house and Kara is in the kitchen, picking at a mince pie. 'Ye didnae really shag—'

'Not now,' I snap, and continue straight past her into the hall.

Thom is halfway up the stairs, cleaning up puke. God, it reeks, and the lavender scented disinfectant isn't much helping. 'Do you need a hand?'

'I'm good,' he says, not looking up.

Where to even start? 'I'm so sorry.'

'Not your fault.' This time he does look at me. He looks slightly hollow. 'I think your little sister is a bit of a twat, though.'

I wince, because we're all so used to protecting Will, but I'm not going to deny that right now. That said, I'm fairly evil when I'm hungry too, and she's been starving herself for about five years.

Thom gets to his feet and picks up the bucket by the handle. 'OK, I'm done. I wanna go find her. Do you know where she's gone? Has she texted or anything?'

I check my phone again to be sure. 'No. But I think I'm the last person she'd text right now.'

'Second to last.'

'No,' I say, following him downstairs towards the utility room off the kitchen. 'This predates you, I'm afraid. Fern believes, unfairly I feel, that I am the favoured twin.'

He gives me serious side eye as he tips out the vomitty bucket water.

173

'I'm not! If anything, Fern is the overachiever! I'm the mutant flamer they keep locked in the attic like Quasimodo!'

'That's not the way she tells it.' He washes his hands and shakes them dry. 'Do you know where she *might* have gone?'

I rack my brain for a coffee shop; a special bench in the park; even a best friend. I don't really know who she's still in touch with. 'She had a few friends at school. She was like B-List, not the scary girls, but she was on the netball team, if you know what I mean.'

'Do you remember their names? Or where they lived?'

Yes, I remember their names but no, not where they lived. I was never invited to those house parties. 'Not really. We had different friendship circles. I hung out with the cutters and queers, obviously.'

'She can't have got far. Let's just ... head out and make a plan up as we go.' He pushes past me towards the hall. All I can do is trail after him like a needy dog.

'Together? Is that a great idea?'

'Rowan, I don't know where I am, and I don't have a car.'

A good point. Dad enters the hall, car keys in hand. 'Maybe you should leave it to me,' he says, grim. 'I'm not sure she'll want to see either of you at the moment.'

Thom looks mortified. 'I'm so sorry, Mr McAllister.'

Dad throws his hands up, so far out of his depth. As if any parent wants to know the literal ins and outs of their kids' sex lives. 'To be honest, Thom, I'd rather not think about it. I just want to make sure Fern is OK.'

I sigh. 'Why don't we split up? I'll take Mum's car. We can cover more ground.'

Dad nods. 'Fine.'

I go to get the car keys from Mum. She's with Willow in the kitchen. I scowl at my sister, but she looks away. 'What you did was very not cool.'

'Rowan …' Mum starts.

'No,' I hit back. 'No more excuses. You crossed a line, Willow.'

'I know,' she says quietly. 'I'm really sorry.'

'It's not me you need to apologise to. You just outed Thom in front of the whole family. You're no better than Perez Hilton.'

She starts to cry. There's a little bit of my heart that isn't stone yet, and it does feel bad for coming in so hard. 'I'm so embarrassed,' she sobs.

And that last bit turns to stone. It's all her, all the time. We have that in common. '*You're* embarrassed? How do you think Thom feels?'

'Stop it!' Mum slams her mug down on the counter. 'Just stop it! I've had enough!'

I feel the words form on my tongue. I could destroy her. *Oh, I'm sorry, maybe you could go fuck someone who isn't our father.* I won't, though. Today is already bad enough. Next year, I'm going back to France, I swear. 'Can I have the car keys?'

'How much have you had to drink?'

'Just one mulled wine.' And I certainly feel more sober than I have in years. 'We're going to find Fern.'

Mum hands over her keys. 'Drive safe. It's freezing out there, and the radio gives a thirty per cent chance of snow.'

I tell her I will, and return to Thom in the hallway. He's ready and waiting, in coat and scarf. 'Let's go,' I say, plucking my own jacket off the hooks next to the door.

We step outside and it is brutally cold, the kind of cold that really spears your chest. Did Fern even take a coat? I didn't really see her go. Dad's car is already pulling out of the drive and turning left, so I guess we'll go the other way.

'Get in,' I tell Thom, striding to Mum's silver Fiesta. It's so frosty, the door is almost sealed shut with ice. I have to yank it open.

'What am I supposed to say to her if we do find her?' Thom asks, his face sickly.

I slam my door shut and start the engine. I crank the heating up to full blast. I'll need to warm the little car up. The windscreen has a glittery crust all over it; I'd be driving blind.

I turn to Thom as we wait a minute. 'Listen,' I say, 'you have nothing to be sorry for.' He looks confused. 'What you're feeling is called shame. You slept with a boy a year ago. You were single. So was I. Despite what you might have learned in church, we've done absolutely *nothing* wrong.'

'But ...'

'No, but nothing,' I interrupt. As the car heats up, so does my certainty. It's fitting, nay predictable, that everyone is rallying around for her heterosexual tears. Oh, poor girl, her boyfriend once slept with a boy. How simply *awful* for her. 'You've done *nothing wrong*. Maybe it's *Fern* who needs to apologise for being a lil bitch.'

FERN

On reflection, storming *upstairs* instead of out the door might have been wiser. It's effing freezing and I didn't think to bring a coat. A bitter, cruel breeze cuts through the flimsy silk of my dress. I grip my arms tight with pink fingers.

I also didn't think where I was going. It's after seven p.m. on Christmas Eve. Everything is shut. My phone was in my pocket as I left, so at least that's something. *This* is why girls enjoy dresses with pockets. If I get really cold, I can just call Dad. He's the last person left off the list of people I'm furious at.

But if I skulk back now, tail between my legs because I'm *chilly*, that'd be so embarrassing. Perhaps I should have consulted with my more dramatic siblings about how to pull off a flounce successfully. Squeezing myself, I head towards Leith, pounding the pavements. My breath hangs in vast lanterns. I'm *Scottish*, we scoff in the face of girls who wear coats on nights out. I pass the Tesco Metro and contemplate heading inside to see if Hamish is working, but I suspect I'd cry on him.

I don't want him, of all people, to see that the rosy Instagram pic of my life is so heavily filtered.

I am still fizzing inside. I can't put my finger on what the emotion is, however. I am *furious* at Willow; I am *disgusted* at Thom; I feel queasy, on a cellular level, that Thom and Rowan have …

Urgh.

I almost puke again. I slurp in some freezing air and it takes the edge off my nausea.

I am *not* homophobic. I am not. I have *literally* marched on parliament for trans rights. I have partied at Pride. I have *checked my privilege*. What I do take exception to is my *brother* shagging my *boyfriend*. Who *would* be OK with that?

I could scream.

I have told myself many times this year that Thom being bisexual doesn't make him any more or less likely to cheat than a straight guy. Hell, look at Hamish, he cheated on me *at least* once, I'm sure. Three drinks for him, and he gets very matey with random girls he meets on a crowded dancefloor.

So why does it bug me so much?

I *trust* Thom. When we go out, I don't know if he notices both boys and girls *staring* at him, drooling, but I definitely do. Do ridiculously good-looking people *know* they're beautiful? The worst ones do, I guess. Thom *seems* oblivious. As his distinctly ordinary girlfriend, I feel those stares acutely. OK, that's not fair. I'm like a *seven* on a good day where I bother with eye make-up. Thom is a solid *nine* even on a hangover, an easy ten in his gym kit.

But still, I do trust Thom.

When we first got together, I had to check myself constantly. Two years worrying about Hamish really left my trust like swiss cheese. I found myself teetering on the verge of '*Who's messaging you? Where are you? Who are you with?*' territory.

Checking his phone if he left it alone. Control, coercion – those dark arts are in me, and I wish they weren't. It was a struggle. Luckily, because Thom is so laid back, it meant I was able to recognise my crazy for what it was – crazy.

Until he told me he thought he was bi.

The truth stinks. I don't like thinking about my boyfriend doing things with men. So maybe I am a bit homophobic? I am full-on crying now. I wipe my cheeks. I don't want to think like that, to be that person.

That said, does the thought of him doing stuff with girls *also* make me feel weird? Also, yes.

This is a mess. I am a mess.

Without quite realising it, I'm on Becca's street. I could, in theory, be popping around to wish her a merry Christmas, couldn't I? Without a coat and only my phone? Sure, that looks really sane. It's been a few years since I've been to her place and all the houses on Denham Green Terrace look very similar. I seem to remember hers had a red front door and it was definitely on the left-hand side of the street. I cross over and peer through a couple of windows intently. One has a red front door and a huge Christmas tree illuminated in the bay window. It's familiar.

I decide it's worth a go. I reach into the middle of a pretty holly wreath and knock the knocker. I must look like a tragic orphan. On the other side, I hear footsteps as someone comes to the door.

I'm greeted by a wave of artificial heat and Mrs Ramsay. She looks surprised to see me – well, why wouldn't she? 'Fern!' she says. 'Goodness! How are you? Come inside out of the cold!'

I step into the toasty hallway of their chic townhouse; smaller than ours, but more fashionable with its parquet floors and mid-century modern furniture. I'd love to live in a house like this one day. It's a Pinterest house. 'Thank you. I'm OK, thanks. Merry Christmas.'

'You too. Where's your coat? Aren't you cold, pet?'

'Freezing, yeah. Is Becca home?'

'She is. Is she expecting you?'

Awkward. 'No, I just thought I'd chance it.'

Mrs Ramsay looks a bit bewildered. I guess it is weird showing up uninvited. I haven't seen Becca since ... the summer before I moved to London. I did *mean* to see her last Christmas, but with all those trips to the unit to visit Will, it just didn't happen. Over the summer, I had to work and Becca was travelling around Australia. This is a good reason for a reunion, I guess. 'Well, you remember where her room is. Head on up.'

I thank her and trot upstairs. Feeling starts to return to my frozen fingers. This is a bit odd. SURPRISE! I knock on her door. She's listening to Christmas songs at volume. 'What?' she yells from within.

'It's Fern ...' I say.

The music stops and a second later, door opens. She too looks stunned. 'Oh my god! *Fern*! I thought someone had said "it's burned"! What are you doing here?'

We embrace stiffly and I enter her bedroom. Not much has changed since we used to hang out. The One Direction posters are gone, although I note Harry Styles is still present, a discreet picture tucked into the rim of her mirror. 'That is a long story …' Around the foot of her mirror is all the paraphernalia of a night out – curling tongs are on, make-up bag emptied out across the floor. 'Oh, are you off out?'

She looks at me like I'm speaking Mandarin. 'Of course! It's Christmas Eve! Aren't you having your big family Christmas thing this year?'

Once upon a time, Becca was invited every year. There's no big drama to why we drifted, it's just that when I started to date Hamish he became my world really. I know. It wasn't healthy, and maybe it makes me a Bad Feminist or something. In a moment of clarity, I realise I'm doing the same thing with Thom. Most of my friends are actually *his* friends that I adopted.

'Fern?'

'Yeah. I sort of just, um, ran away from it actually …'

She frowns. 'Are you OK?'

'No,' I say, my voice almost breaking. I pinch the bridge of my nose, as I heard it's supposed to stop you from crying.

'You poor thing … sit down.' Becca plonks me on her bed. 'Do you want to talk about it?'

My bisexual boyfriend shagged my twin brother. 'I … I can't …'

'That's OK. I don't have to be anywhere until eight-thirty. You can hang here.'

'Where are you going? Can I come with you? I can't go home.'

She doesn't look exactly delighted at this suggestion and that stings a bit. I know I should have been better at staying in touch, but I didn't think we'd grown *that* far apart. I wasn't that bad, was I? Yes, I liked to be in charge back in the day, but who doesn't? We still had loads of fun. I organised the fun!

Becca was always much more interested in boys and gossip than I was. She wanted to be one of the pretty, thin girls: one of Heather Morrison's vapid little clique. They didn't want her, though; back then, at five-eleven and somewhat stocky, she wasn't nearly petite enough. Then Becca underwent something of a glow up during S6; throwing herself into CrossFit and kickboxing. These days, she looks like liked a finely tuned fitness soldier – all rock-hard Instagram abs and Lycra. To be fair, her peachy bum does look amazing.

'Um … yeah, I guess. We're having a few drinks at Farah's and then heading to that party at Leith Volcano.'

'The rave?'

'Yeah.'

'Hamish is going.' The thought sort of plops out of my brain. I don't know why.

'Hamish Bell? God, is he still alive?'

'He very much is. He works at Tesco around the corner.'

'He didn't leave?' In the mirror, I see her screw her face up. 'Figures.'

My instinct is to defend him, but I remember that horse has bolted. 'Do you think Farah would mind if I came too?'

Another pause. 'Yeah, I don't see why not? It's not like she even celebrates Christmas, is it – it's just a night out.'

I remember the Hosseinis being only very loosely Muslim, in the same way I'm Christian in name only, but they do celebrate Eid. Farah was always happy to come over to our party on Christmas Eve, though. As with Becca, we were just so shit at keeping in touch after we left Edinburgh. Becca is at Loughborough (wherever that is) while Farah is at York.

'Is … Farah cross with me or something?'

Becca turns and looks over her shoulder. 'No! I don't think so …'

'So what is it then?'

She shrugs. 'I don't know. We thought … well, you haven't spoken to either of us in so long. You sort of broke the Girl Code, Fern. You dumped us for a guy.'

I look at my feet. 'I know. I'm sorry. I …' As if either of those bitches wouldn't have done the same. But I am guilty as charged.

'Hey, it's fine!' Becca relents. 'Tonight can be like a school reunion! Let's surprise Farah. It's awesome to see you, Fern, it is. I just wasn't expecting it … it's been so long.' She swivels around to face me. 'So tell me all about this gorgeous man I see on your Insta!'

And I burst into tears again.

WILLOW

When I was in primary school, there was this kid: Kyle. He had behaviour issues. I remember once the whole class had spent weeks making this massive partridge in a pear tree for our Christmas show; all papier-mâché and glitter and tinsel. Kyle's behaviour in rehearsals was so bad, he was told he wasn't allowed to play the role of Drummer Drumming any more. That break-time, Kyle snuck into the classroom and threw red paint all over the pear tree. Miss Cullen sent him to the headmistress and I couldn't understand why he'd done it. Now, maybe, I do. If he couldn't enjoy the pear tree, neither would anyone else.

I just threw red paint all over Christmas.

Dad, Rowan and Thom are gone.

Shelly and Kara are watching *Mrs Brown's Boys Christmas Special*, and I want to die. Mum is essentially throwing dirty plates at the dishwasher.

I don't know who's madder? Her at me, or me at her.

I shouldn't have said what I said, but she did have an affair. Now the dust has settled, there's a taste like sour milk on my tongue. The thought of your parents having sex is like maggots burrowing under your skin at the best of times. Mum is a stranger now. I don't know her. She's not what

I thought she was.

She's not just a mum, she's a woman. A woman with a secret side-life. Or maybe me knowing this makes *me* a woman. I'm not seeing her with child's eyes any more. The umbilical cord is truly severed.

I leave them all and head upstairs towards my room. I'm gonna Rapunzel it out I think. I wonder if the demon did this on purpose? Sabotaged Christmas so I didn't have to sit down for a feast. Who knows what tomorrow's gonna look like now.

'Hey, Willow!' Syd runs up the stairs to catch up with me.

'I thought you'd gone with Ro.'

'He asked me to keep an eye on you actually. So this is my eye, on you.'

I'm not in the mood for cute. 'I'm fine.'

They smile. 'Is that like the McAllister family motto? *I'm fine* through gritted teeth? I'm not sure I'm buying what you're selling …'

I demi-laugh. They're right. As long as everything *looks* fine, that's always been enough for us.

'So what we doin'?' they ask.

'What do you mean?'

'Were you planning on sulking alone in your room on Christmas Eve?'

Well, now you mention it. 'Pretty much.'

'No way. You wanna watch a movie or something? We could try *Muppets* again?'

Well, that depends, I think. Is it because they genuinely want to hang with me, or because Ro asked them to? 'You don't have to babysit me.'

'I'm not getting ten quid an hour to be here ...' Syd smiles.

I relent. 'OK. We can watch on my laptop, I guess?'

Syd nods. 'Excellent. Let me grab a beer. It's Christmas. You want one? Are you allowed to drink?'

I honestly forget I'm not legally allowed to. I tend *not* to, though, because alcoholic drinks contain a fuck-ton of calories. But it *is* Christmas and one beer feels right. And I don't want Syd to think I'm a loser. 'Yeah. OK.'

While they fetch the beer, I quickly tidy my room and wonder where to put the laptop. I'd normally rest it on the bed, but that feels like I'm inviting Syd *into* bed, which feels inappropriate. Instead, I set it down in the centre of the rug and pull some throw pillows down off the bed to make a cosy little area.

Maybe I should light some candles? Create a cinema-like environment? I switch off the main light and turn on the fairy lights that are wrapped around my bedframe. I then light a couple of candles on my windowsill. God, maybe this is too romantic, like I'm trying to—

Syd taps on the door. 'Come in.' Too late to worry about it now.

They enter, carrying two bottled beers and a bowl of snacks – popcorn and pretzels. 'Ah, this is cute,' they say. 'You made a nest.'

I could not feel more like Rowan's dorky kid sister. Like I said, it doesn't help that I could easily pass for about twelve. Syd snuggles into one of the cushions and I take my place next to them. They hand me a beer.

'Cheers,' they say.

I clink the neck of their bottle with mine. 'Cheers.'

Maybe Christmas isn't cancelled after all.

ROWAN

'Where are we going?'

I tell him I have no idea. Because I don't. 'We should go *somewhere*. I feel like a kerb crawler.' Which is literally what I've been doing since we left the house; driving at about five miles an hour. We've had some funny looks and rightly so. It doesn't help that the streets are full of merry – in both senses of the word – people noisily making their way into town for Christmas Eve drinks.

'Where?' Thom's questions aren't helping, but he really doesn't know Edinburgh – or my sister it seems – very well.

I take a deep breath. This is *Fern* we're talking about, so she's hardly gone to a chemsex party or a crack den, has she? Although, in fairness, I've been to both of those things, and I made it out in one piece. I have only one rule in life: Don't Do Meth. That shit is poison, and I'm scared, genuinely worried sick, at how many gays my age are getting swept into it. Like, HELLO, IT'S FUCKING METH. Just Say No.

Her old friends seem like a logical place to start. 'Does she ever mention Becca or Farah any more? They were her friends at school.'

I scan his face for recognition, but he just shakes his head. I can't remember where they live either. I know Becca lives somewhere near us because Fern used to walk over after school. 'Is anywhere even still open?' Thom asks.

Yes. There is. Somewhere very PG-13 for Fern: 'Ocean Terminal,' I say, quickly changing lanes.

'What?'

'It's like a big mall, and it's open until midnight tonight.'

'I never get people who leave all their shopping to Christmas Eve.'

'Right?' I agree. 'The elves should unionise.'

It's about a ten-minute drive from ours to Leith docks where the shopping centre is. Fern could have easily hopped on a bus *or* even walked most of the way there by now. It's got all the usual chain coffee places. If I was storming out, I'd either want a drink or a cake, and I think Fern is more likely to head for muffins than shots. There's a definite whiff of pumpkin spice latte about my sister. It's definitely worth a look.

The car park is predictably busy and I can only find a bay about a mile away from the entrance. I step out of the car and feel something land on my forehead. 'Is that …?'

'It's snowing,' Thom finishes.

I look to the streetlights and see dandruff flakes idling through the beam. 'Oh wow. Was it meant to snow? I suppose we are in Scotland.'

'It hasn't snowed since …' He trails off.

'France?'

'Yeah.' For a moment we both let the flakes lazily waltz around us. He breaks first. 'But, um, I've never had an actual white Christmas at home.'

'That's because you're mixed race, babes.' He laughs, despite

189

everything. 'Come on, this is a needle in a haystack job.' I take his hand and pull him towards the bright lights of Ocean Terminal. I thought nothing of it but, he wriggles his gloved hand free. Oh yeah, I don't suppose that'd look too great if we do find her here.

We enter via one of the department stores and, big shocker, there's a lot of lone men prowling the levels of the mall, and they all look very harassed indeed. They have no one to blame but themselves. There's an actual queuing system outside the toy shop. 'Oi! Get to the back of the fucking queue!' a red-faced man shouts at a poor guy who's about to swan straight over the threshold.

'Wow. Intense,' Thom mutters as we pass. God, he has long legs. I have to stride to keep up as he marches along the ground level. 'Do we split up to cover more ground?' he asks.

'No,' I say as we reach the central atrium, with a gargantuan Christmas tree that stretches all the way up to the vaulted ceiling. 'Then we'd only end up searching for each other. Let's check out the coffee shops?' All the chains are scattered evenly around the shopping centre.

He nods at a wall-mounted speaker currently playing Bing Crosby. 'Maybe they can do a tannoy announcement?'

That's actually a really good idea, although it occurs to me she might not want to see us. 'But what if once she knows we're here, she legs it again?'

'Do you think she would?'

'I don't know, Thom, I've never fucked her boyfriend before …'

He stops dead in his tracks. 'Rowan …'

I stare him down, hands on hips. 'What? Ashamed?'

'No … just …' He points to the small children sitting at the foot of the Christmas tree about a metre away. They look up at me, blank expressions on their gormless faces.

'Oh. Hi, kids!' They continue to gawp up at me. It's a bit unnerving. 'OK, what's their deal?' I ask Thom.

'Rowan!'

Someone calls my name across the concourse and I look over, hoping to see my sister. Instead, I see a familiar face dressed in a very unfamiliar elf costume. 'Oh my god! Lesbian Lara!' She looks ace – still very booby, but is now rocking super-cute lavender hair.

She runs towards us, weaving her way through the crowds. 'You call her Lesbian Lara?' Thom asks under his breath.

'Well, there was already a Lara, so …' She reaches us and throws herself into my arms. 'Babes! How are you?'

'Aye, I'm grand, how are you?'

I tell her I'm well. 'Is this like a professional elf gig, or have you transitioned permanently?'

'God, I wish I was a real elf; Santa probably pays better. I'm working at the grotto.'

An idea occurs to me. 'Hey, you haven't seen Fern tonight have you?'

'Here? No. But I've been handing out candy canes to kids all afternoon.'

'Shit.'

'What's up?'

'We've lost her.'

'Can you, like, do an announcement?' Thom asks.

Lara nods. 'Sure. I've just come off break. Come to the grotto with me and I can radio it in. We do it for lost kids all the time.'

We quickly catch up, Lara filling me in on her long-distance relationship with a girl in Belfast, and I'm suddenly very glad Thom and I didn't try to make something stick. It sounds like torture. We follow her through the mall until we reach a cute, snow-topped Alpine cabin plonked outside Marks & Spencer. An animatronic reindeer's head bobs up and down through the window. I can hear its neck creaking which somewhat spoils the illusion. The grotto is pretty quiet – I guess most families with little kids will be getting ready for bed before long.

I remember us before all this decay set in. Me and Fern and Will, so, so, so excited to leave out those carrots, a mince pie and a glass of milk for Santa. Mum and Dad took sleigh riding very seriously and wouldn't let us leave him sherry or a dram of whisky. In the morning, the reindeer would have chewed off the carrots and Santa would leave only a few crumbs on the plate.

Simpler times. I miss simple. Puberty is truly Pandora's box. Once it's open, there's no going back.

'Are we allowed in?' I ask, gesturing at the grotto.

'I don't know,' Lara chuckles, 'have you been a good boy this year?'

I share a glance with Thom. 'Definitely on the naughty list to be honest.'

Lara checks the coast is clear, and beckons us into the grotto. There's an instrumental version of 'Carol of the Bells' playing and it's faintly menacing. I was always quite scared of being taken to see Santa; there's a bunch of photos of little me looking pure terrified sitting on his knee opposite an angelic Fern, who was always happy to "do smiles".

We jump the winding queue all the way into Santa's cottage. Santa's living room has a fake fireplace and another robot reindeer. The man himself is lounging in an armchair, holding a huge Starbucks cup, next to an artificial tree surrounded by presents. 'Have you got the radio?' Lara asks.

'Stone the crows! Is that Rowan McAllister?' Santa says in an Australian accent.

I blink and try to see past the huge white beard. He pulls it down his chin to reveal a face I recognise. 'Davey! What the fuck?'

He gets up and gives me a wet kiss right on the lips. I pull back slightly. Bit forward, Santa. 'Little part-time gig before panto season starts. How the fuck are you, man?'

'Aye, I'm grand. Davey, this is Thom …'

He shakes his hand vigorously. 'This your fella?'

Thom looks a bit more mortified than I'd like. 'Oh – no – I'm his sister's boyfriend.'

'We've lost her,' I explain.

Lara speaks into a handheld radio. 'Hiya, it's Lara at the grotto, can I get a tannoy announcement for *Fern McAllister, please make your way to the grotto*?' There's a crackle of something indecipherable. 'Aye, thanks, Mark. He'll do it now.' I thank her, and she heads outside to monitor her position at the entrance.

I turn my attention back to Davey. I'd have been far keener

to see Santa if they all looked like him. 'How are you, darl? How's Al?'

'Yeah, he's all good. You know him, nothing gets him down.'

'Still playing the rugby?'

'For now … knee injury keeps playing up … and this gig isn't helping.' He grins. You wanna come sit on Santa's lap, boy?'

'Thought you'd never ask!' Davey returns to his throne and I plonk myself – gently, he did just say his knee was bad – into his lap. He takes the opportunity to cup my arse with his hand, which is characteristically Davey. Very dominant indeed. I feel a certain awakening and remember where I am. That only makes it worse.

Why am I like this?

He growls in my ear. 'And what would you like Santa to do this year, boy?'

I bark a laugh. Thom blushes deeply and looks away. Prude. 'Well, Santa, I'd like you to find my twin sister; erase her memory of the last two hours; cure my other sister of anorexia nervosa, and then rescue my parents' marriage?'

Davey looks taken aback. 'Fuck, mate. Tall order.'

'Uh-huh.'

'How about a candy cane instead?'

I laugh. 'Aye, it's a start.'

He plucks one from the tree and hands it to me. 'You want one too?' he says to Thom and gives him a smirk. 'I've got a spare knee for you too, mate.'

Thom scowls. 'I'm good, thanks.'

'Suit yourself.'

'Don't mind him,' I tell Davey, stroking his fake beard. 'He's having a rough night.'

Lara pokes her head into the pretend living room. 'We've got customers, D.' She ducks straight back out.

'Ah, bugger.' He slaps my arse off his lap. 'Hey, how long are you up for? You should come over. Al would love to see you too.'

'Yeah, maybe,' I say, non-committal. Bigger fish to fry first. 'We'll wait outside for Fern. Fingers crossed she heard the announcement. Merry Christmas.'

'Same to you, mate.'

We leave via the exit and circle back around to the front of the grotto. I don't see Fern anywhere as yet. I hope she hasn't scarpered – Lara didn't say *why* she had to report to the grotto after all, though I guess she could probably work it out. I find a prime spot on the pretend brick wall at the front of the cottage. There's a letterbox built into it for kids to deliver their letters to Santa.

'Is there anyone you haven't fucked?' Thom asks, distaste all over his face, and I almost spit out my candy cane.

'I beg your pardon?'

'You fucked Santa.'

'Well, if we're going to get technical, he—'

'Yeah, I get it. He's like *fifty*.' Thom takes a seat next to me on the wall.

'Calm down, Mumsnet; he's thirty-five, a certified silver fox, and I didn't realise you were such a massive prude.'

He shoves his hands in his pockets. 'I'm not …'

'Yes, you are. I saw the way you were staring at us.'

He does at least look a bit ashamed. 'He's so much older than you.'

'Oh my god, Thom. When you go to the ice cream parlour, do you only ever get one flavour? No. Of course not, because that would be boring. Sometimes, you crave a bit of vanilla, yes, but sometimes you want mint choc chip, or raspberry ripple, or all of those things together in one big cone. If humans could just admit that we're mammals, we'd all be a lot happier. We're not supposed to mate for life! That sort of thinking is what led my mother to shag her PhD student behind my dad's back. Davey and Alastair have an open relationship; we are all consenting adults; so please do tell me: what's the big fucking deal?' Well, that told him.

He looks wounded. 'So what, are you saying you wouldn't ever have a boyfriend?'

I half shrug, because I'm not sure that's my destiny, child. In a world with so many men, why on earth would I want just one?

'Wow. You aren't the person I thought I met last Christmas.'

I rubberneck around to give him daggers. 'And what's *that* supposed to mean? That I'm a gross whore? You didn't seem to mind last year when we—'

'Don't put words in my mouth.'

'Words like slut? Whore? Jezebel? Floozy? I don't believe in those words, Thomothy, but I am very aware of puritanism, morality, shame, judgement … and they're not for me. They are fugly polyester cardigans, and I refuse to wear them, so good luck with that.'

He sighs, and scans the mall. 'I'm sorry.' He seems sincere.

Thom is always so sincere, so straight-up, and maybe that's his problem. I prefer chicanery. That was stupid. I sorta … I just thought we had something special. I'm embarrassed that I … misunderstood so badly.'

I take a breath. 'We did,' I confess quietly, under duress. 'Remember the snow-globe analogy? It's still true. What we had was perfect, but it's trapped in that little glass bubble.'

He looks sad.

'What we did or didn't have is neither here nor there because you are with my sister.'

'I know!' he says, highly defensive. After a second he adds, 'I don't believe you, though.'

'Don't believe what?'

'That you'll *never* have a boyfriend. Everyone wants to find … a *connection* or whatever.'

'Babes, I want multiple connections, thank you very much. You're *queer*, Thom, whether you're with a girl or not. Embrace it. It's freedom. Take the rule book and burn it. We're on the outside. Picket fences and church weddings aren't for the likes of …' I tail off.

'What?'

A thought breaks in my head like dawn. I know exactly where my sister would go, and I should have thought of it first. 'Church. They have a big carol concert at the parish church on Christmas Eve.'

He considers this. 'She does love a carol …'

'She loves Christmas full-stop.' It all makes way more sense than Fern coming to a shopping centre now I think about it. I guess I can ask Lara to call if Fern *does* turn up. 'Let's try it.

C'mon. I'll let you take me down the aisle after all.'

I reach for his hand again. This time he takes it, and I drag him up off Santa's wall.

FERN

The snow is properly coming down now. It's gone from talcum powder to fat white feathers since we left Becca's. As Mr Ramsay drives us to Farah's, it's starting to settle on the grass verges and on the rooftops. I can't help but feel cheated. This would have been so magical if tonight had been different. I imagine how beautiful it would have been to watch it fall from the warmth of home.

Instead, it just feels like an inconvenience. A pretty inconvenience.

Farah's dad is minted. The family own a chain of bouji health-food stores all over Scotland. Their house, while very stylish and modern, looks a bit like a sports centre – all huge windows and straight lines. I think I'd prefer to live in a house that looks like a house. It's a goldfish bowl, and I can already see wee fishies swimming inside. I thought it was just a quick drink, not a full-blown house party?

'OK, girls, have fun,' Mr Ramsay says – still very much the Dad We All Fancied. 'But not too much fun, Becca, your nana is arriving at ten in the morning, remember?'

Becca rolls her eyes. 'Yes, I know. Don't wait up!'

We head towards the house. I'm weirdly nervous and I don't know why. These were my friends. 'I didn't realise it was such a big party,' I tell Becca.

'Neither did I … Oh well, the more the merrier, right?'

The front door is unlocked and we head inside to be greeted by the bassline of a disposable club banger from when we were at school. It was in this very house that I lost my virginity on a pile of coats in Farah's bedroom. So classy. That's such a stupid phrase: 'lost my virginity' … I know exactly where it went, thank you very much, and I didn't so much misplace it as I did gleefully cast it aside while drunk on vodka and cherryade.

We enter the open-plan living space. It's very *Selling Sunset*. Farah sees us and runs over. Her thick black hair is still trailing down her back to her bum. 'Fern!' she says, giving me a kiss on both cheeks, but she looks more than a little confused. 'What a … surprise! How long has it been?'

'Too long,' I admit.

'We thought you'd forgotten us.' Farah always could hold on to a grudge for dear life.

'I know, I'm sorry …'

She waves off my apology, but I can tell it'll take a lot more than that for her to forgive me. 'I'm glad you could make it. Sorry I didn't invite you … I just figured you'd be busy.' I take the barbed dig on the chin, and don't tell her that I was.

Farah leads us through the house to the kitchen. I say hello to some other people who were in our year at school. I try to suppress the knowledge that I wasn't invited to this little gathering when half of our year at school was. I know exactly what Rowan would say: he'd say it was *shade*. I remind myself I would have turned the invite down, so I shouldn't be too salty.

200

It's odd how we all look a bit more weathered. The boys in particular look like men now. Phil Johnson has grown into his features finally and looks like a catalogue model, whereas Stan Fletcher's years of habitual pot smoking have caught up with him. Pretty much all the guys are trying on stubble for size. I think it's true that girls grow up faster than boys – we don't look all that different from how we looked in S7.

'Where's your boyfriend, Fern? Isn't he up?' Farah asks and Becca makes an emphatic SHUT IT DOWN hand gesture.

'We had a fight,' I say, and decide to leave it at that. They don't need to know what the fight was about. I don't want to admit to my friends that my boyfriend is bi. Partly because I know what they'd say. You'd be surprised at how many seemingly woke people have a bisexuality blind spot (*greedy, slutty, confused*).

But if I'm honest, I also don't want them to think I somehow turn men gay with my toxic vagina.

I'm going to need to drink quite a lot tonight, I think.

Thankfully for me, the Hosseinis are the sort of Muslims who do drink, unless it's Ramadan. Farah ladles Christmas punch into plastic cups for me and Becca. I take a sniff – it's been spiced with cloves, whatever it is.

I gulp back a big mouthful. 'God, that's strong.' I drink the rest.

'Take it easy,' Becca tells me. 'We have a long night ahead.'

And that's when I see Hamish Bell walking through the front door, peeling off his coat. He turns and our eyes meet from opposite ends of the party. I see him and he sees me.

FERN

I watch him in the bathroom mirror, doing me from behind. He really pounds me. I grip the sink for dear life. I'm four cups of punch in, and my dress is up around my waist, tights around my ankles.

It took only eight magic words.

Twice in two days, how lucky am I?

I can't look at my face, so I watch him. His hands hold my hips, slamming himself into my body. His jeans are around his ankles. He was good, and he's got better. *Touch yourself*, he commands and I do as I'm told.

And it feels so good. My whole body pulses and throbs to the beat of the music downstairs. My hair falls over my face and into my mouth.

He whispers in my ear. *You always were a wrong-un, Fern McAllister.*

I'm spiralling, up and down.

I laugh and I cry.

We get our breath back on the bath mat, staring up at the ceiling. Someone tries the handle, but the door is locked. My heart bumps up against my ribs. Is this real? Did I just do that? It felt good, but it didn't feel like me.

I just had sex with my ex against a sink. *We are each our own devil, and we make this world our hell.* If it wasn't me, then it wasn't the girl with the boyfriend. It was Past Fern. No, Past Fern didn't know it would be that good, Present Fern knew.

I chose that. In order to feel like I was the one making the choices.

Thom can't hurt me if I hurt him first. Or if I hurt myself pre-emptively.

Hamish pulls his jeans over his bum and does up his fly. 'Fucking hell, Fern. Where did that come from?'

I sit up and try to tip the last drop of punch out of my cup on to my tongue. My throat is tight, sore. 'You haven't lost your touch,' I tell him.

He and I had many, many issues, but sex was never one of them. Because Hamish was my first, it was only after we broke up that I learned it doesn't always come so naturally. Lucky, in a way. It was always so easy, always so much fun. I was never nervous or awkward around him. I took that for granted too.

'Hey!' he says tenderly. 'Climb down out of your head. I can feel you on the verge of freakin' out.'

I say nothing, and that says it all.

'Well, don't. It was what it was, OK?' He grins. 'It was fucking hot.'

I can't look him in the eye. 'We should get back to the party or people will talk.' Though to be honest, I doubt they've even noticed I'm missing.

Hamish pushes his hair off his face, and then tidies mine for me too. I brush his hand away. It's somehow more intimate than what we just did up against the sink.

He pulls me in for a kiss. It reminds me, fleetingly, of the sugar high I felt back then. Fern and Hamish! Every text message was a firework; the thrill of nipping at his heels all the goddamn time. 'Don't! What's that for?'

'Because I know you, and you're going to feel really, really guilty any second now, and you shouldn't.'

'Um, you *think*?' I say, incredulous. I'm drunk, but I'm not that drunk. I remind myself it was a choice. 'I don't know *what* that was,' I say, although I fully do.

'Ah, that was one for old times' sake – every couple is entitled to that. Consequence-free nostalgia. Even Edinburgh's own Taylor Swift is allowed a night off from her perfect wee life.' A sob chokes me, totally involuntarily. Hamish frowns. 'Are you OK?'

'No.' I let the tears come, reaching for the toilet roll. Hamish pulls me into his arms. 'If you think I have a perfect life you are so wrong. I'm not Taylor Swift, I'm a … fraud. It's hard. I'm … I try to hold things together. I'm so tired … oh my god, I'm so tired.'

And I am. I don't want to be the ringleader. I want to be the clown for once. I want to be Rowan, just for one day. I'm so tired of running the show. My life; Thom's life; Rowan's life; Willow; Mum and Dad; this year I singlehandedly created Christmas. I just wanted everyone to be happy, for once in their poxy lives. I'm so tired. I want to get off.

I want a night off. Tonight I'll be Rowan.

WILLOW

The credits roll on the Muppets. I don't say anything because I don't want the night to be over. It's still early – almost nine.

'OK, I actually thought that was pretty tight. You got *Elf*?' Syd says. 'That's my favourite.'

I don't wait to be asked twice. I reach for the laptop. 'I think I can stream it, let me look.' I'm sure I've seen it on one of the NINE streaming platforms we signed up for, but which? This may take a minute.

'Me and my mum used to watch that on Christmas Eve,' they say and I hear a bit of homesickness in their voice. You heard it a lot in the unit; people looking for any excuse to talk about the comforting routines they were missing – pets or siblings usually.

'Is your mum …?'

'Dead? God, no, she's in jail.'

I wasn't expecting that either. 'Oh. OK.'

Now they look surprised. 'Are you seriously telling me Rowan actually kept a secret? That's a first. I assumed you all knew.'

'No!' I say, putting the laptop to one side. 'Mum thought you couldn't go home because …' I don't want to finish that sentence.

'Because I'm non-binary? No. Well, they don't *get* it. My stepdad misgenders me all the fucking time, but I don't think it's from a malicious place, if you get me? He's just fuckin' thick.'

I nod.

'My mum was *better*, although I'm pretty sure she thinks I'm being difficult.' Oh, I'm familiar with that one. *Attention seeking*. Syd rolls a cigarette as they talk. I can't stop watching, oddly fixated on their nimble fingers.

'What did she do? Am I allowed to ask?'

'You could literally google it, so … She got busted running a fake MLM scheme with one of her friends. They both tried to pin it on each other, it's a whole big mess, and they both went down for fraud. So I didn't really want to go home to a house with just my stepdad and, like a million boxes of knock-off perfumes.'

I don't really know what they mean, although I remember Mum once ranting because Auntie Shelly tried to get her to join one last year. 'Is that, like, one of those things where you con people or something?'

Syd nods. 'Yeah, so they recruited a bunch of women to sell these shitty perfumes on Facebook and stuff. But they didn't actually have enough perfume to go around, and the "genuine perfumes" were also fakes from the Ukraine. She got twenty months. She'll probably get out early, though.'

I'm tongue-tied again. What to say to that? 'I'm sorry. That sucks.'

Syd shrugs. 'She had it coming. She made her choices. Like, I can't feel too bad for her.'

'Are you sad you're not going home this Christmas?'

Syd downs the last of their beer. 'Honestly, no. It's a queer thing. I sort of made peace with leaving home and never going back. The fact I *can* is a privilege.'

I wonder if Rowan feels like that too. I hope not. It makes sense, though. And of course, Thom, who I just outed to the entire family. Man, I owe him a massive apology. 'I'm so sorry you've had to see all our mad family shit.'

Syd laughs, picking themselves off the rug and crossing to my window seat. 'You mind if I smoke out your window?'

'Go ahead.'

'No, man, it's good for me.' They take a prime spot, looking out over the botanic gardens and the glowing windows of the grand old tenements beyond. You can see the Christmas trees and twinkly lights in some of them. 'You know how you always think you're the main character? All that stuff with my mum. It was such a drama. You forget that everyone else has drama too. Like all those little houses over there. Fuck knows what they've got going on. Little dramas in every house.'

They're pointing at the tenement buildings on the far side of the gardens. I stand over their shoulder to see what they're looking at, and as I do I get a whiff of their cologne or whatever. They smell *amazing*, so clean and zesty. I've never smelled anything so good. I find myself almost sniffing their shoulder.

Wow, it's really snowing now, the gardens turning white almost as we watch. I wonder where Dad, Rowan and Fern are. I hope they all get home soon.

Syd's eyes remain fixed on the night. 'It's a struggle, life.

Everyone is struggling with something. It's why we've got to be kind to each other, even when it's really fuckin' hard. You just don't know. You can't tell by looking.'

You can't tell by looking.

ROWAN

I've never really driven in snow. The cars are starting to crawl through the streets, everyone trying to stick to the black tracks made by other drivers. The back wheel spins a bit, like the tyres aren't quite gripping the road.

'Should we head back?' Thom asks, frowning between the road and the weather app on his phone.

'What's the app say?'

'It says "light snow showers" so ...'

It isn't light snow showers. It's like God's dumped a bag of flour over Edinburgh. But I can see the lights of the church from here, and people making their way into the carol concert. 'Let's do a quick check, and then head back.'

He nods. 'Sounds like a plan.'

The trip has taken twice as long as it should have, with traffic moving at three miles an hour. I see an empty parking space on the side of the road and pull in. I swing my Adidas hi-tops out into the snow. It's deep enough now to make a satisfying crunch. I zip my baseball jacket all the way to my neck.

I like the idea of churches; they're very camp. They're basically insane fairy-tale palaces, covered in pure histrionic pictures of half-naked men and statues. Churches have zero chill and I love it. Like, when I think about it, it blows my mind. Can you imagine if everywhere had half-dead men hanging off crosses? But in a church, it's totally normal, nay, expected.

What I like less is what they represent. My rant at Thom is still fresh in my throat, and the reason I'm a pariah is because of this tower. It was this place that decided, however many hundreds of years ago, that I'm an aberration. It was this place that decreed sex the enemy. A perfectly natural thing our body does – no different from breathing, eating and pooping – became something to be ashamed of.

And I can't think why. Why, of all things, did they decide to make sex bad? And let's be honest, it was only ever bad for women and gays. Like, were the men of history so scared of women that they had to invent all these batshit rules to keep them tethered to the kitchen sink? *Sex is just for reproduction*? Sure, Jan. That's like saying food is only for fuel. They're both there to be enjoyed.

Thom leads the way, joining the procession of people filing into the church. It's busier than I thought it would be. I guess Christmas brings out fair-weather Christians. I trail behind him. 'What's up?' he asks.

I look up at the stone cherubs over the door. They don't want me for a sunbeam. 'Aren't you worried you might spontaneously burst into the flames of hell?'

He laughs. 'Not especially. I sometimes take my mum to church.'

I nod up at the spire as we join the back of the queue to get inside. 'They're not mad on the gays, you know?'

Thom grins my way. 'Let all bitterness and wrath and anger

and clamour and slander be put away from you, along with all malice. Be kind to one another, tender-hearted, forgiving one another, as God in Christ forgave you.'

I blink. 'I beg your fuck?'

'I grew up on scripture. I once had to do a reading in front of everyone at Sunday school. That's from Ephesians.'

'Ephes Ian? I don't even know Ian.' I smile. 'So what? I'm supposed to forgive the systemic persecution of my people for hundreds of years? Have they accepted my innate love of cock?'

Thom shrugs. 'Some have.'

I'm not ready to let the bitterness and malice go. 'I love a grudge. They're like a hobby.' They are, however, collecting for a homelessness charity on the door, which feels like a cool thing to do. 'Do you have any money?'

Thom digs into his back pocket for a beat-up leather wallet.

'Why do straight men always carry ...' I tail off, realising what I've done. Again.

Thom frowns at me. 'For the supposedly woke one, you're very into labels.'

'Sorry.' Thom's ability to 'pass' works even on me. He 'passes' as a straight in a way that I never ever will. I resent him for it, and resent myself for resenting him. God, it's complicated. Sometimes I start trying to rank privilege and it melts my brain: rich white straight cis men first, everyone else second.

And on top of everything, I'm in a sodding church. A blast of warm air hits us as we enter. It really is *packed*. A table next to the door is selling mulled wine – which admittedly smells hugely inviting – and mince pies. I'll begrudgingly admit the church is impressive; twin Christmas trees either side of the altar and fairy lights entwined around the stone columns. 'Do you see her?'

'It's heaving,' he replies.

Most people are squeezing into the pews, looking for any available remaining seats. 'This time, I think we should split up. You take the left side; I'll take the right and I'll meet you back at the doors. If she's not here, I say we go.'

Any straight line should be treated like a catwalk, so I do my best strut down the aisle, scanning the rows for my sister. I struggle to remember what she was even wearing, and it doesn't help that half the girls in here have her haircut. I'm surprised how many young people are here – I assumed it'd be the silver-top army.

I do a full lap around the right-hand side of the church. It's standing room only now and I have to weave through the audience. I don't see her anywhere.

I clock Thom approaching from the other side and he shakes his head. Well, I guess that's it then.

The big double doors are slammed shut, almost in my face, and I'm suddenly trapped. 'Just stand at the back, love,' a kindly old woman tells me.

'Oh, but …'

'We're starting now, find a space.' She returns to her duties elsewhere.

Thom arrives at my side. I turn to the altar and see a choir filing into position. They're all men, all wearing ghastly sequinned waistcoats and red AIDS ribbons. A man with a bright red beard steps up to a central mic. 'Welcome to tonight's carol concert in aid of Four Square, Edinburgh's charity supporting the homeless. We have the very great pleasure of kicking off proceedings tonight. Ladies, gentlemen and everyone in-between, we are Edinburgh Gay Men's Chorus …'

'Oh great …' I mutter.

'Let's listen,' Thom says.

I'm about to argue, to say that Fern might be freezing to death in a ditch, but Redbeard joins the chorus and a younger, very handsome man steps forward. The piano starts to play. I think I spy Gabe standing in the third row of the choir – a trans guy I know from out and about on the Edinburgh scene.

Oh holy night, the stars are brightly shining. It is the night of our dear saviour's birth …

I recognise the carol from *Home Alone*. Some more men join in. As they sing together, I feel a weird swell inside.

A thrill of hope, the weary world rejoices, for yonder breaks a new and glorious morn …

And then the whole choir joins in. It's a wall of sound, moving through me. It rattles my soul in its cage, all glittery and golden. Proof, I guess, that there's a soul in there after all. I'm not strong enough to resist it. The choir reaches a powerful crescendo, and I feel like I'm floating.

Fall on your knees! O hear the angel voices!

I start to cry. It's all too much. I think of Fern, somewhere out there in the city, confused. I think of Mum, alone at home, after we all shamed her. I think of Willow, still so sick. And Thom, poor Thom. He doesn't deserve this.

A sob breaks from my mouth.

Thom takes my hand. 'Are you OK?'

I pull my hand back and shake my head. I cannot bear the beauty of it. 'I hate it. Let's go.' I turn and push through the double doors, and out into the cold.

FERN

It feels *very* early to be heading to a rave, but Farah has become convinced that we're going to get snowed in. To be fair, the bus that takes us to Leith does struggle – more with traffic congesting the roads, rather than the snow itself.

It seems we're not the only ones to think this way. There is already a queue to get into the old church. Thankfully, Becca has lent me a shaggy blue faux fur coat. Very not my style, but at least I won't freeze to death. Hot pink neon lights illuminate the exterior of the building and I can hear pounding music from within.

This is, truth be told, my idea of hell. Perhaps I've made my point and it's time to go home. I must be making my displeasure clear on my face because Becca says, 'Are you sure this is your jam, Fern? We can get you a cab home if you want?'

'No!' I say defensively. 'I just think I need to get a lot drunker, very quickly.'

'Even better,' Farah says, sidling in close. 'I've got some pills in my bra if you want.'

'What?' I hiss, scandalised.

'It's a *rave*, Fern. What did you think was going to happen?'

I suppose people in glass houses shouldn't throw stones, not least after what I just did in that bathroom.

'Don't worry, babe,' Hamish whispers in my ear. 'I'll protect your virtue.'

That's very like trusting the fox with the keys to the henhouse. I don't want to look like a total stiff, so try be as casual as possible as we head inside the venue. Drugs, cool! No one ever dies of them! I hear an actual nervous laugh in my mind. We get frisked down by security – but only in the most half-arsed fashion. Certainly no one is checking inside Farah's bra, look at it that way.

Inside, the church does look very cool. Huge fluorescent yellow smiley faces hang from the rafters, all with either Santa hats or angel wings.

'You don't have anything to prove, Fern,' Hamish says. 'If you want to go home, it's cool.'

'This is fun!' I lie. 'Let's get drinks.'

Because everyone is arriving at the same time, the queue at the bar is about four deep. I'm not actually fun-Teflon. I *like* fun. I actually love clubbing – but I hate dance music. I much prefer cheese, which is why, despite what he says, I prefer clubbing with Rowan. Gay clubs usually stick to chart stuff I recognise and can sing along with. The music here is … a lot. I can see why you'd need narcotics to appreciate it.

I have a sudden pang for my brother. I realise I'm not mad at him any more, like the bruising has gone down. How was he to know Thom had previously dated me? If I have one drink here, maybe most people will be in bed when I get home. I'm acutely aware that by staying out I'm now crossing into the place where I'm being callous; making them worry to hurt them. Hurt people hurt.

I take out my phone and turn it on. It loads up and sure enough I have voicemails from Mum, Dad and Thom. Some messages come through from the family WhatsApp group, and from Thom and Ro. I send a message to the group chat: *I'm fine. Out with friends for drinks. I'll be home before long.*

I feel drunk. Another drink and I'll be quite drunk. Two more and I'll be very drunk.

I might need to be very drunk to face going home.

What have I done? Now the dust is settling, I can see that technically neither Rowan nor Thom did anything wrong. Not a single thing that warranted the extreme reaction in me.

But I have done something very wrong. Topical: I "took back control" and now feel totally out of control. Hamish is right behind me. I can smell him. He still wears the same Hugo Boss I once bought him.

Truly I'm in deep shit. It's all very well for Hamish to keep repeating *it's no biggy*, but it goes beyond me feeling like Lady effing Macbeth. There are CONSEQUENCES. I could go back and confess what I've done, but a rather more honest part of my head will pretend it didn't happen. I'll lie. I'll avoid sex with Thom and get an STI test the second we get back to London. We used a condom, obviously, but can you imagine?

My stomach crunches. I have made a terrible mess.

Hamish slips his arms around me, but I shrug him off. 'Don't!' I call.

'What?' he replies. 'Oh, I see. Is the conscience kicking in?'

I whirl to face him. 'Of course it is! I have a boyfriend.'

He looks a little wounded. 'I know. What happens in Farah's bathroom stays in Farah's bathroom.'

'But what if you have chlamydia or something!' I scream as the beat drops out for a second. Yes. Quite a lot of people hear that. 'Sorry.'

'Gee, thanks for the wee vote of confidence, Fern,' he says, unimpressed. 'FYI I had a test a couple of months back and got the all-clear.'

'I'm sorry,' I say. 'I just feel terrible.'

'That's because you're not a bad person.'

'I am.'

He gently takes hold of my shoulders. 'Fern … just for one night, be human. You don't have to be perfect. We all make mistakes. I'm willing to bet your boyfriend makes mistakes.'

I laugh.

'What?'

'Nothing.' I finally slither my way to the front of the bar; a sticky hatch in one corner of the chapel. 'What do you want?'

'Just a Diet Coke, please.'

I turn back to him. 'What?' He didn't drive here so, why …?

'Diet Coke,' he shouts over the thumping bass.

'I heard. Why aren't you drinking?'

He now looks a little bashful for the first time, surprising given what we just did. 'I've given up drinking.'

I laugh. He always did have a slightly off-kilter sense of humour. I don't really get it, but no one likes a drink more than Hamish, so I guess he's being ironic. 'Sure! OK! Vodka and Diet Coke?'

He looks at me, and I realise he's stone-cold sober. 'I mean it, Fern. I'm in recovery. I'm an alcoholic.'

218

ROWAN

'What was that about? I was enjoying that.' Thom trails behind as we follow the church path back to the car.

I point back towards the building with an accusatory finger. The entire churchyard somehow glows with the sonorous melody within. '*They* shouldn't be singing in a church!' I argue. 'It's perverse.'

'You're perverse,' Thom calls after me and I give him a deathly glare. 'Why can't you enjoy nice things?'

'Why can't you fuck off?' As I say it, I slip on the freezing snow and crash down hard on to my butt. 'Ow!' The pain, then the cold, spreads through me.

Thom reaches down to me. 'Are you OK?'

'No!' I yelp, and hold back frustrated tears. 'That really hurt.' He grips my hand and helps me up. 'I think I've broken my ass bone.'

'That bad?' I nod because I want to cry, but don't want to cry – again – in front of him.

Inside the chapel, the song ends, and we're surrounded by the silence of snow.

'Oh, come here,' says Thom. He tries to hug me, but I push him off.

I brush the snow off my bum. 'I'm fine.'

'Rowan …'

I allow myself a very brief look into his eyes. I don't know what he wants from me. I don't know what he ever wanted from me. 'What?' I mutter.

And then my phone buzzes. Thank Baby Jesus, saved by the text alert. I check and *finally* it's Fern messaging the family group chat. Well, thank fuck for that. I relay the message to Thom, and he breathes a deep sigh of relief. I read her whole message. 'She's gone somewhere for a drink?'

'Where?'

'She doesn't say. Could be anywhere. But she's OK.'

It's like a ten-ton weight lifts off us both. I swear I can see the miasma ascending into the night sky. 'So what do we do?' he asks.

I have no intention of tracking her all across the capital city of Scotland. 'I think we go home. We'll wait for her there with a cute scotch to warm us up.' Thom nods and we get in the car. I type a quick reply, explaining we're out looking for her but will head home and meet her back at the house.

Even in the few minutes we were in the church, the snow seems deeper. How is that possible? I say nothing, I don't want to jinx the ride home. I turn the headlights on and snow now swirls through the beams. Thom must read my mind. 'Are we gonna be OK?'

'Yeah. I don't know. Let's take it really easy.'

Thom digs his phone out. 'I'm gonna text Fern too. Maybe we can pick her up on the way. I don't want her to get stuck.'

'OK.' This shouldn't be that hard. We're only a ten- or

fifteen-minute drive away from home. I carefully pull out, but the back wheel's spinning a bit. I don't know if Mum's little car is built for snow.

Again, I must be powerfully psychic because my phone starts to ring – an incoming call from my mother. 'Can you get that?'

Thom takes my phone out of my pocket and answers. 'Hi, it's Thom …'

He puts it on speaker. 'Did you get the message from Fern?'

'Yes, I just replied. We're coming home now. The snow is pretty bad.'

'I know. Drive very carefully, Rowan.'

'I will. Mum?'

'What?'

'Sorry for being a dickhead before.'

'Which time?' she says, and I laugh a little.

'All the times. I love you.'

'I love you too. Get home safe.' She hangs up.

I focus on the road. I can't really see much ahead of the car. It's all a blobby orange blur, the snow somehow shining the streetlights back at me. I find myself squinting, leaning forward in my seat. I can dimly see the little pink brake lights of the car in front of us.

'I hope Santa can fly over the weather,' Thom says.

'OK, this is quite scary. Anything from Fern?'

'Left on read.'

'Wow. Brutal.' I flash him a brief glance. He looks pretty gutted. 'She's being a bit of a dick now, Thom. She needs to come back so you can talk about it.'

He nods and exhales deeply. 'We do need to talk.'

There follows an awkward silence. 'Can I ask a difficult question?' I ask.

'Don't see how I can stop you.'

'OK. Like … is it working? You and Fern?' I mean, I've observed them together all day and – knowing my sister – I wonder how it works. Thom *does* seem laid back, which Fern would need, but wouldn't that also mean they're opposites? She has so much *drive*, so much ambition. And that's not a bad thing, but I always saw Fern ending up with some mad stockbroker type: someone with as much determination as she has.

That said, she dated Hamish for ages, and he's as Chaotic Good as it gets, so maybe *that's* her type?

Another big sigh. 'It seems to work,' Thom says. 'It's easy.'

If someone said that about my relationship, I'm not sure I'd be thrilled. 'Wow. High praise.'

'Something needs to change,' he half-mutters under his breath. 'I'm not …'

Happy?

'It's always Fern's plan, you know? Not mine. It sometimes feels like I'm along for the ride.'

I actually laugh. Of *course* it's Fern's plan. 'Well, duh! My sister is a lot. Actually, that's not fair. She's *strong*. And she needs a strong man or she'll steamroller him.' I'll say that for Hamish – he called her out on her shit constantly, and she didn't like it one bit.

'Rowan, stop!' Thom suddenly reaches for the wheel. I try to slam on the brakes and we career forwards.

'Shit!' We halt just millimetres from the car in front, which has stopped for some reason. Someone honks a horn and I dimly hear an engine revving. I roll down the window and stick my head out into the night. Oh shit. It's uphill to ours, and a car ahead of us is struggling to get up. They are trying to move forward, but their wheels are spinning in the snow, the car sort of rocking from side to side in the middle of the street – and blocking traffic in either direction.

That's the thing with Edinburgh – it's slap bang in the middle of two hills.

'What's going on?'

'Someone's stuck.' I look behind us. We could take a long way around and turn back, but we'd risk getting stuck on the other side of town too. There's no way to make this journey without tackling a hill. I guess we wait.

'I'll go see if I can help.' Thom gets out of the car and zips his coat up. God, I hadn't even thought to offer. That's why he's a good person, and I'm not.

I switch off the engine, but decide to wait in the car. I don't see how I'll be much help in my trainers anyway. He soon vanishes into the blizzard.

Half a Little Mix song later, Thom returns. 'Not a lot we can do. There's another stuck halfway up the hill too. She's gonna turn back and maybe we should do the same. Is there another way?'

I nod. 'OK.' I twist the key in the ignition and nothing happens. The car makes a tragic, asthmatic wheeze, but won't start. 'What the fuck?' I switch it off and try again. It stutters again. Doesn't start. I shut off the engine.

We both sit in stiff silence for the longest second ever, both of us knowing exactly what this means.

I look at Thom. 'Told you,' I say. 'God hates the gays.'

WILLOW

And now *Elf* finishes too. Dad is home, and Fern has at least messaged, but Rowan and Thom still haven't returned. It's getting late. I check my phone again. It's been at least ten seconds since I last looked. Syd picks up on it.

'Hey, it's OK. They'll be back soon. All of them.'

'But the weather …'

'My therapist calls it catastrophic thinking,' Syd says. 'Do you always jump to the worst possible scenario? I had to train myself out of it.'

They are right. I nod.

'What's the worst that can happen? Fern stays at a friend's tonight? Rowan and Thom park the car and walk home? It's all gravy.'

I nod again. 'How do you do that?'

'What?'

'Be so wise.'

They smile broadly. 'I have had so much therapy. So much! Literally hours. What you just saw was me channelling a middle-aged dude called Paul.'

I'm going in, boys and girls and anyone beyond the binary. 'Did you … did you have an eating disorder?'

'No,' they say with certainty. 'Although when I got really

low, I'd lose my appetite for three or four days at a time, which is literally what anorexia means, I guess. I have OCD.'

My mouth opens then closes, uselessly.

They go on. 'Like actual OCD, not Monica-TV-comedy OCD where you like things clean. I actually, um, had a checking disorder. That's where, like, your brain gets stuck on all these weird thoughts and shit. I started to worry – all the time – that I was going to say or do the wrong thing. And it would … it would just cripple me, you know? I had these mad ideas in my head that I was going to say something racist or homophobic. I developed a tic too – I would constantly ask people to repeat things I'd said. Eventually I just stopped going out. It was easier. I was frozen.'

I nod, processing what they've said. 'I … um … yeah.'

Syd smiles. 'What?'

'That … yeah. The way I feel … it's not about food any more. Not really. I'm scared of feeling a certain way. I'm scared of what might happen if I don't win.'

Syd nods too. 'It took over my life for like a year. There was no Syd, only the sickness.'

'Oh my god, *yes*.' They are putting into words exactly how I've felt for years. A fat tear rolls down my cheek and splatters on to my knee.

'Hey, it's OK,' Syd says. 'Can I give you the best piece of advice I was ever given?'

I wipe my eyes on my sleeve. 'Yes.'

'You are not your thoughts.'

'What?' I need to focus. My head and heart are racing too fast and I can't concentrate.

They twist to face me. We mirror each other on the rug. 'OK, hear me out. Your thoughts are something that happen *to* you, or *in* you, but they are not *you*. Does that make sense?'

'OK ...'

'When I was sick, I thought that that was it for Syd Curtis. I was just a mad person who'd never get better. And the thought of it never ending ... fuck. But therapist Paul pointed out that those beliefs weren't *real*. They were just thoughts in my head. They were drowning me out.'

I nod along. People have told me similar things in the past, but coming from Syd, I *believe* it.

Syd taps my head with a finger. 'And it's a bastard because the sickness sounded a lot *like* me, but it wasn't *me*. I was under attack. So I fought back.'

'Did you win?'

They consider this. 'I don't know if it's something you win. I still have negative thoughts a lot of the time, but I know it's not *me*. I'm fine in here. I'm a whole person – I like olives, I hate bananas. I can't sing, but I'm really good at video games. I love myself, and other people love me too. But sometimes, little gremlins creep in.'

They have gremlins, I have a demon. Seems fair. 'What do you do with them when they do?'

'Track and trace, man! The trick is in spotting them, tagging them, and filing them in a mental box of bullshit negativity.'

I laugh a little. It's kinda like the patented WAIT method, but I prefer Syd's method. 'I am not my thoughts.'

'Too right you're not. You're Willow McAllister.'

I half-laugh ruefully. 'I ... I'm not sure who she is any more,'

I admit. I have been Little Miss Anorexia for so long now. Like *what do I like?* I like secretly exercising and thinking of ways to avoid food. *What do I dislike?* Food, being told I can't exercise. *What do I do?* Just think about food and exercise mostly. There's nothing else in here. I'm a seashell.

Syd frowns. 'Babe, you can be whoever you want to be. I'm self-made. I remade myself from scratch. If you met me four years ago, you wouldn't recognise me, no way. No one else gets to decide who you are except you.'

I don't want to be Little Miss Anorexia any more. I don't. I am bored of myself. I want to be anything else. Although I know what that means. Immediately the demons in my head swarm … *no, not that, not food.* All of a sudden it's stunningly clear that food is not the issue: those demons are.

Syd gets to their feet. 'It's getting late, I might call it a night. Santa won't come if we're awake at midnight.'

I jump to my feet. *I am not my thoughts.* I want to live again. I want to be free. I want to be in the world if there's people like Syd in it. 'Wait!' I say.

I grab their hand to stop them. 'What?'

I've seen this in the movies, how hard can it be? I step close and place my lips on their lips.

FERN

Rowan always says that the real party is in the smoking area, and he might not be wrong. I huddle next to one of the heat lamps, keeping my ex-boyfriend company. He still has one disgusting habit, and I'm quite grateful because I was starting to think he was a clone or an alien body-snatcher.

'What do you mean?' Hamish asks, borrowing a lighter off some random guy and then handing it back.

'How can you be an alcoholic? You're not even twenty years old yet.'

He looks at me like I'm simple. 'And I've been getting thoroughly shitfaced since I was twelve or thirteen. I remember getting wasted in Gareth Evans' basement, and everyone filming me because it was so funny. It became my whole thing, didn't it. Hot Mess Hamish.' He takes my hand. 'Don't deny it. You fucking hated it.'

I see no lies. 'You were never *that* bad.'

'I was never that bad around *you* because were one of the only people who did call out a lot of my shit. When we broke up it got worse.'

'Are you saying it was my fault?'

He recoils. 'No …'

'Why do I have to be Lisa Simpson all the time?' I don't want to make his stuff about me, but am I really such a killjoy?

'That's my point! Everyone needs a Lisa! Without anyone pointing out how much I was drinking, I really went for it. I knew there was a problem when I needed a little "morning drink" so I didn't get shaky hands. I was like *fuck* …'

Wow. I had no idea things had got that bad. I guess I was halfway to London by that point. I have to ask the next question. 'Wasn't your dad an alcoholic?'

Hamish nods. 'Aye. He was. He is, and therein lies the problem. I thought "an alcoholic" was someone like him; someone older. I didn't really connect the dots about how he got to where he did. He didn't start out as a slurring middle-aged mess at the bookies, did he?'

'Hamish, I'm so sorry,' I say, my heart aching for him. 'I had no idea.'

Well, truthfully, I did worry about his drinking, but – like him – I didn't think a seventeen year-old could call themselves an alcoholic and mean it. 'Neither did I until recently. Tell you what, though, I feel proper amazing. I was either constantly drunk or feeling like shite. Now I feel like a new man. Fern, I go to the gym!'

I laugh. 'No way!'

'I swear.'

'Well … good for you.' I had noticed back in the bathroom how toned his tummy was, those little ridges running over his hips. He's always been a skinny legend, but now he's hard and muscular with it. 'How long have you been sober?'

'My first anniversary will be New Year's Day.'

That figures. 'That's seriously amazing, Hamish.'

He shrugs. 'I'm a little worried about leaving home, and meeting new people, but I'm determined to stay sober ...'

Huh? 'You're leaving?'

'Aye. I start at Roehampton in September.'

This is news to me. 'You never said ...'

'Pretty sure I did.'

'You definitely didn't, but that's ... amazing. What are you studying?'

'English and Philosophy.' This is a total change from what he was *supposed* to be doing at Oxford. He was always freakishly good at maths and science, and was supposed to be studying engineering.

My mind is blown. Twice in half an hour. 'But what about the band?' Trash Bandits are everything to him. I was always second fiddle. That was made very clear.

Hamish shrugs. 'Nothing lasts for ever. Dom is studying in Glasgow now ... it's been hard to carry on ...'

'Oh wow.' This is huge for him. I don't think going to university is the *only* path to success, but Hamish was always *that* infuriating bastard who just rolled up to exams without a minute's worth of revision and somehow managed to get a high B+. I always wondered what he'd achieve if he actually put the work in.

'Fear not, I'm still a just above average drummer, and there are plenty of bands in London ...'

He's selling himself short, he's actually very talented. I wouldn't ever take that from him. He's moving to Roehampton, which is just outside Waterloo. 'You're gonna be in London,' I say, almost to myself, and then wish I hadn't.

He looks puzzled for a second and then guffaws. 'Och, calm those cogs, McAllister. You're a married woman, remember?'

'I'm not married!' I snap.

Hamish grins. 'I'm kidding, Fern!'

'I should go,' I say, feeling the cold cut through me all of a sudden. The guilt is starting to feel like the flu, something horrid in my marrow.

'Stop beating yourself up. He doesn't have to know. I'm not going to say anything, I promise. No one else knows. No one else will ever know.'

A new thought occurs to me. 'My god, you did that *sober*,' I say. What's my excuse? Two cups of punch? 'I need to talk to Thom. Things are … weird.'

'Fair. I'll walk you out.' The smoking area is out the back of the church so we have to go through the chapel to get to the exit.

A sweaty, slightly farty, wave hits us as we enter. Hamish explains MDMA can have that effect on people: the Molly shits. The music is pounding and the crowd seems to bounce up and down, arms aloft. They almost seem to be in a trance, possessed by the beat.

Becca sees us and waves us over. 'There you are! This song is *so* S6!' I dimly remember it. 'Come dance!'

'I'm heading out!' I shout.

'No!' Becca cries, clearly now quite high and/or drunk. Her pupils are like saucers. 'I love you, bitch! I miss you!' She wraps her arms around me and pleads with me to stay.

'One last dance?' Hamish says, offering me a hand on to the dancefloor.

232

The Lisa Simpson in me grumbles that it's well past time to go home, but I don't want mine and Hamish's last dance to be what happened in that bathroom. 'OK.'

My old friends have formed a messy circle at the heart of the room under the giant smilies. I join in, trying to find my rhythm. I feel something on my head, and I look up to see fake snow falling from a net on the ceiling. 'Oh my god!'

Hamish laughs and brushes the snow off my head. I get a load in my mouth and scream, which only makes the situation worse. Hamish coughs up a mouthful too and I laugh even more. Becca spins around and around like a snow angel.

Maybe I'll get just one more drink after all.

ROWAN

Thom slams the bonnet down and heads back to the passenger side. 'What did they say?' he asks, taking his seat. In neutral, we've already pushed the Fiesta to the side of the road so people can get past us, but now *all* the cars are struggling to get up the hill. Tyres spin and horns are honked and nerves are fraying. People just want to be home for Christmas. I get that.

'They said to stay with the car and wait. They'll be with us ASAP but we should expect them to take a while.'

'How long?'

I gesture at the blizzard. 'I'm guessing *quite* some time. Did you get through to Fern?'

'Straight to voicemail.'

I'm half-cross and half-worried. I guess she's in a pub somewhere, but I wonder how she'll get home. Thom blows into his frozen pink hands. I turn the car's power on and whack the heating up to full blast.

'You shouldn't do that,' Thom says, switching it off. 'Without the engine running, you'll run the battery down.'

I give him a look and turn it back on. 'So what? The engine is already fucked.'

Thom switches it off again. 'You don't wanna pay for a new battery.'

I turn it back on. *Again*. 'I'm cold, Thom! You want to huddle for warmth instead?'

'Funny.' His coat looks a lot warmer than mine; it might come to snuggling. We are clumsily silent for a moment until he turns to me, a vinegary look on his face. 'You know, I can't figure you out.'

I hold my hands up in surrender. 'What have I done? It's not my fault Mum's car's shit!'

'You know what?' He backs down. 'Never mind.'

I twist to face him. 'Um, no. Say your piece, babe. All ears.'

Thom shakes his head. 'I ... I've met your family, and I've seen how supportive they are of you. I don't understand how you've become so ... hard.'

Excuse me? 'I'm not hard ...'

'OK, *cold*.'

I actually laugh. I mean, what else am I meant to say to that?

'See? It's like you're a machine. I saw it in France, I saw it in that church. It was so *beautiful*, and you just don't *feel* anything. Don't you *care*?'

Oh, clamber off my dick, I implore you. He doesn't know me. He doesn't know what it was like. I remember where I got every last scar and bruise from Finnians: the changing rooms, the rugby pitch, the canteen. The popular kids lining the footpath leading to the school gates. Every day for seven years I ran the gauntlet; head down, pretending to be deaf.

McAllister takes it in the arse.

I knew even then that to *show* them my wounds, all that gore, would be to let them win. And so I never did.

And I won't start baring my neck now.

'You don't know shit,' I say, staring out into the night. 'I can feel.'

'Then why isn't this bothering you?' he raises his voice now, eyes wide.

'Why isn't what bothering me?'

'You and me?' he says angrily.

'What about you and me?'

'Didn't you like me at all? Did I imagine everything about last Christmas?'

Oh, Thom, you stunning novice. I'm going to have to school him. I take a breath and look him squarely in the eye. 'I never really tell people how bad things were for me at Finnians. I don't even think Fern knows what it was like for me in PE. For the last two years, I wore a neck brace so I wouldn't have to do it. I sat outside the PE office and read Jackie Collins paperbacks.'

Thom frowns. 'What does that have to do with us?'

'I'm not a robot, Thom, I just have really, really thick armadillo skin. Because otherwise I wouldn't have survived high school. I mean that. Every single day, I had to pretend that being called a faggot or a gayboy or a girl didn't bother me, but guess what? It did. Every day for ten years. But I had to keep going, it's not like you can decide not to go to school, and my skin got thicker and thicker and thicker. It's like armour.'

That shuts him up. 'I'm sorry it was so shit,' he says eventually.

I offer a smile. 'Yeah, but I had my secret identity, didn't I?'

'What?'

'At school I was shamed homosexualist Rowan McAllister and by night I was "Callum, 18". That was my fake Grindr name.'

His head flops back against the headrest. 'Oh my god ...'

'Go ahead, judge all you want, but I realised there were boys out there that didn't hate me, didn't want to kick my head in, or spit at me. Well,' I admit, 'some of them wanted to spit on me, but in a different way ...'

'Got it, thanks.'

'I realised I was ...'

Thom considers me through his insane lashes. 'Hot?'

'I was going to say *worthwhile*, but I prefer yours.'

He smiles meekly. 'You're not *just* hot, Rowan. You've got more to offer than your ass.'

I cackle. 'Thanks, hun! Is that the moral of the story?'

'No!' he says. 'What I mean is, I get that you had a shit time at school, but I don't see why that means you can just switch off your feelings.'

'Because I had to! That's the thing with the Feelings button. Once you learn how to flip it off, you can't feel the good ones *or* the bad ones.' I take a breath, quite pleased with the notion of the Feelings button. 'I knew in France that if I let myself ... go *there*, I'd wind up getting hurt, or hurting you. Like, what was the point? You were leaving!'

'But now I'm here.'

'Yeah, and you're going out with my sister!' I actually clap out the last two words because I feel like he's forgetting that wee factette.

The seat creaks as he twists his whole body around to face

237

me. 'I know! Fuck, I know! And I'm sorry. I think I'm missing the button. I can't turn my feelings off. I've tried, but I can't. I really liked you. I *like* you. You've been in my head all year. And I know I shouldn't admit that, but it's true.'

He is close now. Dangerously so. The car feels airless, the windows steaming up. Snow is settling on the windscreen, sealing us inside our own private igloo. I need to let some of the air out of this bubble. I boop his nose with my index finger. 'There you go, I turned off your Feelings button …' I quip.

'You're doing it again, trying to shut me out.'

'Because we can't …'

And then, very quietly, he says, 'I can't help it.'

Another creak and he's kissing me. I'm kissing him too. It feels like falling, both of us powerless against gravity.

I have reminisced many times about our night in Courchevel, but my memory hasn't done him justice. He's a very, very good kisser, his lips so perfectly warm and soft. I've never needed much encouragement and I'm rock hard in mere seconds.

This is very, very bad, but very, very good. Is there a word for lovely terrible?

As intoxicating as it is – my head feels like it's full of brilliant, angelic white light – a sense of Fern soon bleeds in around the edges. She is my *sister*. And this is wrong. 'Stop,' I say pulling away from him.

Thom, too, looks guilt-ridden. 'I'm sorry.' He screws his eyes shut. 'I don't know what's wrong with me.'

'Nothing! Nothing is wrong with you!' I cup his warm cheek in my palm. 'But Fern and I have a very simple rule: *I licked it so it's mine.* Fern licked you first.'

Thom laughs. There follows a very long silence. It gets too much to bear. 'Rowan. I want you.'

I find that I don't want to lie to him. I perform a brief emotional peepshow. 'I want you too.'

Fern might as well be sitting between us in the backseat.

'What now?' he asks.

I just shrug. This is impossible. And normally I fucking live for drama, so it's weird that I feel so deflated. 'It can't happen. She's my sister and I love her.'

The car fills with a different kind of light, and Thom's skin turns amber. It takes me a second to realise he's not actually radiating golden light, there's a vehicle approaching from behind us, orange lights flashing. We are rescued.

But I don't want to go.

As soon as we leave this car, it's all over.

WILLOW

Syd pulls away from the kiss, wiping their lips with the back of a hand. Am I that repulsive? Am I a bad kisser? I've never really … 'I'm sorry,' I say, mortified.

'Don't be,' Syd says, looking pretty much stoned.

'I … I … um.'

They seem to snap out of it. I must look panic-stricken because they take my hand in both of theirs. 'Willow, I'm just surprised. I was *not* expecting that.' I say nothing. They tilt my chin up. 'Look at me. You don't want to kiss me.'

Huh? 'I … do, though?'

'Really?'

'Yes.' I can't remember the last time I felt like this. I can't remember the last time I felt anything, though, so …

Syd smiles kindly. 'Babes, listen. We did a real fuckin' deep-dive up in here tonight. It stirs shit up inside, you know what I mean?'

I pull away and turn the lights on. I want the romance gone. Shoo, romance, out you go! I'm so embarrassed. 'It's fine. I get it.'

Syd sort of winces. 'Willow! It's not like that, I swear, man …'

I'm so stupid. Of course they don't want me. I'm Gollum.

That's what Jake Bradley called me at school once. It stuck. People used to call *Precious* at me at school, or ask me to look after their rings, until word travelled that I was properly sick, and everyone changed their tune. Then they started buzzing around like flies, asking what they could do to help. #BeKind. 'It's no big deal,' I tell Syd. 'Just forget it.'

If eating three meals a day feels like a long way off, then being happy enough inside my skeleton to, you know, *have sex*, feels like a million years away. I mostly assume I'll be a confirmed virgin, like Queen Elizabeth. But, right now, if Syd hadn't stopped us, I'd have been ... at least listening to the suggestion. This is super new.

But I've fucked it. Big shocker.

Syd says, 'Actually – if things were different – you're very my type.'

I'm not sure that's helpful, TBH, or true. I wait at my bedroom door willing them to leave, but now I have to ask. 'If what things were different?'

'You're my best friend's sister for one thing ...'

Don't see what difference that makes. Not like they're a thing. 'And for ... two things?'

Syd plonks their behind down on my bed and pats the space beside them. I reluctantly join them. 'You know Rowan?'

'Vaguely,' I say sarcastically.

'You know he's an obnoxious dickpig, right?'

I laugh aloud. I really wasn't expecting that.

'Well, I'm about as bad as he is. I'm kinda shitty, cannot lie. And it's all my own stuff – commitment or whatever.'

I didn't buy that toxic shit in *Bridgerton* and I don't buy it

241

now. The whole *oh, you don't want me, I'm so fucked up* thing. Meh. It's so arrogant to think that a girl can't decide what's good for her or that she'll fall blindly in love after one kiss. I shake my head in a slightly pitying way. 'I didn't think we were going to, like, get married …'

Syd sighs. Maybe that was a bit harsh. 'I'm explaining this all wrong. I know our experiences are different, but I remember what it's like. When you realise there are other people like you in the world, that you're not alone, you start to confuse those feelings for other feelings.'

I am suddenly very interested in a frayed hole in my jeans. They are right. I don't know how I *feel*, but I know I wanted to kiss them. Really what it boils down to, what it always boils down to, is that I am not trusted in my own mind. 'I'm not a child. I'm so bored of people treating me like I'm made of china.'

Syd smiles. 'Girl, we *all* have hearts made of china. We have to put ourselves first. Always. And us making out is not good for you, trust me.'

I shrug. 'Don't I get to decide that?'

Maybe that's exactly what I need: to be a normal – whatever that means – seventeen-year-old. I don't have any friends. They were great at first, but soon got bored of me trying to scrape margarine off sandwiches. Maybe what I need are some things a doctor can't prescribe: a bad boyfriend to pester me for pics of my tits; a hundred group chats to slag off my friends from other chats; an intense and toxic girlfriend who compels me to steal shit from H&M. Everyone else is making mistakes, why can't I?

That may be true, but I'm not going to *badger* Syd into a make-out sesh, am I. I don't have *much* dignity left after this afternoon, but I'll take what I have and save it for New Year's.

And now Syd shrugs. 'This … this is not our time.' Does that suggest there *will* be a time? They climb off the bed. 'I'm gonna turn in. You gonna be OK, though?'

I don't know but I nod, letting them off the hook. This is so embarrassing. I wish I could erase their memory with witchcraft somehow.

Syd gets to my door and turns back to face me. They are beaming. 'Hey; that was a good little kiss, you know. You're a good kisser.' They slink out.

Huh. Well, I think, that's something. I'll take that and stick it under the tree for tomorrow.

ROWAN

I sit between Thom and Bartek, the enormously easy-on-the-eye pick-up driver, in the cab of his tow truck. His arms strain against his overalls and his sleepy expression is pleasingly dim. Under any other circumstances, we'd have already had sex I expect, but tonight I've only given him a passing glance. Sign of the times.

I feel sad. I don't like it. I preferred feeling nothing. Feelings are for stupid people with time on their hands.

The first little van couldn't do a roadside repair, so then we had to wait *another* forty-five minutes for Bartek in his big pick-up, all the while not kissing or even looking each other in the eye. To kill the mood, I resorted to thinking about dead people and Mum having sex with her PhD student, who – in my head – is played by Jabba the Hutt.

Mum's car dangles behind us, but this truck is making light work of the snow which, sod's law, is tailing off. It's now just fine powder on the wind.

Thom and I have barely said a word. I hope he didn't see me checking out Bartek's arms. 'So … what happens now?'

'I take the car to garage,' Bartek says as I point out which our house is. He pulls the truck over and hands me a card. 'Here is address. Call on twenty-seventh.'

I tuck the card into my pocket. 'OK. Do you need money?'

'Not today. When you collect.'

'Well, thanks, man,' Thom says. Why do men do that? Add 'man' to everything? Syd does it too, and they don't even *have* a gender. Thom disembarks first and I follow him out, trying to catch Bartek's eye as I go.

The house looks dark, although there's a light on in Mum and Dad's room. Or is that just Mum's room? Or Dad's room? Are they even in the same bed? God, what a sloppy prolapse of a day. There's a horrid swamp gas feeling in my stomach, but, despite all the dramz, I am glad to be home.

It's still bitterly cold, I want to get inside. 'Do we need to talk about what happened in the car?' Thom asks.

I shake my head. 'No. No autopsy, please. I can tell you what killed it right now.' I look at the house. 'Back to real life.' My heart sinks further than ever. I wish we hadn't kissed. It feels like a relapse and now I'm a junkie off the wagon.

'But what about—?'

'What about *nothing*!' I say vehemently, prodding his chest with a finger. 'You've got to stop this, Thom! It's not fair! You are with my ...'

I stop on hearing my name. 'Ro!' The voice echoes down the snowy street.

As the pick-up truck rolls away, I see my sister with her arms around Hamish Bell halfway down the street. I squint and realise ... Fern is *drunk*. He's basically dragging her along. Talk about reality kicking in. What the hell? 'Oh my god, are you OK?'

245

'A hand would be gratefully accepted ...' Hamish says through a tight jaw.

Thom and I meet him in the middle. 'Is she all right?' Thom asks.

'Aye, just a few too many sherries down the rave.'

I laugh, despite everything. '*You* went to a rave?' I ask her directly – she's drunk, not dead.

'Rowan ...' she says with a gravitas like she's not seen me for ten years. 'And Thom ... oh my god, Thom ... I'm so sorry ... I was such a megabitch.'

Hamish unwraps Fern's arm from around his neck and sort of hands her to Thom. 'So you must be Thom. You're very tall. I'm Hamish.'

Thom frowns. 'Ex Hamish?'

'The very same,' I add. It's weird she'd go to him, of all people. Things did not end well between them.

'Good to meet you, man,' Hamish says – another *man*er.

'Fern?' I say. 'Are you OK?'

'I just need a pint of water and I'll be *fine*.' Ah yes, my sister believes any hangover can be averted with a thoughtful glass of water before bed. Oh, I think she might be wrong on this occasion.

I note she's wearing Hamish's coat too. 'Come on, let's get you inside. You want your coat back?'

Hamish nods and I try to peel the puffer jacket off my sister. 'No!' she argues. 'It's warm! And it smells like Hamish!'

I wrestle it off her and hand it back. 'Come on, Drunkerella. Let's get you inside before you turn into a pumpkin.' I turn to Hamish, who seems oddly sober for him. 'Thanks for getting her home. You wanna come inside for a nightcap?'

'I tried to get a cab but … snow … and …' He gestures at my highly inebriated sister. 'And no, you're OK. I should be getting home.'

'Done raving?'

'Aye, I think so.' He offers Thom a weirdly chivalrous hand to shake. 'Good to meet you, dude.'

Thom looks bewildered, but shakes it anyway. Fern almost stacks it and I grab her other side. 'God, Fern, I thought I was the messy one …'

'Say hi to your mum and dad for me,' Hamish says and sets off, never once taking his eyes off Fern. For a second, I wonder if her gave her something stronger than just sherry, but while Hamish was always a ropey drunk, he was never a total villain.

'Will do,' I mutter, already guiding Fern towards the front door. 'OK, Fern, pick up those little trotters. Aye, that's it.'

'It's freezing!' she says.

'Yes, it is …'

'Were you looking for me?' God, she's loud. If my family were sleeping, they're not now.

'We've searched half the city,' Thom says, without judgement. I sense he's feeling her out, but she doesn't seem overly angry at either of us. That's a good sign, although tomorrow will bring a very different version of her I'm sure.

We reach the doorstep, and Thom and I lift her over the threshold. The door is unlocked. I actually breathe a huge sigh of relief as we step inside. The grandfather clock in the hallway has just struck midnight.

I'm not sure of the state of play, but we're all home for Christmas. We are *safe* and warm, and I remind myself that's a gift that not everybody gets. I am, although some days I struggle to remember it, lucky. Very lucky indeed. The gratitude makes me teary for some reason.

See? There is a soul in here.

Thom wraps an arm around Fern and they start up the stairs together. I watch them go, and I'm left alone in the hallway.

CHRISTMAS DAY

The house on Arboretum Road had now seen 121 Christmas Days since its completion. Much is said of the one in 1914 when soldiers downed their weapons, but the house found that each and every Christmas heralds its own pause. Time is different on Christmas Day.

Down the years, the house had welcomed countless guests; cooked many turkeys; stood tall in gales and snowstorms and hail. The house had heard many voices raised in anger, felt plates or glasses smash against its walls, but – on Christmas Day – a calm seemed to reign. For twenty-four hours, a benign quietude fell over the house. An armistice.

They do say Christmas is a time for peace to all mankind, and this Christmas was no different.

The mother and father are up first, working together in the kitchen. Both in dressing gowns, she puts on a pot of coffee while he checks over his list of timings. They have a job to do. The house knows better than most that marriages are work, and the mother and father have been working together for a long time. They will do so today.

The aunt soon follows, and asks if she can help. The mother tells her it's her Christmas too, and to relax. The aunt steps across the snowy lawn in her slippers, smoking a cigarette over a cup of black coffee. This is not how she imagined her Christmas would be.

251

The younger daughter is surprised to find an ember of love for Christmas still glows in her heart. She wakes up with dawn, as keen as she was all those years ago, to see if Santa's been. She tries to go back to sleep but finds she cannot. Staring at the light creeping in around the curtains, she makes a silent vow to herself. Today is the first day of a new beginning.

She tells herself, over and over, that she is not her thoughts.

And she will not let them win. She too is deserving of joy.

The boy wakes early too. His first thought, the same he's had since he was very young, is to wake his twin sister and race downstairs to see what's under the tree. But he cannot, and he does not like this gulf that yawns between him and his better half.

Instead he tiptoes to his friend's room and snuggles alongside them on the sofa bed. He assures them that he's OK. Merry Christmas, they say.

The young cousin finds, overnight, she has bled. At any other time, this would be a cause of great embarrassment. This morning, however, she looks to the ceiling, because this can only be a Christmas miracle. She gives thanks and promises she will be better from now on.

The elder daughter is the last to awaken, her head full of cobwebs and regret. She remembers everything and sleep is the only place it didn't happen. Her boyfriend waits for her to come to, patiently. She feels very sick. She cannot look at his face. She pretends to be asleep long after she wakes. Eventually she can avoid him no longer. Can we have one day, she says, can we pretend yesterday didn't happen? Yes, he says, it's Christmas.

Peace on earth.

After breakfast, during which it's wordlessly established that no one is to discuss the fraught events of the day before, the family gather in the drawing room, around one of the most beautiful trees the house has ever seen. As is tradition for this generation of McAllisters, they are still in their pyjamas. Their friends were warned of this custom too.

It's time for presents. The house can't believe how old they are now, parents and children alike. It feels like only yesterday three small children tore wrapping off with gay abandon, screaming at their parents to look at what Santa had brought. Today, it's a more civilised affair. The aunt crouches at the foot of the tree, reading the tags and handing out parcels.

The boyfriend gives the elder daughter a charm bracelet she admired in a flea market in Camden. Her eyes fill with tears because she knows things have changed now. This bracelet is perfect, it represents what could have been. She gives him a cashmere sweater and realises she doesn't really know him at all.

The son gives everyone an early edition of their favourite novels: Little Women; Matilda; A Wizard of Earthsea and Animal Farm for the father. For his best friend, a thoughtful pair of headphones to replace the one's he'd thoughtlessly left at a gentleman's flat.

Their parents had asked what they wanted in advance – a mixture of gadgets and gizmos the house couldn't begin to fathom, and the seasonal usuals in the stockings over the fireplace: socks, gloves, scarves and hats. That hadn't changed in over a hundred years. An orange, made out of chocolate, for all of them as well.

The house soaks up the gratitude. The fire crackles.

While the turkey roasts, the house thick and hazy with that familiar aroma, the youngsters watch a film called Frozen. The elder

253

girl sips mint tea, gradually shrugging off the night's sickness, if not her guilt. The adults weave around one another in the kitchen, an efficient hive, making space in the oven, mashing and stirring.

At two in the afternoon, the children – for to the house they are all infants – are summoned to the dining room. The younger daughter faces her fate with great dignity. She repeats her new mantra and takes a seat next to her brother, knowing – together – they will get through this. The pair pull a cracker, and he crowns his little sister with a paper crown that almost falls over her face.

Their father, with help from his wife and sister-in-law, has outdone himself. There's a nut roast for those who don't eat meat, and a regal, ten-kilogram turkey for those who do. The younger girl lets herself smell the food, just be amongst it. And it does smell good. She is very scared, but she is NOT her thoughts. Sprouts and honeyed parsnips and perfectly crisp roast potatoes. Tiny sausages wrapped in bacon. Sage stuffing.

The son watches his twin and her boyfriend through the candlelight. They are together, shoulder to shoulder at the table, and he acknowledges a certain melancholy. One day will he bring a boyfriend to this house for Christmas dinner? He would like that. Someone who is just his, and he just theirs. It is a nice idea; belonging. This craving takes him by surprise.

Next comes Christmas pudding, alight, dowsed with brandy cream. Trifle too, and everyone finds room.

The elder daughter is surprised to find she's hungry despite the excess of the night before, and that things seem peaceful with her boyfriend. Perhaps yesterday is something that doesn't need speaking of, ever again. Let Christmas Day be a rebirth.

As the sky turns violet, easing into night, the family play board

254

games. In one, they pretend to hold a seance for clues – not the first seance the house has seen. In another, the players must 'escape the room'. There is much laughter, and any disagreements are in jest. The boy rolls on his back, laughing. His twin threatens to pack the game away if he won't follow the rules and the house has seen this argument many times before.

And as night falls, the mother makes turkey sandwiches for anyone who's hungry and even the younger daughter asks for a bowl of trifle. She finds it isn't as scary as she thought it might be. She claims a small victory over the things in her mind.

Come on then, Fern, *the father says,* let's do this. *The daughter takes her place at the piano, flexing her fingers. The baby grand piano has been in the house for three generations now, brought into the building by the father's mother's father. The elder daughter pleaded for lessons as a child and plays rather beautifully once she's warmed up.*

The aunt and her daughter start – both excellent singers – with a song by someone called Mariah. The mother and daughter sing 'Oh Come All Ye Faithful' and then everyone implores the son to sing. He has a lovely voice, but doesn't consider himself a singer. He was not properly encouraged at school.

Tonight, he agrees. He speaks to his sister to ask if she has the music. She does. He clears his throat and the sister begins. He sings a carol called 'O Holy Night' and he sings it for the boyfriend. He remembers the effect it had had on him the night before. It is his gift to him.

Fall on your knees! O hear the angel voices!

The boyfriend wipes away a tear before anyone sees.

The son is not religious, but he feels something move through him.

Something that is not quite earthly, something transcendent.

In the kitchen, a quiet moment away from the frivolity in the lounge, the aunt cries on her sister's shoulder. She misses her husband. She is trying to be strong, but she's not sure she can juggle life all alone. Her sister tells her she is not alone, and never will be.

As for the mother herself, as she goes to bed alongside her husband, she wishes more than anything that the day didn't have to end. Their ceasefire is off at midnight. She wonders again why she gambled this wonderful thing she had for the thrill of something new. Her husband cannot forgive her betrayal for the sake of this one blissful day.

Although he is reminded that they together put down roots, and their buds have blossomed now. They are their own people now; exciting and unexpected characters. They each bring him such joy. If he could have this day for ever, he would.

And in the next room, the daughter and her boyfriend return to bed. Should we talk? *he asks.* No, *she says.* Let's let today just be perfect. It's like one of those snow globes with glitter in. Perfect. The most beautiful day. We can talk tomorrow.

But the boyfriend has heard that one before, and he doesn't want to live in glass bubbles. They turn away from each other in bed, facing opposite walls.

BOXING DAY

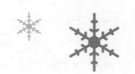

FERN

Two hangovers in two days. I am paralysed. I lie very still, staring at the ceiling, so as not to wake Thom. I know once he's awake I can't avoid my fate a second longer.

Oh, I feel sick.

I hate Boxing Day so much. It is literally the day furthest away from Christmas. I truly loathe it. It's a problem. When I was younger, Mum and Dad used to reserve one final present to tempt me downstairs, knowing how wretchedly miserable I would be. Christmas methadone to wean me off it.

Still, what an anticlimax, honestly. Where do we go from here? The story doesn't end on Christmas Day. Just ask Jesus.

Yesterday was perfection. I got my wish. A Christmas Day of peace and harmony and laughter.

And it was all pretend. So much went unsaid. No, that's not fair. It was real. But it was temporary.

Everything is such a mess. I should tell Thom what happened with Hamish or I'll rot inside. I believe that; the stench of what I did will find its way out through my mouth as stale, dead air.

I could pretend it never happened. I believe I can get away with it, but I don't think I should. All day yesterday I waited. I waited for Hamish to text, knowing that he couldn't in case

Thom saw. But there wasn't even a *Merry Christmas*. I wanted so badly to text him. I typed in *thank you for getting me home safe*, but I never hit send.

I rub my temples.

Out of nowhere, I feel a rush of energy. I want, no need, a cup of tea. Once I have that cup of tea, and maybe some buttery toast, I will be cured. I will be Fern McAllister once more, and if Fern McAllister is good for anything, she is good at fixing things.

I can do this. I can mend us, mend us all.

But I won't start with me.

I fling the duvet back and swing my legs off. Thom stirs. 'Hey … morning …'

'Wait there,' I say, throwing my dressing gown on over my pyjamas. 'I'll be back in a sec.' I leave the bedroom and thunder down the hall to Mum and Dad's room. I knock on the door, three short raps.

'Hello?' A muffled voice comes from within.

I open the door and get a poison whiff of night breath. Woof. 'What time is it?' Mum croaks from somewhere in the shadows.

'It's just gone seven,' I tell them. 'We're doing the walk, right?'

'Oh, Fern …' Dad grumbles.

'Actually that wasn't a question. We're doing the walk. All of us. Arthur's Seat. So get up. I'll stick the kettle on.'

The Parent Trap. I'm getting them back together. If I can't fix Thom and me, I'll fix them. But I'm going to need reinforcements. I'm going to need my brother.

260

WILLOW

The snow is starting to melt. From my bedroom window, I can see green tips of grass poking through the white crust. Everything is stark and real again. Yesterday was slick with a soft-focus honey glaze. Today is HD life once more.

And I'm scared.

I ate a lot yesterday. I had turkey and potatoes and sprouts and gravy and trifle and toast and tea and mulled wine. More calories than I can keep track of. I consider purging but know it's way too late. My stomach feels hard and round, like I've swallowed a bowling ball. I hear the others gathering downstairs for breakfast but, as yet, no one has come for me.

It's OK that I ate yesterday because no one will watch me today. I'll eat nothing, and nothing tomorrow, and then I'm even.

No! Fuck off! My head is fucking full of thoughts.

I am not my thoughts.

I am not my thoughts.

But it's like I'm in the middle of the sea, and the waves are coming up at me, and my head keeps going under. Those thoughts are rubber rings, or driftwood. I can get hold of them to stay afloat. The best way I know to stay alive is to starve myself.

261

I didn't want to be here today, but here I am.

There's a knock at my door. 'Will?'

It's Syd. I go to let them in. 'Hey.'

They're wearing the beanie hat my parents gave them and a woolly sweater that looks like they've come straight off a Norwegian fishing vessel. 'Morning, hi. You good?'

'Yeah.'

'No guilt carried over from yesterday?'

I say nothing. God, they're good.

'Yeah, thought so. Christmas is tough for addicts – no routine, loads of temptation. Don't feel too bad.'

I still say nothing.

'You coming on Fern's big walk?'

Oh god, how could I forget? The annual Boxing Day walk. I groan. 'Yes. There's no escaping it.'

'Cool. Breakfast first?'

'Give me a minute.'

I rummage through my underwear drawer for some thick socks so my Docs won't rub my ankles. There's no escaping the McAllister traditions – least of all with Fern around – and there's no escaping these thoughts. I am not my thoughts. OK. But are these hitchhikers going to be in my fucking head *for ever*? Do I charge them rent?

If that's true, I'm the landlord. They're living rent-free in my skull which doesn't quite seem fair.

I guess I smoke 'em out. And the only weapon I have is food. I'll have to take my meds, and eat my food, until they get bored and move out. I did yesterday. I ate more than I *had* to and I didn't die. I didn't *enjoy* it, it's always oddly mechanical, but perhaps in time …? Maybe if I just *keep going* it'll get better. I need to prove to myself that food isn't the enemy.

The thoughts in my head are.

FERN

I find Rowan in the kitchen, eating peanut butter direct from a jar with a teaspoon. 'Well, that's revolting. Don't you dare put that back in the cupboard after.'

'I licked it so it's mine,' he says, almost wistfully.

'Are you coming on the walk?'

'Do I get a choice?'

I smile. 'No.'

He tosses his spoon in the sink and leaves the peanut butter on the counter with the lid off. I tut, and screw the lid on before moving it to one side where no other poor soul will smear Rowan's mouth on their toast.

'Do we need to talk?' Rowan says.

'Probably. But no.'

'We don't really do heart-to-hearts, do we?'

He's right, of course. It goes without saying that I would die for him. I'm less certain he'd return the favour.

'I want you to do something for me.'

He says nothing, but he seems open to suggestion. 'Talk to Mum and Dad. Make them see sense.'

'Fern ...'

'No! I know I flipped out, but this is stupid. If it's all over with PhD guy, I think they should try and make it work.

Soon Willow will be moving out ...'

'Will she?' Rowan says doubtfully.

'And then they get their lives back. I feel like they got so close and fell at the last hurdle. Don't you?'

Rowan rolls his eyes. He's smeared them with black eyeliner today. It does look pretty cool, really bringing the blue out. 'What am I supposed to do?'

'They listen to you. You know they do.'

He shakes his head. 'It's not gonna work.'

'Please ... just try.'

He purses his lips. 'Very well. But if I do that, then you need to talk to Thom.' And now I roll my eyes. 'I mean it. He loves you and you hurt him last night.'

For a second it feels like my heart falls through a trapdoor, and I then I realise Ro only means how I left them in the lurch. 'He hurt me first,' I whine.

'Not on purpose. I know we don't talk about real things, but I think you've got a really good guy there, Fern.' He looks me squarely in the eyes, not trying to wriggle out of the emotion the way he usually would. 'Believe me, there are a lot of really shitty guys out there. I've shagged about sixty per cent of them. Guys like Thom are as rare as rocking-horse shit and you'd be feckin' mad to let him go. Make it right. OK? Please?'

I nod, and he heads out.

Oh my god. My heart stops, just for a split second, because I know him, and I see him. I don't know what happened last Christmas, but I know this: my brother is in love with my boyfriend.

265

ROWAN

Each year, rain or shine (or indeed slush), we walk from ours to Arthur's Seat, along with half of Edinburgh who have exactly the same Boxing Day ritual. We've been told since we were toddlers that it's a dormant volcano, but let's not dick about, like, it's a hill. Perspective, people.

I borrow a coat of Dad's, and style it out with one of Willow's voluminous scarves so I don't accidentally look heterosexual. The snow is receding on the pavements now, but still frames the tops of cars and rooftops. It's cold, but not bone-crunching cold like it was on Christmas Eve. It's tempting to make a snowball to pelt at Dad, but then I'd be stuck with wet gloves for the next four hours.

Gosh, is this adulthood?

A hand slips into mine as we reach the end of Arboretum Road, and Kara pulls me back. We let the others pull ahead. I'd already started planning how I can separate from the pack to go get her a new pregnancy test.

'Aye, I'd not forgotten,' I tell her. 'I'm thinking I'll say I want some weirdly specific drink, like Campari or something, and I'll bob into Tesco on the way home.'

'Ye dinnae need te!' Kara says gleefully. 'I'm on the blob!'

I feel a mighty wave of relief crash into me, and it wasn't

even my uterus. 'Oh, praise Jesus! It's a Christmas miracle!' It's fitting, I think. At Christmas people remember the birth of Jesus, and today we celebrate a little egg dying inside Kara. Cute.

'Nae feckin' kidding, Rowan. This is the best Christmas ever.'

'Well, I hope you've learned your lesson, young lady. Condoms!'

'I know, I know. Dinnae tell my ma, OK?'

'Of course I won't. I didn't tell a soul.' I make a mental note to pass the information along to Fern. And Syd. And also Thom.

I take some time to chat to my cousin now her crisis is over. I think things are pretty tough with Uncle Rabbie gone, but – at the same time – they seem to be getting on with it. Kara is going to finish this year at school and then either go to college to do hair and beauty, or train to be a flight attendant, which I think sounds highly glamorous. They have such cute uniforms.

She already seems more like herself again. I suppose any of those future options would have been a bit fucked if she had been knocked up.

We reach Prince's Street, and Auntie Shelly and Kara peel off to go check out the sales in the shops rather than come with us. The rest of us carry on, the remainder of the way uphill. Now that Shelly's gone, Mum and Dad are alone together at the front of the procession. Right then; this is my chance.

Everyone knows gays walk faster than regular humans, and I

power-walk past Willow and Syd – who are thick as thieves, oddly – and then Thom and Fern.

I notice they are holding hands so I'm assuming the crisis is very much over.

'I'm going in,' I say to Fern, ignoring a weird jealous niggle as I pass them.

'Good luck,' she replies. '*Make* them.'

'I can't *make* them,' I say over my shoulder.

'I believe in you.'

I stride onwards until I catch up with my parents. 'Hello,' I say brightly.

'Rowan,' Dad says under his breath. 'Have you smoothed things out with your sister?'

'I'm not sure there's anything to smooth out,' I say.

'Oh good,' Mum says.

'I know this might come as a shock,' I say, 'but I didn't actually do anything wrong. On that occasion. Just wrong place at the wrong time.'

'Such a coincidence,' muses Mum.

I slept with a lot of people's boyfriends last winter. Statistically one of them was bound to belong to *someone* I knew. 'Anyway, never mind me, what about you two?' I ask, ripping off the plaster.

'What about us?' Dad asks, cradling a coffee we picked up en route.

'Don't gaslight me! I haven't forgotten the whole divorce thing.' I shrug my shoulders up to my ears. 'I don't know. Is this *really* what you want?'

I sense them both squirming. I too am squirming.

The parent/child dynamic is about to be thrown all the way off. We don't talk about feelings in our family, which may be how we've ended up in such a mess. 'Ro, I'm not sure it's a case of *want*,' Mum says.

'Yes, it is!' I say indignantly. 'OK, hear me out. Like, who says you *have* to break up?' They look to one another, puzzled. 'I mean it. Like, is there a rule? Someone cheated so now you have to get divorced?'

'That is usually how it works, yes,' Dad says.

We pass Edinburgh Castle and Arthur's Seat is in sight now. 'I think that's bullshit,' I tell them.

'Rowan …' Mum scolds.

'No, listen. Literally every gay couple I know is in some sort of open relationship.'

'We aren't gay,' Dad adds, stating the plainly obvious since he is wearing a wax jacket.

'Evidently. You aren't nearly so evolved. But listen: monogamy didn't exist ahead of Christianity, and that's basically when you got together.'

'Thanks for that, son.'

'You met when you were younger than I am now. Do I seem ready for marriage to you?'

'Do you want a serious answer?' Dad asks with a grin.

'It is insane to me that you expected to only … *sleep with* … each other for all your adult lives. Talk about setting yourself up for a spectacular fail.'

Mum says, 'Rowan, we took vows.'

Well, that was your first mistake, I think. Making a promise to love one person for ever. What are you, five? 'Do those vows say anything about what happens when one person fancies someone else? Because in fifty years, I think it was fairly likely one of you might get your head turned. And actually, I played a groom in a play once and the wedding vows said shit about monogamy.'

'One day you'll …'

I wag a finger in his face. 'No! Don't pull that one. I'm being the mature one here. I don't know how bad things have been because you haven't actually bothered to tell us, but I know that yesterday you were happy. I saw it with my eyes.'

They don't try to deny it.

'So if you still believe you can be happy together then you should think about it. Not for us – we'll be fine – but for you. Don't split up just because you think it's what you *should* do. That's bullshit. *Should* is worrying what other people think. I stopped caring what people think of me years ago. It's chaotic, but beautiful. Just do what you want.'

'Rowan,' Mum says, 'it's really not as simple as that.'

'Yes, it is. Like the Prophet Miley once said, if you're not hurting no one or taking nothing, where's the harm? Just do what you want. Do you actually *want* to break up?'

Neither of them are willing to answer that question which I think it really telling. Dad wraps an arm around my shoulder. 'You know what, son? Wee glimmers of that actually made sense. If this acting thing doesn't work out, you could be a therapist.'

'Dad, I *need* a therapist,' I say. 'And why wouldn't my acting work out? How very dare you?'

Oh god, maybe I quite *like* my parents. Who knew?

270

We'll never be *friends*, but I do look forward to seeing them. I walk between my mum and dad, a strip of human Velcro, hoping that somehow it's enough to keep them together.

WILLOW

'Are you cold?' Syd asks. I thought I was hiding my intense shivering well, but apparently not. They could probably hear my teeth clattering together.

'Freezing.'

Kids are making the most of what's left of the snow, sledging down the hillside, screaming at the top of their lungs. I didn't even think; we have a sledge – a bright orange plastic one – somewhere in the garden shed. That would have been fun.

The families all look so *happy*, so worry-free. But then, walking in our cute procession towards the overlook, we probably look like a bog-standard family too. Yesterday *was* utopia. I wonder what it would take for every day to be so easy: literally Christmas?

'Here.' Syd wraps an arm around my shoulder and rubs vigorously. Without the rubbing, it could be a sexy thing, but it's more like they're trying to dry me off. Still, Fern and Thom are behind us on the footpath to the top of Arthur's Seat; I wonder what they make of it. I think they'd like to see me do normal teenage girl stuff.

'Better?' Syd asks.

'Yeah,' I say. 'Um, did you … tell Rowan about the other night?'

'Nope.'

'Thanks.'

'That's our business.'

'I'm sorry …'

'Hey!' they say. 'Don't be. It was a mood.'

It's pure embarrassing really. I was punching. Syd is … cool and sexy and really, insanely well-dressed, and I'm the scrawny runt no one wants from the dog-rescue place. If I wasn't me, I wouldn't take me on. I'd get one of the nice puppies with a glossy coat and shiny nose. I'm *that* dog, the scary-looking one from memes with patchy fur and mental snaggleteeth.

I wonder if Syd reads my mind because they carry on. 'I said this wasn't our time, but what I meant was, it's not *your* time.'

'What do you mean?'

'OK,' Syd says, 'what I'm about to tell you may disturb you in the short term but help you in the long run.'

I laugh a little. 'Trigger warning. Go on.'

'People are shit. I really mean that.'

'OK …'

'I came to this conclusion when the psychologist who was treating my OCD had a nervous breakdown and got signed off for six months.'

I laugh, again, nervously this time. 'What?'

'I'm not kidding. The person who was supposed to be fixing me needed fixing. And that's when I realised that I couldn't rely on anyone else. I had huge crushes on people too – other people with OCD I met online and stuff. I couldn't rely on them either, and you know I couldn't rely on my mum or stepdad.'

'That … is shit.'

'Told you. At first it was scary because I was like, *Fuck, I'm in this all alone*, but then I was like, *Well, who the fuck else is going to fix this for you?* I'm not gonna tell you how to live your life, but no one is going to save you but yourself, Willow.'

That's bleak. I want Wonder Woman or Captain America to teach me a very important lesson.

'Maybe I'm getting this wrong,' they say. 'I don't mean there's no help out there, because there is. My friends are amazing – even Rowan, when he's not on a comedown. I get therapy from college once a week; that's pretty sweet. But I know that all those people who help me need help too. I can't lean on them too hard. It has to be me.'

They seem very strong, though. I don't know if I have that strength inside me.

'Give me your phone,' Syd says.

I reach into my pocket and hand it over. 'Why?'

'I'm giving you my number. Message me whenever your head is fucking you over. Seriously. You know in Alcoholics Anonymous people have a sponsor? I'll be your sponsor.'

I shake my head. 'But you just said – you have your own stuff to deal with.'

'I know! And if I don't have the mental capacity to provide help, I'll tell you.' They hand my phone back and I'm weirdly excited that I have their number stored. 'That's why you also need a Plan B, and a Plan C and a Plan D. You know you have a brother and sister who'd move heaven and earth for you, right?'

I know that's true, but I also know they're sick of me.

274

That's not even speculation. A lot of social media posts are keen to tell me YOU ARE NOT A BURDEN, but I really think I might be. Truth be told, I'm fucking sick of myself, so it doesn't feel fair to expect any less of anyone else. 'So … what you're saying is: I can't do this alone, but I have to do this alone?'

Now Syd laughs. 'Exactly.'

'Great,' I say wryly.

'But you have me,' Syd says. 'I swear. My phone is on noisy all night. I promise.'

And knowing that does make me feel a little better. Knowing that, even when the night gets really dark, there's a little candle burning for me down in Bristol.

FERN

Thom finishes his tale. I had to tease it out of him. I wanted the unedited, director's cut. It plays out like a Richard Curtis Christmas rom-com. Picturesque French backdrop; a broken leg; a case of mistaken identity; a cute bartender; twenty-four hours of happiness in the snow, and then a bittersweet farewell. I would watch that literally every Christmas if it was on Netflix.

Some of it was hard to hear, but at least now I know the whole story. Thom doesn't know half of it.

'I know this isn't the right thing to say,' I say after taking it all in for a minute or two, 'but I just don't understand how you can fancy both me *and* Rowan.'

Thom gives me a *for real?* expression. 'Fern, the reason you don't understand is that you're not bisexual.'

'Fair, I guess.'

'Like, how do you describe having a crush on someone? You just do or you don't. When I saw you in that coffee queue, I fancied you. When I saw Ro in that bar ...'

'Yeah, got it.' I think back to the early days. Seeing Thom in lectures, then later in the coffee shop where I finally plucked up the courage to say *hello*. I did fancy him. He caught my eye. I looked back and kept looking. I started fantasising about a future with him. I remember the first time his name popped up on my phone and how excited I was. I almost dived across the room to reply. That's what it's like to fancy someone.

A kid on an old-fashioned wooden sled cuts across us and cries SORRY at the top of his voice. Thom puts a protective arm in front of me. We're on the last leg now. We'll soon be at the top, where we'll get the traditional McAllister Boxing Day photograph, then start the walk back down, possibly stopping for lunch somewhere.

Only then do I remember this year's Boxing Day photo may well be our last as one unit. Next year will we have to alternate days between Mum and Dad? My heart sinks. This Christmas – however perfect yesterday was – can get in the sea.

Up ahead, I see Willow with Syd, and Rowan gesticulating frantically between Mum and Dad. I wonder how he's getting on. My instinct is to wade in and do it my way, but I need to trust him. I do hope he's not extolling the virtues of open relationships or something wild like that.

I feel acutely vomitty, but Thom has done his part, and now I need to do mine. I'm not, and I'm aware this is on the controversial side, going to tell him the whole truth. I think telling him what happened with Hamish would be partly selfish; like, just to unburden myself of guilt. I don't want to hurt him, and I think the best way to do that is to not tell him. Thom trusts me, so how would he ever guess? I feel a twist in my gut. I need to say what I'm about to say because the problem is Thom and me, not Hamish Bell.

'Do you think this is working?' I ask. 'You and me?'

'Yes …' he blurts out, and then, '… no,' he concludes.

'Right?' I say, oddly glad to hear him confess. I thought I was going mad for wanting something more. 'Like, it works, but …'

'Something's missing,' Thom says. 'But it's like I feel greedy for admitting that.'

Precisely. Something like the intense fire I felt in that bathroom on Christmas Eve. Not just that; that does Hamish a disservice. If I'd never been out with Hamish, maybe I'd never have known that urgency, that all-consuming, giddy, hunger for someone. That obsessive need to touch someone, to be all over them like glue. I have had it once and I want it again.

And I don't have it with Thom.

That feels WILD to admit because it's like being given a free Ferrari by the universe and then turning my nose up at it because it's too red and sporty, but …

Now I've said it, I already feel lighter, easier, like I've been holding up an enormous Jenga tower. Letting it go is as easy as gravity. All the bricks come crashing down. It's noisy and then … nothing.

'I think we're too young to settle on each other because it just … works,' I tell him. I might cry. My eyes sting.

He nods. His eyes look shimmery too. 'Do you think we're better as friends?'

'We *are* friends,' I say emphatically. 'Thom, I do love you.'

'But not like *that*?'

'It's a different kind of love, I guess, but it's definitely love. I would go to war for you.'

He smiles. 'So would I.'

'I think … if we'd met when we were, like, thirty, we'd be endgame …'

'Fuck. Thirty.'

'Exactly. I'm not ready for endgame. Not yet.'

'Me neither.'

Becca and Farah used to joke that I was the most middle-aged sixteen-year-old they'd ever met. My student house is the cleanest in London. I hand in all my assignments well ahead of deadlines. I am Lisa Simpson. I don't think it's a bad thing that I've always known what I want in life. I want what my parents have. Had. A marriage; some children; a nice house; a good job. What's wrong with wanting that?

I'm just not sure I want it *yet*.

'What about Rowan?' I say, my voice a dormouse squeak.

'What about him?'

I shake my head. 'Thom … c'mon. There's something between you.' And there is. There seems to be less air in the room if they're both in it. Like the house is holding its breath in anticipation. I don't know if it's the same as what I have with Hamish: that *folie à deux*.

Thom kicks a clump of ice down the path. 'I don't think that's what Rowan wants.'

'Is it what you want?'

'Fern …'

'No. It's OK.' I steel myself. I'm shivery and I don't think it's the cold, I think it's all the adrenaline. 'You want what you want.' I know that better than anyone, don't I?

A tear rolls down Thom's cheek. 'I don't know what I want.'

'Go talk to him.'

'I can't.' He covers his face with his gloves. I didn't mean to make him cry. I pull him in for a hug and he slumps on to my shoulder, hiding his face. I hold him tight. A million years have passed since we ran for that train at Kings Cross.

ROWAN

We have to wait our turn at the top of the hill. Everyone wants their picture overlooking Edinburgh. It's a clear day and I can see it all from up here: the castle; the Forth Bridge; all the city. I know it's a bit Brexit to love your hometown, but I do properly fancy Edinburgh. He is a sexy beast, and I'll come back for him one day. I'm too young for him now, and he's too distinguished for me. He's a full salt-and-pepper beard, scotch-on-the-rocks Daddy Bear. I'm not ready to settle down. If Edinburgh is Brando, Bristol is James Dean, and I'm not done with him yet.

It's blowing a gale. Every year we stand here for a goofy picture. I've more or less mastered how to face into the wind, so you look like Beyoncé on stage, and not merely windswept.

'Syd? Will you do us the honours?' Mum asks, handing Syd her phone.

'Sure.' Syd backs up ready to take the picture.

Fern beckons Thom into the picture. 'No,' he says, downbeat. 'Should just be family.'

I frown. Both he and Fern are subdued. 'Are you OK?' I breathe in Fern's ear.

'Fine.'

'Fern …'

'Leave it, Rowan.'

She means it. I drop it. At a safe distance from the edge, we take our places in front of Mum and Dad. Dad drapes an arm around our shoulders.

'I'm not squatting down again,' Willow says, and I laugh. It became a tradition that she'd squat at the front and it always looked ridiculous.

'You have to!' Fern says. 'It's tradition.'

'You do it then!'

'Don't start!' Dad clips. 'No one has to squat.'

Mum and Dad bookend us. I hope they heed what I said. I still see, no *feel*, a lot of love between them, the sort you wouldn't walk away from. That said, Willow is almost eighteen now. What if *we* were the thing they had in common? And soon we'll all have moved on. Maybe I should get them a dog?

'OK, you ready?' Syd shouts.

'Everybody try to look normal, please,' Mum says.

'Ew!' I say loudly and everyone laughs. We are normal. What even is normal? A Tory politician; his cheating wife; gay son; anorexic daughter and the uptight one. But everyone has their shit, I really believe that. Even the most muesli, beige-looking suburban families have their mutant incest babies locked in the attic.

I accidentally catch Thom's eye. He's standing at Syd's side, looking desolate. I think he's been crying. There's a weird ache in my chest. I want to help him, but I can't.

Our kiss in the car on Christmas Eve pops into my head, and I push it out again. Who am I torturing more, him or me?

He's well and truly been sucked into the McAllister vortex.

But he's gorgeous, and young, and smart. He'll untangle himself from our family thorns, and go on to wonderful things, I have no doubt. The sea parts for you with a face like his.

He'll be fine.

And so will I. Give me a week or so, and I'll be over him like I would a mild gastric flu.

Oh, but I want him, though. That's what the ache is. It is want. Humanity's little addiction. We all *want*. I want him every way you can have someone. I dig my nails into my palms. I've wanted all sorts of things my whole life, and I've been disappointed before. When I was a tiny proto gay I wanted a nice, handsome boyfriend. Of course I did! The fantasy brought me so much comfort when I was scared of who I was, in bed at night. All that shit I got at school; potentially being thrown out by my parents would be worth it once I was with Troy Bolton. Then I got a bit older and realised the fantasy doesn't really exist. It just hurts. You get close to guys and they fuck you over unless you fuck them over faster.

I can't have him. I can't. I can't take Fern's boyfriend, and then fuck it all up – which I inevitably would based on past evidence – and make even more mess.

I'll take a tip from my *other* sister. I'll starve myself.

We – as usual – decide to head down the hill the quicker, but more perilous, route. Maybe Thom will get a broken leg two years in a row. I set off with Syd, but Fern grabs my arm. 'Wait up. Can we talk?'

'Sure.' We can, although I'd rather not. It's alien, feeling so distant from her. When Willow was born, we were like two and a half, and decided to punish our parents for bringing an interloper into the mix by creating our own secret language. Much like Keisha and Mutya did when Heidi joined the Sugababes. That's how close Fern and I have always been. We have grown apart since we left home, and I'm sad about that, well aware I'm chiefly responsible.

When I got to Bristol, I was off the leash, truly, for the first time in my entire life. Kid in a candy shop. I didn't want to FaceTime Fern. Sorry, I didn't.

'Don't worry,' Fern says as the rest of the entourage pull ahead of us on the zigzagging pathway. 'Thom has already told me everything about Courchevel.'

'Ew, not everything I hope.'

'He left out the gory details.'

I take my sister's hand, the way we did when we used to cross the road. 'Look, I am sorry I boffed your bf, but you can't be mad at Thom for being bisexual.'

'I'm not.' I give her a look. 'I'm not! Mad is not the right word. I've been processing it for over a year and yes, I know it's obviously way harder for him! God, whatever I say, I sound like such a bitch!'

Bitch is too strong a word. Too fabulous a word now you mention it. 'You're not a bitch. Uptight, yes. Bitch, no.'

'Can I tell you a secret?'

'Of course.'

'I slept with Hamish on Christmas Eve.'

I stop dead in my tracks. Holy fuck. Still, I will not give her the satisfaction of out-slutting me. 'I knew it.'

'You did?'

'I knew there was something when he dropped you off.' I don't actually believe twins have psychic intuition, but it gives me great joy to freak Fern out and pretend that I do.

'I feel awful.'

And she looks awful too. Her face is as white as the hillside. 'Oh, girl, don't do that to yourself. These things happen. Usually to me, granted, but ...'

'Please don't tell anyone.'

'I won't. Have you told Thom?'

'No. Things are bad enough. We just broke up I think.'

So ... Thom is single? But that means ... That means nothing, chill the fuck out. 'Because of Hamish?'

She shakes her head. 'No. And not because of you, either. Because of *us*. There's just ... no magic. I know that sounds vague, but I don't know how else to describe it. Being with – you know who – reminded me that something was missing. Do you think I'm evil?'

I link my arm through hers. It's odd to hear my sister – the sensible one – talk of something as abstract as magic. That sort of swirly-whirly chaos theory stuff is much more my style. 'No. I think you're human.'

'Well, I think I'm evil.'

'Fern, your problem is you try to control everything, and you can't control all the fun stuff: love, sex, hate. Otherwise love would be like shopping. It would be too easy. You'd just go down the high street and pick a boyfriend you liked the look of off the rack and take him home.'

Fern grimaces. 'I think that's slightly what I did. I wanted a nice boyfriend, so I went out and got one.'

285

'Yeah, it doesn't work like that. Look at Charles and Di.'

'I love him, though,' she says sadly. 'I do. More than anything, I want the people I love to be happy.' There's a long pause, and then she says, 'So, if it makes you both happy, you should go for it.'

For the second time in five minutes, I freeze. My whole body goes into spasm. 'Are you on crack?'

'No. I mean it.'

And then I remember who's talking. 'I'm not going to be some consolation prize for him, to make you feel better about noshing off Hamish Bell.'

Her eyes widen. 'Oh my god, that is so not what I meant.' And then she gives me a different sort of look, one of mild disgust. The sort of expression I'd reserve for a pigeon pecking at vomit on the pavement. 'Did you like him at all when you were in France? Or was he just another convenient random?'

'Fuck off, Fern.' I head down the path faster but she trots after me.

'No, you come back here, Rowan, you wanker!' She grabs my arm. 'Thom said he really fell for you ...'

I'm hardly going to tell the truth, am I? *Oh, I thought about your boyfriend all year, I just didn't know he was your boyfriend.*

She speaks with kindness, and she very much reminds me of our mum. I try to yank my arm free, but she's freakishly strong. 'Rowan, stop, please. I love you and I love Thom. The only question is whether you love each other.'

I swear a dark cloud rolls over the sun at that exact moment. Everything goes dark. It's like the earth splits and I fall into the abyss. It was safer when I couldn't have him. The thought of having him is so much scarier.

I cannot love him.

FERN

Conveniently, I used the last caffeine-free teabag last night which gives me a watertight excuse to pop into Tesco Metro.

I just want to see him. I know it doesn't make any sense, but I've ended things with Thom and there's only one person in the world I want to tell.

I scan the aisle and, for a moment, I think he isn't here. I try to shrug off the disappointment, but my heart feels somewhere near my socks. Only then he emerges from the storeroom, pushing a cage on wheels, seemingly filled with milk cartons. He's so bloody sexy. Why couldn't I ever admit that? Even in a blue Tesco fleece he's delicious. He sees me and I take a deep breath.

'Hey,' I say.

He pauses for a second and then continues to wheel the trolley past me. 'Hey there, you,' he says.

'Christmas Wrapping' comes on the sound system and I realise with horror they have the same songs on a constant loop. What fresh hell is this? I block it out and think what to say. I should have written a script. 'I hoped you were going to be here. I didn't want to turn up at your house.'

'You're looking for me? Or tea?' He nods at the decaf Yorkshire Tea in my hands.

'I wanted to see you.'

Hamish smiles, but he seems deflated. I suppose I would be if I was working at Tesco on Boxing Day too. 'You fancied a quickie in the dairy section?'

'Hamish ... I wanted to say thank you for getting me home on Christmas Eve. I was a hot mess.'

He nods. 'No biggy, I owed you one. You put me to bed more times than I can count.'

He starts unloading bottles of milk on to the shelves in the fridge cabinet. I hover at his side. 'And, um, I wanted to say I broke up with Thom this morning.'

He stops and checks his boss isn't watching from the checkout area. 'Because of us?'

'No. And yes. I realised that he and I don't have what you and I have.'

'And what's that?'

'You know ...' I lower my voice slightly as an old lady reaches past us for some semi-skimmed, 'that *thing*.'

Hamish looks at me a moment, his expression blank, and then goes back to unloading the milk cartons. 'Right, so one amazing orgasm and you want to get back together?' His tone is always jovial but there's something behind it. He lowers his voice. 'Fern, I haven't seen you in almost two years.'

'What? No!' I'm not sure I'd given it that much thought because it's simply so ludicrous. How would that even work? Also, arrogant much? The orgasm wasn't *that* ... actually I can't lie, I was genuinely shook. 'That's not what I'm saying ... I don't really know what I'm saying ... but don't you think we should talk about things?'

'I ... don't know?' He frames it as a question and I realise I can't rely on my memories of Christmas Eve. Did I imagine the whole thing? There's a scintilla of *pity* in his expression. Oh god, this is like poking pins under my nails. I wish I could evaporate into thin air.

'Look, Fern,' he goes on, 'I can see why this is happening. It's because I've finally changed in a way that suits you. I'm sober, I'm coming to London, I quit the band.'

I say nothing because these thoughts *have* crossed my mind. I stare at the floor.

'I've changed, but you haven't. Fern, can't you remember what we were like? We were, um, pretty fucking toxic? You trying to control everything I did; me trying to take back control by doing fucked up shit all the time. Why would you want to go back to that?'

He says *we* were toxic, but he means *I* was toxic. I'm actually winded, like I've been punched in the gut. 'I ...'

He relents. 'Fuck. Shit. I'm sorry. That came out way harsher than I meant.'

'No, it's fine,' I say, backing away towards the tills. I waggle the teabags in his face. 'I don't think we should get back together. That would be crazy! I just, um, came to say thanks for the other night.'

'Fern,' he says sadly, 'don't do that.'

'Do what? I'm seriously fine!' My voice does not sound fine, it sounds unhinged. Well, this is what you get for trying to be spontaneous. Guess I'll go back to being a controlling, uptight shrew! That's what everyone thinks of me! There's a new year's resolution to work on as a single gal about town in

290

London. You have to laugh, right? 'I'm … I'm happy you're happy, though, Hamish, I really am. Um, maybe we can get a pint in London when you're settled?'

He nods, although I think we both know I have more chance of waking up tomorrow with a mermaid tail. 'That'd be good.'

'I'll see you, then.' I turn and join the queue for the express tills. I suck back the overwhelming urge to sob. God, I hope I'm not on CCTV. I'm such a wanker. Did I really think it was going to be that easy? That I'd maturely end things with Thom and walk into a cinematic reunion with my ex? It'd be the end of the movie; a big kiss in the middle of Tesco, then cut to credits. Yeah, I really did, although I was pretending, even to myself, that I didn't. I'm an embarrassment.

What's even scarier is the panic creeping in. A voice in my head tells me it might not be too late to race home and beg Thom to reconsider. ANYTHING BUT SINGLE. The terror takes me surprise. I didn't think I was that girl, but it also occurs to me that since I was about fifteen years old, I've only been truly single for about four months. I have forgotten how to do it. What fills your time if you don't have someone else to think about?

I have no Thom, no Hamish and, worse of all, I don't really know if I have myself. Who am I all by myself? I have no idea. My only hobby is 'boyfriends'. I'm going home with nothing.

'Doll, you in the queue or not?' the lady behind me barks. I didn't realise it was my turn.

'I'm sorry,' I mutter, and take my tragic decaffeinated teabags to the self-checkout.

WILLOW

Fern arrives home and places a box of teabags on the kitchen counter next to me. I'm helping Mum make bubble and squeak with the leftovers from Christmas dinner. I squash a mixture of cold mash, shredded cabbage and sprouts into little pancake shapes and hand them to Mum to fry. Maybe I need to engage with food more, like, spend time preparing what I eat instead of having it forced upon me. I cannot deny they smell very, very good as Mum places them in the oil.

That said, I am wary of that oil. I don't like the way it's looking at me.

'Where's Thom?' Fern asks.

'He's outside with Syd,' Rowan tells her, nodding towards the back garden. 'They're talking video games.'

Fern grimaces. 'Got it.'

The front door goes again, and I lean back to see Auntie Shelly and Kara bustle down the hall, arms full of Primark and New Look bags. Shelly hands the bags to Kara. 'You go on and get these all packed?'

Kara heads upstairs while Shelly continues towards us.

'Did you get some bits?' Mum asks.

'Aye,' Shelly replies. 'Some real bargains. New leather jacket for a fiver in New Look. Not real leather like, but nae bad … look listen, hen, we're gonnae head back to Glasgow in a wee bit.'

I say nothing, but I thought they were heading back tomorrow.

'Why?' Mum asks.

'It's Rabbie …'

Rowan and Fern stop chatting at the kitchen table and instead listen for whatever this development is. 'Oh Christ, what now?' Mum prompts.

'He's back,' Shelly says. 'I changed the locks so he cannae get in.'

I sense Mum tense up, the way an angry cat arches its back and puffs itself out. 'Back back?'

'I dunno. He called jus' now in town.'

'Shell …' Mum warns.

'Aye, I know.'

Mum thought Uncle Rabbie was a steaming pile of shite long before he ran off with someone the same age as Fern.

That's what stings. Mum and Dad are *not* the same as Shelly and Rabbie. They're not. My auntie and uncle *despise* each other; constantly picking at each other in that passive aggressive *well maybe SOMEONE shouldn't have left the milk out* fashion. Pure bitter, the pair of them. That's not what Mum and Dad are like. I know I've been wrapped up in myself, but I'm not totally blind.

Mum reaches into the basket on top of the fridge and pulls down a tote bag. 'Well, I'm sending you home with some food, OK? We've got enough here to feed an army.'

'Thanks, Chris.'

Mum loads up the bag with a panettone; a box of Roses; some cold turkey cuts; half a ham and a bottle of Baileys someone from the university had gifted her. 'Yer a sweetheart,' Shelly says. 'I'd best be getting packed up if we're gonnae get the five o'clock train.'

I finish off the bubble and squeak. 'Does everyone want eggs on top?' I ask, feeling oddly useful for me. Everyone says that they will, and I fetch the eggs from the fridge.

'I'll take over,' Mum says, plucking the spatula out of my hand. I take a seat with Fern and Rowan at the table.

'Is she OK?' Rowan asks, picking up, I think, on Mum's tight-lipped concern.

Mum sighs, taking out her frustration on the bubble and squeak, jabbing it in the pan. 'Ah, I don't know, Rowan.'

If it weren't for Shelly's constant drama, I'd be the only thing Mum had to worry about. A sharp slice of guilt cuts through my ribs.

'I wish …' Mum goes on, breaking eggs into the frying pan as she talks, 'I wish that Shelly could settle, you know? It's been the same since we were kids. One shitty man after the next. Don't get me wrong – she is the thing the shitty men have in common. I wish she could … realise she deserves a man who treats her better. Find some sort of peace. You know?'

We all nod. Mum turns to look at us. She points the spatula at each of us in turn. 'I hope you know how lucky you are to have each other. Friends and boyfriends come and go, but brothers and sisters are for ever. I mean that. We're chalk and cheese, but your Auntie Shelly is the best friend I've ever had.'

I look to Fern and Rowan. Despite his surly mood, Rowan

boops my nose with his finger and I roll my eyes. With them being twins, I always felt like the 'spare', but now more than ever, I'm so glad I'm not an only child. I feel *it*. That sameness. I wonder if they've finally let me into the psychic network that Rowan always jokes about.

'Look. Whatever happens, we're still a girl gang,' Rowan says listlessly, before quickly adding, 'I'm the Beyoncé ...'

'I'm Kelly!' Fern adds at once.

'Fine, I'm *Solange* ...' I say smugly. I think that's a definite victory.

'Ooh, an intellectual ...' Rowan grins.

'I don't know what literally any of that meant, but whatever keeps you quiet ...' says Mum as she starts to plate up the brunch.

We used to fight all the time. We were so, so horrible to each other. Nothing was off limits: scratching, biting, farting and then wafting the smell in their faces. Rowan once farted in a Tupperware container and made Fern open it. Fern once locked Rowan in Nana's shed and didn't let him out until he ate cat food. I used to tell Fern to kill herself almost weekly. Ro and Fern were worse – thick as thieves one second and then screaming abuse the next. There's a black skid mark on the wall in the hallway where Rowan once hurled a Doc Marten boot at Fern's head.

I think that era is over, though.

None of us knows what's going to happen next, but I strangely look forward to us all being grown-ups. Friends even? I don't really have other friends, so I suppose by default Ro and Fern are my best friends. No one else speaks our language.

I wonder if – now we're not here for Santa – *this* is what Christmas is for. It's a universally agreed date for getting us back together. A pact. Who will we be next year? In ten years? In twenty?

I hope I'm here to see that. I really do.

ROWAN

I need some time away from them. I've hit my limit. My family can be *sweet*, but as with actual sweets, if I eat too many I get a weird furry feeling in my mouth and want to vomit. I stuck around for some curry, and then retreated to the quiet of the top floor.

Like any self-respecting queer, I went through my witchy phase when I was about fifteen. I thought my tarot pack had long since found its way to a car boot sale, but, by some miracle, it's still in my desk drawer.

Fucked if I can remember what all the cards mean, but I make it up as I give Syd an impromptu reading. It's pitch black outside my window and I've lit a million IKEA tealights all around the room for added atmosphere. I flip over the Eight of Wands. 'The Eight of Wands is a sign of great mysticism. It's telling you to believe in the power of nature over capitalism.'

Syd fixes me in a highly sceptical glare. 'Are you making these up?'

'No.'

'So, "The Devil" really means Satanic forces are presently doing my bidding?'

I smile. 'Well, I'm in your life, aren't I?'

Syd throws my Spongebob Squarepants at my head and I

duck out the way. 'You're such a shit! You could have literally googled!'

'I preferred my way!' There's a knock at the door. 'Helloooo?'

The door opens and Thom pokes his head through the gap. 'Hey.'

'What's up?' I ask, not looking at him. 'Has Fern concocted some sort of organised fun for us all to hate?'

Syd agrees. 'If someone suggests charades, I'm hitchhiking home.'

'I think things are wrapping up down there. Everyone is really tired.' Thom half-smiles. 'Um, no. I wondered if we could talk for a sec …?'

See, this is why I don't give guys my number. 'Yeah, sure.' I look to Syd. 'Can you give us a minute?'

Syd knows their cue. 'Sure. I'll be downstairs. I'll suggest charades.' They gather their hoodie and glass of wine and vacate past Thom, who hovers awkwardly.

'Come in then,' I tell him. 'Does Fern know you're up here?'

'It was Fern who sent me up.' He perches next to me on the edge of my bed. 'She thinks we have unfinished business.'

Meddling cow. I collect in my tarot cards and give them a shuffle. 'You want a reading?' I can tell him I don't see a Scottish twink in his future.

He cups his face in his hands, rubbing his rough jaw. 'Now I'm here, I don't know what I want to say.'

I take pity on him. 'Look, I get that breaking up with Fern must be a headfuck, but …'

And he launches himself at my face. The kiss almost knocks me off the side of the bed. He smells so good. His lips are warm and soft. I kiss him back for a second before I get my head together and pull back.

'Easy, cowboy.' He tries to kiss me again, and I put a hand on his chest to stop him. 'I mean it.'

'What?' he asks, confused. 'I thought ... I thought you'd prefer it if we ...'

I smile. 'Fuck the pain away?' Peaches. Timeless.

Thom looks so lost, so green. A fledgling. It hurts in my chest. I feel waterlogged inside somehow, and I can't save him when I'm struggling to stay afloat myself.

'I can't do this, Thom. I'm sorry.'

'But now that me and Fern ...'

'I can't,' I say again.

He takes my hand on the duvet. My first urge is to yank it away, but I like how his skin feels. 'Rowan, I don't want to hurt you. I don't want *anything* from you. I just ... I just want to be with you tonight.'

I shake my head. I don't want to shame him for being so open with me, but I know myself well enough to know I'm not great with resolve. 'If we start something, we won't stop.'

'We don't have to do anything. But can I stay with you tonight? Just as friends?'

I fix him with a highly doubtful glare. This is me we're talking about. 'Is that a good idea?'

'Please? I can't stay with Fern. It's too confusing.'

I don't tell him that sleeping with me will probably make things ten times more confusing.

'No funny business if that's what you want,' he says. 'I swear. We can even go top and tails.'

I laugh. I haven't done that since I was about eleven. 'Now Shelly and Kara have gone we have a spare room, you know.'

He half shrugs. 'I don't want your parents to think there's something up.'

But there is. Although I see why he doesn't want the gossip mill to start turning. 'I guess you can stay in here if you want. But promise to keep your hands to yourself?'

'Scout's honour.'

I bet he was a Scout, too, so I take his word. I know I *should* exile him to the guest room. But I don't want to. I know this is madness, but after this weekend, I'll never see him again. This is it.

Where's the harm in a sleepover? I get ready for bed, and then he does. He returns from brushing his teeth and strips down to his boxers. In the candlelight his body almost glows. I avert my eyes, already feeling myself getting hard. Why am I putting myself through this? I try to think about sad and/or gross things again to kill the boner.

'Did anyone see you come up?'

'I don't think so. Well, only Syd.'

'Syd is cool.'

'Shuffle up, then,' he says and I scoot over to the left side of the bed. He slides in alongside me.

It's half-ten, and I should be cream-crackered after all the fresh air. I find myself wide awake and ready for action. I turn to the Bert to my Ernie. 'Maybe this is a bad idea.'

'What? We're behaving,' Thom says innocently. 'Look, I'll keep my hands above the sheets if you want.'

300

'Fine.' I snuggle down and blow out the final candle on my bedside table. 'Goodnight, Thomothy.'

'Goodnight, Rowan.'

There's a velvety silence, and then the bed springs shift. I feel his body press against my back. 'Thom …? That had better be a ghost because I thought we had an agreement?'

'Is spooning not allowed?' I can hear a smile on his lips. It's good to hear.

'Probably not, no!'

'Do you want me to stop?'

I feel his dick pressing against my butt cheek and it takes everything I have not to roll over. 'Go to sleep, scamp,' I tell him. It's quite fun being the prude for once. I feel like a Victorian maiden, fending off the lusty baron.

'Sleep tight,' he whispers. 'I really like cuddling you.'

I don't *not* like it. He wraps his arms around me and as his hands touch my torso I nearly spring clean out of the bed. 'Oh my god, your hands are like ice, what the fuck is wrong with you, are you dead?'

He pulls them back. 'Sorry! I get really cold hands and feet! I don't know why!'

'Give me them here.' I take his hand in mine and give it a rub. 'Better?'

'Much better.' In the darkness of my teenage bedroom, his breath tickles my ear.

'Now shut up, you deviant, I need my beauty sleep.'

He chuckles. 'You're already beautiful, Rowan.'

He kisses my neck fleetingly, just below my ear, and I gasp. He falls silent. As the minutes pass, I hear his breathing grow deeper, like the tide shivering on the beach. It's hypnotising. With Thom Simpkins' arms wrapped around me, I fall into the safest sleep I have ever slept. No nightmare could get anywhere near me.

27 DECEMBER

ROWAN

His arms are still loosely around me when I awake. White, frosty light creeps in at the edges of the blinds, and I get the sense it's still early.

I stir, and Thom wakes. 'Morning,' he croaks. 'You sleep well?'

'Like a baby,' I admit. I feel weird, though. Like a hangover, but in my chest.

He rolls off me. 'What time is it?'

'Early I think.' I check my phone on the bedside table. 'Just after seven.'

He buries his face in the pillow. 'Urgh, I'm going back to sleep.'

Already, there's a nauseous feeling in my stomach, and my skin feels too tight. *What the fuck have I done?* I should have never, ever let him sleep here.

'I slept so well,' Thom says, his eyes closed. 'I dreamed about you.'

'Oh aye?'

What does he want from me?

My legs twitch. Can I ask him to go? Where's he gonna go? Back into Fern's bed? FUCK. This just made a shitty situation so much worse. I should have been stronger.

I've made him believe I'm someone I'm not. Last night, I gave him the Boyfriend Experience with added Intimacy.

But I'm not here to be had; owned.

I clamber out of bed. I have to get out.

'Where are you going?' he murmurs.

'Just to the loo, babes. Back in a sec.' I cross to the bathroom and lock myself inside. I sit on the toilet and rest my head in my hands. It's too much.

Sometimes I quite like those fantasies: Thom and me in killer Burberry coats and scarves, strolling through a russet, autumnal park with coffees and the ubiquitous French Bulldog. Truly the gayest dog.

I imagine introducing him to my little queer collective of socialist, vegan, poly artists and activists in Bristol. My STRAIGHT-ACTING, BISEXUAL boyfriend who's stepped right out of a Hollister ad. They'd hate him. He's so vanilla.

We don't even like any of the same things! Sex and Christmas – that's it! What are we gonna do for the other 364 days a year?

The sheer notion of dating one person to the exclusion of all others is terrifying and perplexing. What if he's not the one for me? What if it's a mistake? I somehow *know* Thom isn't one for open relationships. Then I'd have to break up with him, and I can just see the broken little look on his face. Why do people do it? Why do they go into these things knowing they'll likely get hurt, or inflict hurt? It's so perverse, and I don't know if the highs top the lows. The overwhelming weight of our future squashes me down like a sumo wrestler, wraps its hands around my throat.

I can't breathe.

'Are you OK in there?' he calls from outside, and even his concern feels like a trap.

'Fine!' I shout back.

I want to escape my own body; even that feels like too much of a cage. I want to be everywhere, with everyone. I will not be trapped. I will not be pinned down.

You'll never meet a man who looks at you the way he does.

No. I won't be contained. *Je refuse.* Even by Thom Simpkins. Even if there is something in me that feels like honey. And even if that honey is love. I don't want it. It's easier without.

I won't hurt me.

FERN

When I get out of the shower, Thom is back in *our* room, getting dressed. It's funny how fast I've let him go. This is like a whole new guy standing in front of me: *Rowan's new boyfriend.* He looks like someone I once knew. *You remind me of my ex.*

'Hey,' I say. Thom looks deeply embarrassed, but he needn't. 'How did it go?' I ask, taking the pressure off.

He can't quite look me in the eye, but he nods. 'I … thank you.'

'For what?' I unravel the towel-turban from my head and shake my damp hair loose.

'For being cool.'

Given how not cool I was when he came out, it feels like the bare minimum I can do. I feel like I'm going to cry, but gulp it back. I shrug. 'It's OK. I want you to be happy. Both of you. Where's Ro?' And now Thom shrugs. His forehead wrinkles and I know that face. He's harbouring a worry. 'What?'

'I dunno. He's being weird. He was in the shower for ages, so I came down here.'

I step into some knickers, not unwrapping the towel. It wouldn't be right to be naked in front of him now. New landscape.

This situation with Rowan feels hauntingly familiar,

however. 'It's like Niall.'

'Who?' Thom asks with a frown.

I shake my head. 'A guy he dated – briefly – in S7. He was a bartender at one of the venues where Hamish, my ex, played. Rowan was *obsessed* with him, going to see like three gigs a week so he could stalk him, and then the second Niall showed any interest in return he ceased to exist. Rowan only wants guys he can't ...' I stop, reading Thom's face. He looks crushed. On reflection, maybe I should have warned him last night before advising him to talk to Rowan.

My brother is a complicated one. He's cute and funny and seriously smart, but actively seems to repel love. And I don't know why. I think we all assumed he'd grow out of it, but he seems to be getting worse. Perhaps that's not quite accurate. He wants to be loved. Who doesn't? If anything, Rowan's problem is a reluctance to *give* love. He wants to be adored. That's why he's so keen on the notion of fame. He wants to stand on stage, basking in love, without having to risk giving a single drop back.

'Did you talk about things?' I ask.

Thom blushes. 'Not really ...'

Actually I don't wanna know. 'Got it.' I can't have it both ways. I can't encourage them and then get squeamish about things. I have to imagine, honestly, that my Thom regenerated into a new Thom, *Doctor Who* style.

I finish getting dressed and then give Thom's arms a squeeze. 'I know my brother. It's not you, OK? It's very much him. Will you let me talk to him?'

'I can't ask you to do that. It's weird.'

I manage a smile. 'Give me this one. You know I like to control things.'

'That's true,' he says, smiling back.

'Wait here.'

I head downstairs and I see Rowan's bag in the hallway. What's that about? He's not physically running away is he? That's next level, even for him. So bloody dramatic. I follow the sound of voices to the kitchen. He's talking to Mum and Dad. '... it's an open return so we can go back whenever.'

'Do you have something to get back for?' Dad asks, inhaling a huge mug of black coffee at the table.

Rowan shrugs. 'Syd is working tomorrow. I just hate the bit between Christmas and New Year – the perineum of the year.'

'You're leaving?' I ask sharply.

Rowan didn't hear me approach and now looks caught out. I know *he* knows what this is about, even if Mum and Dad don't. 'We were going back tomorrow anyway. Might as well get it over with.'

'You absolute pussy,' I say loudly.

'Fern!' Mum snaps.

Rowan glares at me for a second, pure venom in his eyes, and then shouts past me. 'Syd! You ready or what?'

WILLOW

I watch Syd throw their things into their bag, leaning my bum against the warm radiator. I sense that Rowan's decision came out of nowhere, and it's not like Syd can stay here without Rowan, I guess. 'You can stay if you want?' I tell them.

'Nah, it's good. I got shit to do back home. I have a shift tomorrow night.' Syd told me about their part-time job as a theatre usher, but I also wonder if that means *someone* to do back home. I have zero right to feel jealous, but it does zing in my stomach.

I also know they are right. The time is not now. But I love that I have something to think about that isn't my illness. 'Will you come next Christmas?' I ask.

They stop what they're doing and look at me. 'If Rowan invites me ...'

'I'm inviting you,' I say. 'You got me through this Christmas. I honestly didn't think I'd survive it, you know?'

They smile. 'Good. I'm glad.'

'Everything you said was right. I don't know if I believe in fate, but it's like you were my Christmas present.' Wow, that was cringe. Regret that one.

Syd walks to me and kisses my forehead gently. 'You are a gift.'

I stare at a hole in the toe of my sock. 'I owe you one. Next Christmas you can claim hours of free therapy.' They laugh and go back to packing. I go on, 'I'm gonna get better.' Can't take it back now. 'I will. I'm in recovery. As of Christmas Day.'

Syd briefly looks up. 'Don't be scared of relapse. You probably will. Everyone does.'

'I know. But this is me, making a choice. I either live in that … fog … or I do something else.'

'What are you gonna do?'

'I'm not sure yet,' I say honestly. Getting through the day seems like a good place to start. I don't have to be strong for ever, just the next twenty-four hours. Even less than that. I just have to get through the next meal. I will face it head on.

Syd zips up their bag and hoists it on to their shoulder. 'Well, you have my number. Let me know what you decide.'

'I will.' I want to kiss them one last time, but I hear footsteps stomping upstairs. It's Rowan.

'Syd? Are you ready?'

'Just about.'

'Come on, or we'll miss the ten-thirty.'

He sweeps back downstairs, and I share a final glance with Syd as they pass me in the doorway. I feel a little crackle of static, and something inside me that I didn't think existed. I *want* them. It's like those tiny buds sticking up through the snow in the garden. Under the frost, something is growing. Spring is coming after a very long winter.

Some day. Some day we might. How exciting is that? Definitely worth sticking around to find out, I think.

FERN

I watch with great distaste as Rowan hugs Willow and then Mum. Thom waits his turn. 'So … bye! Happy New Year!' Rowan says brightly, playing along with the parental guidance version of events. As far as they know, Thom and I are still together. 'See you later!'

Thom is left with little choice but to play along. 'Yeah. You too, man.' As the words leave his mouth, he turns and walks back to the kitchen. I feel the darkness of his mood, a churning storm cloud. He's been ghosted in the flesh. I didn't think such a thing was possible.

Syd gives my mum a hug. 'Seriously, Chris, thank you so much.'

'You're welcome any time, Syd. And thank *you* for looking after this one.' She ruffles Rowan's hair.

'Are you coming?' Dad shouts from the driver's seat of the car down the drive.

'Come on …' Rowan says. 'We'll miss the train.'

They head towards the car, but I seize my chance and chase after them. 'Ro, wait,' I say.

'I can't,' he says.

'Just a minute. Can I talk to my brother, Syd?'

Syd nods and continues down the drive to the car. Rowan

313

pouts. 'What? Are you seriously going to try and pimp me out to your boyfriend?'

I keep my face stern. He won't cute his way out of this one. I'm not Mum. 'What are you doing, Rowan? You're running away? You're like a child.'

'No. I'm going home.'

'Thom is one of the good ones.'

'Fern, please! I am finding this all so incredibly ick. I cannot.'

I shake my head. 'Who hurt you?'

He looks to the skies. 'Oh, Jesus.'

I boulder on, not letting him off the hook. 'Was it school? I know you think I buried my head in the sand, but I know how hard it was … and … I wanted to make it better for you, I did, but I was fourteen too, you know?'

He balls his fists. 'I am begging you, can we not?'

'Rowan, please! I just want you to be happy.'

'And I can't be happy and single? *Reductive*: look it up.'

I ignore that. And I obviously know what reductive means. 'Maybe we *are* psychic. I know you. You *crave* love. You always have, more than anyone else I know, but when you get it, you push it away. You're basically a cat.'

He sort-of laughs. Behind us, Mum watches with concern from the doorway. She taps her watch, but I'm not done. 'I think it's because to love and be loved you have to open yourself up to the possibility of being hurt. You have to take off the armour. You have to show your soft bits to someone. You have to be vulnerable, and that's the scariest thing there is.' I might be getting through to him. I think I've found the tiniest breach in his rhino-thick skin.

314

I think back to the version of myself who thought she had it all sussed out five days ago. She had no idea what was coming. 'Yeah, sure, that means you get hurt sometimes. Love really, really fucking hurts. I should know. I stand before you a shipwreck.'

His expression softens for a second. I must be a pitiful thing: hair still wet, shivering to death on the front lawn in my slippers.

'I just can't, Fern,' he finally says, a deflating balloon. 'It's too hard. Tell him I'm sorry.' He gives me a tight hug. 'Thank you,' he whispers in my ear. 'I definitely love you. That one's a given.'

'I love you too. Always.' He then hurries to the car, where he jumps in the back. Dumbly, I watch the car pull out of the drive.

Well, I don't think so. I turn on my heel and stride back to the house and past Mum. 'What was all that about?' she asks.

'Where's Thom?' I say, ignoring the question entirely.

'I'm in here,' a voice drifts down the hall from the kitchen. I charge down and find him making some coffee at the stove.

'Put that down,' I command.

'What? Why?'

'You need to talk to him.'

He looks at me blankly. 'Fern, give it up, he's gone.'

'No he hasn't, and he doesn't leave for almost half an hour.'

I am in my FLOW – the headspace I occupy when fully obsessed by a project or essay. I perceive no barrier to my success in this endeavour. 'He has an open return so we can go for a coffee near the station or something.' Thom continues to look at me like a madwoman. 'Come on, I'll drive.'

Mum hovers on the threshold to the kitchen. 'Fern, what's going on?'

I turn to her and hold out my hand. 'Can I borrow your car, please?'

'I haven't collected it from the garage yet, love.'

Shit. Forgot that detail. 'It's fine. We'll get an Uber. In fact, that means we don't even have to worry about parking. Thom, come on!' He's about to argue but I hold up a hugely decisive index finger as if I were pressing pause on his response. 'Thom. You are allowed to have a say. Rowan is not the final word on how *you* feel. And don't tell me, tell *him*.'

Mum throws her hands up. 'Will someone please tell me what's going on?'

I'm already booking the Uber. There are lots in the area, thank god.

Willow lingers behind Mum, catching up faster. 'Thom and Rowan ...? Is that a thing now?'

'What?' Mum says. I suppose she's had her own shit to deal with this Christmas.

Filip accepts my ride and is a minute away. 'Get a coat,' I tell Thom. This time he nods and abandons the coffee pot. He walks past me to find his coat and I follow.

'Can I come?' Willow says, very much like a kid wanting to come on a road trip.

'No!' I snap.

'Let her come,' Thom says. 'It's probably too late anyway.'

'Fine, whatever,' I say, putting on my coat and scarf. My phone pings as Filip arrives outside. 'It's here.'

The three of us pile into the back seat of the Prius, a bundle of duffel coats and knitwear. Filip has the heating on full-pelt so we all peel off the layers we just put on before we die. 'Edinburgh Waverley?' he asks and I confirm our destination.

As the weirdly silent car pulls out of the drive, I check my phone. It's 10.05. Ro's train is supposed to depart at 10.30. We have time. I hope. Or this is all going to be super anticlimactic.

'Thom,' Willow says. 'I … um … never said sorry … for what I did.'

So much has happened since Christmas Eve, it takes me a second to remember what she's apologising for.

'It's OK,' Thom says, but only because he's a gent. It's very not OK.

I'm about to interject, but Willow goes on. 'It's not OK. At all. I outed you. So not cool.' Thom sort of shrugs it off. 'You seem pretty decent and I was, like, the worst. I, um, I'm gonna try harder.'

I look at my little sister. She seems different. The pilot light has come on in her eyes somehow. She's annoying, but annoying the way she was when she was twelve. The before times.

'I don't care who knows I'm bi,' Thom says, and I see the Uber driver's eyes in the rear-view mirror. He's suddenly very interested. 'Actually, that's a lie. I do care. But I wish I didn't.'

'You are not your thoughts,' Willow says, and I'm a little taken aback. Has she been reading Rumi memes or something?

'Exactly,' Thom says, pondering her words. 'I'm not going to be ashamed. I'm not.'

As we approach the station from the rear, I see Dad's car

heading in the other direction. 'That's Dad!' I shout, and even the driver peers out of the window.

'We've still got time,' Willow says and then turns to Thom. 'What are you going to tell him?'

'I have no idea. This is all Fern's idea.'

They both turn and look at me.

'The way I see it, I would prefer to say exactly what's on my mind. Otherwise, I'd never sleep ever again, running through all the things I *wished* I'd said. *What ifs* keep you up at night, not facts.' That's also quite Rumi, I think.

I think of Hamish and how I didn't quite manage to tell him how I really felt yesterday. Oh well. I'll just have to live with that, I guess. I hope Thom is braver than me.

The Uber pulls into the drop-off zone and we tumble out. The station is carnage. I've always thought this station was too small for a city the size of Edinburgh, and today must be one of the busiest days outside of the festival. A lot of people are heading back from Christmas holidays today it seems, the concourse is sweaty and crowded; bad-tempered. The magic of going home for Christmas is all gone, and everyone just wants to get home and eat something that isn't chocolate.

I look at the departure board. The 10.30 to Plymouth is now ready to board on platform 1. It's only 10.16, though. There's still time.

'Do you think they already boarded?' Thom asks. 'I can't get on the train without a ticket.'

There are automated ticket barriers *and* a train guard manning one of the gates. Our tickets are only valid on the twenty-ninth. Shit. I should have foreseen that. There must be a solution. He can get a ticket to the first stop on the service – that won't cost much – although the queues at the ticket machines are ten deep …

'Wait!' Willow cries. 'Syd!' She takes off across the concourse, taking hold of my sleeve as she goes. As we race through the crowd, I bump shoulders with a red-faced woman who calls me a slag. Bit harsh. I see Syd emerging from Costa Coffee, two enormous takeout cups in their hands. 'Syd!'

Syd stops and blinks like they're hallucinating. 'Hey … did we forget something?'

'Where's Rowan?' I ask urgently.

OK, maybe that was too intense because now Syd looks genuinely scared. 'He's on the train. He went to get us seats while I got these.' They motion at the drinks.

'Shit!' I say.

'Can you call him?' Willow says.

'Did you guys all drop an Adderall or something?' Syd says with their usual chill.

Thom finally speaks. 'I need to speak to Rowan before you leave. I should have told him how I feel last Christmas, so I'm not going to let him go without a fight this time.'

Even Syd looks a little surprised at that admission. 'Wow. OK. You're cutting it fine.'

'I know. This is not like me.'

A slow, easy smile breaks on Syd's face. 'It's *very* Rowan, though.' They hand me the coffees and reach into their coat pocket. They hand a ticket to Thom. 'Go get him, buddy.'

'Are you sure?'

'Yep. Go. Just get off the train in the next ten minutes

or you're going to …' They look up at the departure board, 'Berwick-Upon-Tweed, wherever that is.'

Thom's face lights up. *Hope.* And I know I'm doing the right thing. I am. This is right. 'I'll be two minutes,' he tells us.

'Coach E,' Syd shouts after him as he runs towards the barriers.

I watch Thom go through the gates and vanish into the crowds. The last smoky traces of sadness leave my body. Christmas, after all, is about giving, not receiving, and if I can give two people I love a really big, beautiful gift then it's totally worth it.

I hand Syd one of the coffees and take Ro's for myself. A gingerbread latte is the least he can do. And now we wait. I cross my fingers on the coffee cup.

ROWAN

I don't even want to know why the train carriage smells of sprouts. It's rank, and almost full, but I have managed to secure us two seats together, albeit without a table this time. I check all my murder podcasts have downloaded. This time, I'm not excited, I just want to get home, but there's a six-hour train ride in the way. I plan to sleep through most of it. That way, maybe I'll have the energy to go out tonight.

I wonder if I should message Ryan or Greg and see if they're back in Bristol tonight. The last thing I want is to be alone in my shitty student house. Jas and Paloma aren't due back until after New Year's, so it'll just be me and the kitchen slugs. We once had a kitchen frog.

I flick through messages on my phone, trying to remember who was in Bristol over the break. It's a tough call. Ryan has the nicer flat and the bigger willy, but Greg *is* a drug dealer so always has plenty of—

'Rowan?'

I look up, expecting to see Syd and a much-needed coffee. Instead, Thom looms over me in the aisle. Is this a dream? Am I *that* tired? This makes no sense. How did he even get on the train? 'Thom … what? Did I forget something?'

'You forgot me,' he says quietly. Thom blushes. A stressed-looking woman tuts at him, squeezing past with her wheelie case to get to her seat. He mutters an apology.

'Thom, I don't ...' I say loudly, over a tannoy announcement about the onboard catering facilities.

He sighs, clearly self-conscious and with half the carriage trying to get around him. 'Can you move over?' he nods at the seat.

I like the aisle seat, but I shuffle to the window. 'You coming to Bristol with me? Thom, what are you doing? Is this like in *Twilight* when Jacob imprinted on the baby?' I hiss.

'Hear me out, OK?'

I didn't think this sort of thing happened to real people. I am Keira in *Love, Actually*. True, *I look quite pretty*, but this is mortifying for him. Still, if he really wants to make a scene, who am I to stop him?. 'Very well. What say you, Thom Simpkins?'

He lowers his voice. 'Last night ... I don't feel like that with anyone else. When I'm with you, it's like when I heard that song in the church. It feels like there's something huge inside me. Something lovely, and light, and warm. And I don't know what else that can be ... but ...'

If he's not going to say it, then neither am I.

'I've never felt it with anyone else ... and I think you feel it too. I know you've been with a bunch of guys, but this feels different to me and, no offence, Rowan, you're not that good an actor. I see you.'

I make an unfortunate clucking noise. Slandering my artistic skill is not the way to my heart.

Let's look at the receipts: Thom and I have had two, three magical nights together. More than a lot of people get, I'm sure, but why play Russian Roulette? Quit while you're ahead.

'Rowan, it's gold,' he says again. 'What kind of idiot would walk away from gold?'

My throat feels tight. I did not think anyone would ever describe me as gold. 'You are so sweet.' I take his gloved hand in mine. My eyes sting. 'But it wouldn't be gold for ever. Eventually we'd turn into brass. We'd turn into my parents. Or you and Fern!'

He shakes his head mournfully. 'I never felt this way with Fern.'

'Let's literally never tell her that, because she would skin us for handbags.'

He looks downcast for a moment. 'How do you know?' he says defiantly.

'How do I know what?'

'How do you know it'd turn to shit?'

'Because it always does!'

'You never stick around long enough to find out.'

I roll my eyes. 'Because I get *bored*, Thom! Happy? What do you want me to say?'

'I don't want you to say anything. I'm asking you to *see*.' He squeezes my hand. 'We have something here. Tell me you didn't feel it when we were in bed last night. Tell me, without lying, and I'll get off this train.'

I can't. I'm not going to lie. 'I did feel something …'

'So …'

'I felt amazing, because it was amazing. But it was one night.'

'It doesn't have to be,' he says with a gleaming smile. 'Let's see what happens. That's all I'm saying. Won't you just … try?'

323

Oh, I can't. It's too scary. It's vast and it has rows and rows of teeth. 'Thom ...' A tear of sheer frustration burns the edge of my eye. 'I would love nothing more than to be your perfect boyfriend, and hold your freezing hands, and have funny in-jokes, and cuddle you on cold nights ... but I don't know if I can do that. And there's a very real chance that I will totally fuck you over.' The tear pops out.

He kisses me. 'I might fuck you over too,' he whispers. He wipes the tear off my cheek with his thumb. 'Rowan, we don't know what tomorrow is going to bring. I'm here now, asking you to get off the train and just ... stay another day, or two. Maybe stay for New Year? Let's see what happens. No promises, no rules, no guarantees, just ... one day at a time.'

'One day at a time?' OK. That might just be doable I guess.

'One day at a time.'

'I don't know, Thom.' I shake my heavy head. 'Even that freaks me out ... like, I am losing my shit here.'

A new voice suddenly interrupts. Across the aisle, a middle-aged lady with a white fluffy chihuahua on her lap has apparently been listening intently to the whole conversation. She speaks like she smokes about sixty a day. 'Och, you young 'uns are feckin' painful! What are ye blathering aboot? He's a good-lookin' laddie! If I was thirty years younger, I'd be up that like a rat up a drainpipe.'

My mouth falls open. Yes, me, lost for words. I want to tell her to mind her own business, but she's frankly too fabulous. Even her chihuahua is judging me. Did she train it to do that?

'I know this is nuttin' to do wi us, like, but ye should go wi'

324

him!' a teenage girl in the row behind us shouts. She has very Kara energy.

'Are you mental, he's well fit,' her friend agrees.

Thom says nothing, but grins at me, no doubt feeling vindicated.

The tannoy ping pongs again. *This is the ten-thirty Cross Country Express service to Plymouth. Will those not planning on travelling with us please leave the train as we are departing shortly.*

'Be away wi' ye, then!' the older woman adds.

'Oh, for fuck's sake!' I say, standing up. I know what the audience wants. I'm an actor, after all. Can you imagine any other ending at this point? 'Let's go then.' There's actually a cheer from the teenage girls. 'One day at a time …' I warn Thom, shoving a cautionary finger in his face.

'One day at a time,' he agrees, reaching for my bag on the overhead shelf.

Today, I am intrigued. Let's see what happens tomorrow. When I think of it like that, it doesn't seem nearly so scary.

'Quick.' Thom takes my hand and pulls me down the aisle towards the door. 'Or we'll end up in Berwick-Upon-Tweed.'

People watch us as we pass, hand in hand. I know I agreed to day by day, but I feel oddly proud that for today at least I am his and he is mine, and everyone can see.

As we leave the carriage, I take a wee bow.

FERN

We manage to get a black cab at the station taxi rank that's big enough for all of us. Nothing has been said, but they did come off the train holding hands ... until they saw us and let go. I suspect that was for my benefit. Rowan said nothing. He just held a sassfinger in my face and said, 'Not. A. Word.'

I am not one to gloat, but whatever Thom said or did on that train worked. Apparently we are now staying until New Year – all except Syd, who *did* board the train once Thom handed the ticket back. They have a part-time job as a theatre usher and they need to be back by tomorrow night for a shift, which really puts things in perspective. However bleak things are for me right now, at least I don't have to watch over a pantomime for the next four weeks. So there's that.

I note, however, Willow hugged Syd very tightly before they departed. Are they shagging too? Why not, everyone else is. It seems this Christmas was possessed by some horny festive spirit. The Wankus. I hope they did. It's like Willow's been trapped in some hell dimension and now she's back with us on this side of the veil. I'm here for it.

The cab pulls up outside the house and Thom gallantly carries Rowan's huge bag up the path. Once more, we pile into the hallway, again greeted by spiced apple and cinnamon candles, Mum and Dad.

'OK,' Dad says, 'now I'm really confused. Shouldn't you be halfway to Berwick by now?'

'They swapped,' Willow says simply, pointing at Rowan and me. She says nothing more and heads to her room.

Dad looks baffled. I'm leaving that one for Rowan and Thom to explain.

'Fern,' Mum says. 'There's someone to see you in the lounge ...'

'Huh?' I peel off my coat and scarf, hang them on the pegs, and head into the drawing room. Hamish is perched on the armchair next to the fire, cradling a mug of tea. He looks so out of place in his torn jeans and filthy Vans. 'Hamish?'

He stands to greet me. 'Hey. I hope you don't mind me turning up without an invite?'

I'm confused but ... 'No ...'

'I got you something.' He motions at a gift-wrapped box on the coffee table. There's no way he wrapped that himself; it's way too neat and has a wee bow on top.

Am I missing something? 'You're a couple of days late ...'

'It's me,' he says with an impish grin, 'what did ye expect?'

I kneel by the dwindling fire and put an extra log on. 'I didn't get you anything.'

'I didn't expect you to. Open it.'

I cross my legs and take the little box. It's light as a feather. I pull off the ribbon and find a small jewellery box. 'Should I be worried?'

'You wish, darlin'!'

I lift the cardboard lid off and laugh aloud. It's a tiny, gold Lisa Simpson charm on an impossibly delicate pendant. 'Oh, that's so sweet.'

'Lisa is the best one,' Hamish says. I take the delicate chain out of the box and unfasten the clasp. It really is lovely. I only wear almost invisible jewellery. I thank him sincerely. 'Here, let me help,' he says.

Hamish kneels behind me and moves my hair off my neck. As his fingers touch my skin I get a shiver all up and down my spine. 'I wanted to say sorry for the way I talked to you in the shop yesterday.'

'What do you mean?'

'I was rude. Dismissive. It wasnae fair.'

He was dismissive, yes, not so much rude. 'I probably had it coming. Like if you turned up in one of my lectures, I'd be less than thrilled.'

'What you did was really brave. No one else I know in the whole wide world would go marching into Tesco, of all places, to tell someone how they felt, and I totally shut you down.'

I say nothing, glancing up only briefly to meet his eyes. He saw through my cunning decaf tea excuse then.

'I, um, think I felt a little out of control, you know,' he goes on. 'Which is scary when you're in recovery. You start to think, *Fuck I could really use a drink …*'

I feel the little Lisa resting in the middle of my collar. I finger her spiky head. 'Do you really think we were bad for each other?'

'I think we were young.' Hamish looks at me. Does he *know* his eyes are a powerful sexual tractor beam? Actually, yes, I think he probably does. 'Fern, no one else has ever cared for me

328

like you did; taken care of me like you did. You care so intensely about the people in your life. You would do anything for them. The problem was, I never gave you anything, I only took. You needed a boyfriend, not a son.'

I laugh ruefully. God, that about sums it up. I keep raising sons. I look away from him, staring instead into the fire. I don't know what to say. I put up with behaviour I shouldn't have tolerated for far too long.

Hamish clears his throat. 'I have no right to ask you this, Fern, because I treated you like shit, but can we ... try again? When I move to London, perhaps we can see a film or something? I know! It's probably madness but ... we're not kids any more ...'

Hamish Bell, my first love.

I kiss him. We click together like Lego. I don't know what weird magic binds us together, but this boy has never been out of my system since the very first kiss. I used to think he was poison, but I wonder if he was more like ... chilli. He powerfully changed my flavour for ever. There's no getting rid of him. Moreover, I really love chilli, however hot it is.

This kiss is light years away from the hungry insanity of Farah's bathroom. It's tender, the heat of the fire on the right side of my face. I could so easily just drift away. I fold my arms around his neck and hold on for wherever the ride is going.

He pulls back. 'I'm different now, I swear.'

I don't necessarily want him to be different, that would mean losing part of who Hamish was, I just need him to be ... honest. Maybe I'm insane, and I may well come to regret this, but I do trust him. 'We're older,' I say, as if that explains everything, and he nods. 'And my answer is yes. We can try again.'

His whole face lights up, like Christmas. 'Yeah?'

'Aye.'

This time, he kisses me and it feels *easy*. I let go and fall into him. If it's love, I expect you don't have to think about it.

NEXT CHRISTMAS

The house on *Arboretum Road* had seen 121 Christmases since its completion, but this was perhaps the most harmonious it could summon from memory.

For the younger daughter, the day starts the way it always does of late. She unfurls a lilac mat across the floor in front of the bay window, and broadcasts herself to thousands of viewers all around the world. She greets them the same way she does each morning:

Hello, and welcome to WillowTree Yoga. I'm Willow and this is a special Christmas morning Sun Salutation.

When this curious routine started in February, the house had looked on, perplexed by this strange behaviour. It soon came to realise, however, the profound peace the girl found in these poses, the comfort, the pleasing repetition of it all. It also saw how this new mission had brought her closer to people all over the world. She speaks of her recovery, the good days and the bad, both of which there have been many. Her listeners take comfort in this community she has created. She is not alone, and neither are they.

This morning she says:

I know – I remember – how hard this day can be if you're in ED recovery or if you are living with an ED. Just last Christmas, I was in full panic mode. Remember, you are not your thoughts, don't let them tell you that you aren't valid or deserving. You deserve joy on this day like anyone else. OK! Let's get out of our heads and into our bodies for twenty minutes. Let's be present, here, and together …

The rest of the house wakes up one at a time. The mother and father appreciate the quiet kitchen at dawn. The worker bees go about the hive and they reflect, wordlessly, about how far they've come since last Christmas. Quite simply, neither of them wanted to leave. In the end, talk of walking away from one another petered out. Love was enough to keep them together.

Once a week, they speak to a therapist via a laptop in the drawing room. They talk of forgiveness. They talk of their son's guidance, but found – once they agreed to change the unsaid rules of their union – they didn't especially want, or need them changed.

They are still the young lovers who met all those years ago, but they are best friends, soulmates, husband and wife. They are architects of something they built together.

As winter turned in to spring, laughter returned to the house on Arboretum Road. This is what keeps them together. With their younger daughter speaking so openly about her recovery, they – for the first time in many years – took a holiday just the two of them in July. They went to Santorini, ate olives and drank wine as the sun set in a way they'd never seen before. In September they went to France without going anywhere near Disneyland. They realised that they have been together for a very long time, but – with their children no longer children – there is much of the world that is new to them.

They also enjoy the newfound friendships they have with their children. The boundaries they once set no longer need their watchful eyes. They are becoming equals who see each other through choice, not the necessity of a last name.

The elder daughter and her boyfriend are the next to wake. Without words, they have woozy, sleepy sex. He holds her from behind, effortless. It's her favourite time. After they finish, they snooze a while longer.

As they do, the son and his boyfriend stampede downstairs from the attic to excitedly wake his friend in the office room. Once again, they have brought the orphan home, and once again they are most grateful for a calm place to be at Christmas. They are part of the family now.

As the morning rolls on, everyone congregates in the drawing room, bucks fizz in hand, for presents and pyjamas around the tree. The doorbell goes for a first time and it's the aunt and the cousin, this time accompanied by a newcomer; the aunt's new partner. Her name is Michelle and they met at the job centre. As an outsider, she feels wary, but the mother embraces her warmly and she feels welcomed at the hearth. The mother believes, for she has told the father, that this time – at last – Shelly has made the right choice.

The doorbell goes once more and it's the younger daughter's new boyfriend. They evolved from friends, to best friends, to unspoken boyfriend, to boyfriend. He's a studious, quiet boy, his voice rarely above a whisper, the house has to strain to hear him, but when he does speak, his asides are hilarious. The younger daughter often cries, struggles to breathe for laughter.

The orphan friend, too, has found love this year. They speak – at length – of an artist from Iceland. They visit each other every few

335

months or so, and so far, it works for them. The orphan speaks often with the young daughter. Last Christmas it seems they found something everlasting.

The elder daughter takes control of the present situation, as was ever the way. A gift has gone missing, accidentally left on the train perhaps, and she loses her composure. Her boyfriend, though, seems to be her antidote. As her frustration spirals, he takes her hand and leads her back to reality: it doesn't matter, we can order a new one and it'll be here for Hogmanay, he tells her. The house has seen this many times, and in many ways down the decades: lovers don't have to match; they have to be in proportion. This year, the elder daughter unwinds.

The son, meanwhile, curls up on his boyfriend's lap in the armchair. He is perhaps the most changed of all. The house has never seen him so still, so serene, so content in the here and now. To the house, it is a most beguiling mystery. The young men have formed a clever code of smiles and glances, a little fortress for two. He and the boy, Thom, don't speak of the secret ingredients that make the recipe work.

It's ample for them to look knowingly to one another, and explain to anyone who seeks to know: we're really happy right now, thank you.

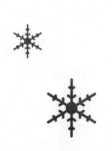

STAY ANOTHER DAY

WORDS
Juno Dawson

MADE WORDS BETTER
Lily Morgan
Emily Sharratt

TIRELESS ADVOCACY
Sallyanne Sweeney

GETTING SHIT DONE
Lena McCauley
Sarah Lambert

MADE YOU LOOK
Emily Thomas
Beth McWilliams

PRETTY COVER
Alison Padley

FILM AND TV RIGHTS
Marc Simonsson

IF YOU'RE READING THIS IN A LANGUAGE
OTHER THAN ENGLISH
Samar Hammam

THIS BOOK EXISTS BECAUSE OF
Dozens of people at Hachette Children's Group

MORAL SUPPORT
Samantha Powick
Max Gallant
Sarah Lea Donlan
Prince

YOU
The reader

Happy holidays!

HELP AND SUPPORT

EATING DISORDERS:

Beat – The UK's Eating Disorder Charity: beateatingdisorders.org.uk

SEED – Eating Disorder Support Service: seedeatingdisorders.org.uk

GENERAL MENTAL HEALTH:

YoungMinds – Young Person's Mental Health Charity: youngminds.org.uk

Childline – 24/7 support line: 0800 1111

GENDER AND SEXUALITY:

Mermaids – For gender diverse kids and their families: mermaidsuk.org.uk

Gendered Intelligence – Improving trans people's lives: genderedintelligence.co.uk

Stonewall – Acceptance Without Exception: stonewall.org.uk

Juno Dawson is the bestselling, award-winning author of ten novels and six non-fiction titles, including *Clean*, *Meat Market*, *This Book is Gay*, and *What's the T?*.

She is also a successful journalist, writing for *Attitude*, *Glamour* and the *Guardian*, a screenwriter, broadcaster and a Stonewall Role Model.

She has contributed to news items concerning sexuality, identity, literature and education on BBC Woman's Hour, Front Row, ITV News, Channel 5 News, This Morning and Newsnight. In her spare time, Juno runs a cabaret night in Brighton.

You can find Juno on Twitter and Instagram @JunoDawson